W9-CJS-829

THE CITY WHERE
WE ONCE LIVED

Also by Eric Barnes:

Shimmer
Something Pretty, Something Beautiful

THE CITY WHERE WE ONCE LIVED

A NOVEL

ERIC BARNES

Arcade Publishing • New York

Copyright © 2018 by Eric Barnes

All rights reserved. No part of this book may be reproduced in any manner without the express written consent of the publisher, except in the case of brief excerpts in critical reviews or articles. All inquiries should be addressed to Arcade Publishing, 307 West 36th Street, 11th Floor, New York, NY 10018.

First Edition

This is a work of fiction. Names, places, characters, and incidents are either the products of the author's imagination or are used fictitiously.

Arcade Publishing books may be purchased in bulk at special discounts for sales promotion, corporate gifts, fund-raising, or educational purposes. Special editions can also be created to specifications. For details, contact the Special Sales Department, Arcade Publishing, 307 West 36th Street, 11th Floor, New York, NY 10018 or arcade@skyhorsepublishing.com.

Arcade Publishing® is a registered trademark of Skyhorse Publishing, Inc.®, a Delaware corporation.

Visit our website at www.arcadepub.com.
Visit the author's site at www.ericbarnes.net.

10 9 8 7 6 5 4 3 2 1

Library of Congress Cataloging-in-Publication Data is available on file.
Library of Congress Control Number: 2017962838

Cover design by Erin Seaward-Hiatt
Cover photo: iStockphoto

ISBN: 978-1-62872-883-5
Ebook ISBN: 978-1-62872-884-2

Printed in the United States of America

For Nora

THE CITY WHERE
WE ONCE LIVED

PROLOGUE

Sometimes, at night, I would light houses on fire. But no one particularly cared. I could sit on a porch across the street from the flames, watching the fire spread from the first floor to the second, and still no one would come. It was many years since there'd been police or fire trucks or ambulances, and I picked houses far away from the few neighbors that remained.

I guess this was so I could be alone.

• • •

There's a point in the fire when the heat and light seem to peak. Even across the street, my hands and face feel like they might burn, and I need to squint my eyes, wet now, heat pushing against them.

But still I watch, till the fire grows larger than the house itself, the house just a shadow, a memory of walls and windows and a roof, all now overtaken by the rolling, rising flames.

And then I walk home.

• • •

There are no people here, not one other person in this twenty-story building. The power works on most floors and the water runs, but the people here, they mostly choose to live in the houses, not the big buildings. Maybe they don't like the idea of living close to someone else. The chance they might run into someone in the silence of a dimly lit hallway. The chance a stranger, a neighbor, might be standing there on the other side of a door.

But the people here don't live apart because of fear. There is no violence here anymore, no danger or crime.

It's more that people want to be alone. It's more that there's so little to say. It's more that people are so tired.

I'm so tired. It makes me think everyone else is too.

And maybe other people don't like being so high up in the air. My room in this hotel is at the corner of the twentieth floor and in the daytime, to the south and east, I can see the gray, still buildings and empty streets of this one-time downtown. This building is the tallest, but there are other buildings too, eight square blocks of low, stone buildings and tall, steel skyscrapers.

The graffiti is faded to gray and white.

To the west there are the factories, brown now, rusted, a massive and disconnected collection of low, long buildings whose hard, straight rooflines bow sickly in places, the rigid sightlines destroyed, the weight of rain from many years bending the structures, sinking them inward.

There's a big iron wheel I can see. There's a gear three stories high. Water towers. Power lines stretching from building to rail yard to warehouse and loading dock.

I have binoculars I found in the hotel's office and now use them to stare out at the remnants of the city. Abandoned excavators in the industrial zone. Trucks parked at the rear of office buildings, their tires now flat, the windows rolled down.

I can see some buildings' windows have been broken, can see doors that have been boarded up, other doors that have been left wide open.

I see people some days, half a mile away, in the neighborhoods beyond downtown, a few men and women walking amid the many houses that stand there still.

When it rains hard, the clouds are so low that I can see nothing from these windows.

When the fog comes, covering the streets and the bases of the buildings around me, it seems that I am suspended alone here in the sky.

· · ·

It's been years now that I've lived here. I sleep mostly on the couch, a few hours a night, then again in the late afternoon. It's hard for me to stay asleep for very long.

The paint peels in wide swaths from the plaster walls and from the ornate moldings around the mantel and door frames. I light fires in the fireplace for heat. It's a very old hotel and this room is in a suite. The outlets on some walls work, so I've set up floor lamps in the three rooms of this place. A living room where I sleep. A bedroom where I keep my clothes. A bathroom and small kitchenette.

There are rugs I've found to cover the wooden floors. Fine rugs, probably, like the fine sofa and table and chair. Yet everything is colorless. In part because it's all so worn. In part because the walls are so pale. In part because these are the items I wanted to drag in here from other rooms.

Pale items, without color or distinction.

Most days I leave the windows open, even when it is very cold. Tall windows that open from the top and bottom, they reach all the way to the high ceiling, the wind blowing heavily, swirling from room to room, and I would rather dress warm than feel the air in this place go still.

Everything here is already so still. I find myself making reasons to create motion and noise. And, even then, for hours and hours at a time, this room will be entirely silent.

There are weeks I don't talk. When finally I do, I don't recognize the sound.

· · ·

Something in the ground is killing us. No one knows this for sure. But it's what people think. There are no mice or rats or roaches here. No cats or dogs. No animals other than the few thousand people spread across many miles.

The trees have died and the plants have died and the grass and shrubs and flowers of thousands and thousands of front yards and small parks are all brown now, crumbling, and slowly blowing away.

3

There are massive chemical and petroleum plants in the industrial zone to the west. You can't help but think this is part of what's driven away all life. Smokestacks and pipes raised to the sky. Beveled tanks and rusted cylinders. Storage pools now dry but coated in a substance somehow rubbery and wet and very faintly green. Substances you wouldn't ever want to touch.

When I walk through the industrial zone, I touch very little.

But the water in my hotel room is like all the water here, icy and brilliantly clear and it tastes like water from a stream, like a childhood memory of running through the woods and finding a stream you believe no one else has ever found.

Except that now, in this place, you can't help but think that the water tastes this way because of something that isn't supposed to be in it.

• • •

I enter the house through the front door. I've walked a long way tonight, in the dark, and I'm not entirely sure where I am. A few miles from my building. Like always I carry a flashlight and a compass, but rarely do I use them.

I flip light switches as I enter rooms, absently, a habit, wondering which houses and neighborhoods have power. Sometimes only parts of a house will work. The decay of this city moves room to room, wall to wall.

Eventually, though, it does seem that everything will finally turn off.

This house was left as it was lived in, dishes in the cabinets and magazines on the table in the living room. The doors are stiff to open, though, and there's dust across everything, thick in the flashes of the streetlight outside. It probably smells old and dank in here, but it's hard for me to know for sure. Everything these days smells old.

In the stairwell I see light from upstairs, cold white light from a streetlight nearby. There are photos on the walls of the stairway. Family and children, captured once in time. I have a thought that I should straighten the photos. But, after doing this a few times, I stop touching them.

4

The light above me enters through a dim window at the end of the upstairs hallway. The steps are wooden, loud under my feet, built of boards that seem to pop with every motion I make.

There is noise here, too, getting louder as I go upstairs. Not a noise in the house, but coming from outside, from above. Like a growing wind, but heavy. Heavy as a storm.

I turn a corner and see another stairwell, to a third floor, and the noise seems to come from there.

On the third floor I flip a switch on the wall and it lights the room like a forgotten daybreak, sudden and painful, and I flip the switch back off, my eyes blinded, the remnants of white and yellow still painful in my eyes.

In a minute, I can see the streetlight just outside a window, through white curtains pulled shut, and there is blue-white light as I move the fabric aside. The window is covered in some sort of filth, inside and out, an oily dust that lets light through, but blocks any distinct shapes or images.

The noise outside is loud, growing, and now I'd like to think that it's just a storm.

I step on something hard and there's a pop and there are voices. I nearly fall to the floor, ducking down, covering my head, light behind me, and it's a moment before I realize that the voices are on a television. A talking man. A woman sitting. I stare at the images like they are foreign and unknown. But they aren't. It's just that I haven't seen this in years. A news report, filled with talk of war in the desert and flooding along distant rivers and school failures in the suburbs, more images than I can process, words and colors I don't understand. But I know I don't need to understand. I know what they say is what they've always said, the news of dread and fear between bright commercial breaks, and I turn back to that window, wanting to see for sure what is making the noise, finding a wooden chair that, in a moment, I throw through the glass. Cold air blows into the room and the streetlight is brighter now, white across all I can see, and the noise outside drowns out the television, and I see now how I've made my way to the edge of this forgotten city, to the wall that marks its end, because I can see beyond the wall, down from the third story of this house into the massive highway, eight or ten or twelve lanes below me, filled with cars and trucks driving fast to some destination of their own and the roar of it all fills the room, one sound, wavering as it seems to peak.

It won't peak, though. The noise will just keep rising.

I see the body then. Next to me. In the white light of the broken window and the blinking blue of the TV. A body on a bed, lying still, just a few inches away. Blackened and sunken into itself, draped in clothes, a woman, looking like the skeletal remains of a fire that touched nothing but her flesh.

But there was no fire. Just time.

You don't see many bodies here. Most people move on before they die. This person, she may have made a choice.

Light from outside and the glow from the TV touch all sides of my body and I hear nothing but the highway and I keep staring at that dead woman, so very close to me, and I can't help but imagine her features.

After a few minutes, I touch her hand.

It's heavy and dry.

This is my apocalypse. My end that won't ever finish. The purgatory of a godless man, alone now, living here, in a city that's been abandoned.

It must be another twenty minutes before I manage to leave the room.

But it does not take long for the house to burn.

PART I

CHAPTER I

Years ago, I would walk into a house that I once owned, back on the south side of the highway. It was the house where we lived when the first of the children was born. The new owners hadn't changed the locks, even many years later, so my old key still worked. But someone finally found me, sitting in the kitchen. I didn't hear the man coming down the stairs. He recognized me. After a moment, he said I could stay for another minute, but then I would have to go.

But I couldn't stay. I told him I was sorry. I told him I would never come back. And I never have.

The worst part is waking up. I'll remember everything I had. Through most of the day, I am able to forget. But in the moments after I wake up, I will always have a second where I find myself remembering. Their faces and their movements, the smell of them before they went to bed. The sounds of their voices every time they would come home.

I came here to the abandoned North End less than a year after they died, returning to this place where I grew up. Where I was born forty-five years ago.

Five miles by ten miles, the North End of this city has nearly completely died. It started decades ago. The closing of dirty, aged factories. The migration from downtown to the suburbs. The rise of crime and the spread of homeless camps in vacant buildings and emptied warehouses. The failure of schools, police, the very streets we drove along. People kept moving away. The cycle, of abandonment and disrepair, it was the only thing growing stronger.

There were once more than a million people here.

Now, even the homeless have moved away.

For a time, there was an effort to tear down whole blocks of houses. The last-ditch effort of a city government that has since evaporated. The power and water and gas were shut off to some blocks. Bulldozers cleared the land. The remnants of the homes were hauled away to somewhere else in the North End. Left behind were the dying grass and a few dead trees, and the flat, concrete outline of a neighborhood.

Otherwise, nothing changed.

Most neighborhoods were left standing, though, even as they too were emptying of people. No buyers of the homes, the residents shut their doors and moved. Some houses still have their porch lights on. Years now they've been untouched.

• • •

There are many things here that you don't need to buy. There are abandoned stores that still have clothing and blankets and towels. There are matches and light bulbs and batteries in most any home or building. There is more here than those of us who are left could ever possibly use.

We get food from a small corner store a half mile from my hotel. It was probably once a liquor store. You enter through the front door and immediately there's a protected room, thick glass and heavy bars and a shallow slot through which you pass your money. The other side of the glass is piled very high with boxes. I can't make out the person on the other side. He or she is a shadow, a muffled voice. Taped to the window is a handwritten list of what's available for the week. Cans of food most of the time. Bread some weeks, just two or three slices in a small plastic bag. No fresh vegetables or fruit. No drinks. No milk or cheese. You say what you want and the person tells you what it costs and after you've slid your money through the slot, the person slides back the food you ordered.

Most days, they can't make exact change.

I don't really eat much. So none of this is a problem.

Outside the store, only the right side of the building is lit, the other side lost in darkness.

There is one last overpass crossing the wide, deep highway. It is the only way to get from here to the South End, where a million people now live. The other overpasses were closed, one by one, over time. Unsafe and crumbling, they are barricaded with concrete blocks and barbed wire on top of fences and signs that point anyone to turn away from here.

It's not clear what will happen if the last overpass is deemed unstable too.

The highway intersects with two other highways, which together mark three of the four borders of this large area known as the North End. The highways were built in straight, deep trenches, cutting through neighborhoods fifty years later, tall concrete walls added as sound barriers in the twenty years after that.

From my hotel room, I can see a few sections of the walls. But I can't see the vehicles down on the roadway.

The fourth border of the North End is the bay, far to the north, many miles away. I haven't been there since I was a child. There were parks there then and boats to rent, but over the years that area was given over to a port. Grain elevators and loading piers and massive fueling centers for the ships and barges that eventually stopped coming as this city died.

The water reaches into the city, though. Via a series of canals stretching down from the bay. Some canals are narrow as backstreets, others are wide, grand avenues of water, with ornate, block-long bridges crossing over them. Other canals run close to the houses, houses that have small docks leading from their back doors to the water. Still other canals are lined by old, wooden houseboats, ten and twenty stationary floating homes, many now slowly sinking into the cold water beneath them.

• • •

I see the police car turn onto the main boulevard when it's still a mile away. There aren't many cars here anyway, but this one is brightly white, the blue and yellow lights flashing, even though it drives very slowly as it makes its way downtown.

Car 4043, painted on the roof.

Some of the traffic lights still work, but the car moves steadily forward, ignoring them. The car crosses the small bridges over the canals, moving straight toward this building it seems, and I wonder for a moment if the police are trying to find me.

I don't think they'd have any reason to do so.

I watch them stop below my building, staring down at them through my binoculars as I lean my head partway out my open window. It's cold today, but not blowing hard. Even as high as I am, I can hear their radios, indistinct words buzzing out from the open car windows.

As they get out of the car and look around at the empty downtown, it's clear they had no idea that this all is here. They keep looking up, turning their heads, talking to one another across the roof of the car.

One is shaking his head.

Disbelief.

The other officer, a woman, is trying to use her cell phone. She presses buttons, holds the phone to her ear, then in a moment stares at it in her hand. It won't work here, but it will take her some time to realize.

I decide I should go down and talk to them.

When I push open the front door of my building a few minutes later, both police officers jerk their bodies, turning around to me, hands on their holstered guns.

I raise my hand. "It's all right," I say, and immediately I try to think of the last time I have spoken.

It's hard to imagine what I look like to them. My hair is long and I don't shave often. I'm wearing a wool blazer and a sweater underneath it and weathered jeans stained in many places. I look as if I'm a tired and worn college professor standing now as the sole survivor of a plague.

"It's all right," I say again, and as I walk forward they keep their hands on their guns.

It hurts my throat a bit to talk. Mostly I notice my lips and tongue, like they are new to me.

The officers are both so very young-looking. Fit, broad-chested, the man's hair closely cut and the woman's jaw seems tightly drawn. Sculpted.

No one here is young or well-groomed and if we're fit it's only in the sense that we are able to continue to survive.

The radio from the car continues to emit the buzzing drone of digitized voices. I see the cell phone in the female officer's hand. I point at it. "That won't work here," I say.

She glances at it. "Why?"

I point up. "The towers have all failed," I say. "Years ago."

It's been a full week since I have spoken. I remember the last words I said. To the person at the corner store. "Thank you," I said.

We stand here, the police officers and me, outside my building, staring at each other. The woman glances around, as if expecting other people to come out and speak to her.

"Do you need help?" the male officer asks me.

I shake my head. "No," I say. It's a moment before I think to say, "But I assume you do."

It has started to rain, very slightly, heavy but erratic drops hitting us here and there, as if a person in one of the buildings above us is throwing down small handfuls of water.

"Someone is missing," the female officer says. "A woman. She's gone missing. And her family thinks she might have come here."

"To this building?"

"To the North End," the man says.

"It's a big area," I say.

He nods. It's clear they had no idea how big an area this is.

"Have you ever been over here?" I ask.

They shake their heads.

"It's a big area," I say again.

We're silent. It seems as if they are unsure what to do or say. The script they usually follow in a missing persons case has unexpectedly slipped away from them.

"There's a newspaper here," I say. "If you have a photo, they will run it."

"Who reads the newspaper?" the woman asks.

"People who live here," I say.

"How many people live here?" she asks.

"Maybe a couple thousand," I say.

They both look around slowly. As if trying to see some of the other people I've mentioned. Wondering, I'm sure, if they are even now being watched.

Probably they are. Me as well.

"Why do you live here?" the male officer asks me, then raises a hand, shakes his head. He didn't mean to ask that out loud. It's just what's on his mind.

"This is where I grew up," I say.

"But why live here now?" the woman asks.

I think about this for a moment. "Do you want to give me some information about this missing woman?" I ask. "They'll put that in the newspaper too."

The woman reaches inside the car and pulls out a piece of paper. I step forward and she hands it to me. There's a black and white photo of a woman who's been crying and a brief description of her. It says she's forty. It gives her name and where she is from in the South End.

There's no explanation of why she is missing. No mention of why she might be here.

"Can we get your name and number in case we have more questions?" the male officer asks me.

I give him a name, not mine. "I don't have a phone," I say.

As they are getting in the car, the woman says to me, "Are you sure you don't need help?"

I shake my head.

She's still staring at me, from the mirror, as they drive away.

• • •

From a room on the other side of my building, I can see the South End at night. The glow of streetlights and homes and buildings and cars, shining upward, reflecting against the clouds, lighting them up with a dull, cold gray.

14

It's a view I only stumble on, not a view I want to see.

A million people living as if they had not abandoned this place where I still live.

• • •

I leave the missing woman's photo and description on a table in my hotel room. It's a week before I take it to the paper.

We move slowly here.

The police did not say she is in danger. They didn't say she is a murderer or a thief. They only said that she is missing. That her family wants her found.

Probably I only asked for the information because I work at the newspaper. Strangely, the paper still functions. It is only eight pages, printed once a week. I write every word and take every picture.

I do finally run the photo, after another week has passed, along with a short article noting that the woman is missing. That maybe she has come to the North End.

I wake up a few days later and find myself thinking that, as much as anything, I've run the article to give her a warning. *They are looking for you. They know you might be here.*

Maybe this woman wants a head start. Maybe she deserves it.

I've always assumed that lots of people here don't want ever to be found.

There are three of us who work at the newspaper. There is the old pressman in the basement who prints the paper and puts it out in the racks and boxes we still have around the North End. And the office manager who comes every day, but doesn't stay for more than a few hours. She is an older woman, probably fifty-five, though she often looks much younger.

Everyone in the North End seems to be a similar age. The people who are younger have aged from being here. The people who are older, maybe there's a way in which this place makes them seem healthier than otherwise they might be. They walk where they go. There is not the kind of food that would make you heavy or unhealthy.

There are, however, no children. I haven't seen a child since I arrived.

The office manager brings me my pay, every week, a small amount of cash in a stiff, gray envelope. It's not clear to me where she gets the money. But she also brings me things that make the office function, paper and pens and notebooks and folders. She brings these items in a brown paper bag that does not look like it came from a store. The pens don't look new. The paper is just a small stack, fifty or a hundred sheets, loose, not in a wrapper.

She brings black and white film for the camera, too, never more than one roll. I take pictures sparingly. We only get the chemicals to develop the film every few months, when the pressman goes to the South End to get the press supplies and the big rolls of paper we use for printing.

I take one picture every week of an old building or home in the area. I write a history of that structure, spending hours at the abandoned library researching the history of the building, its former tenants, its architecture, the history of the neighborhood where the house or building stands.

I write another article that covers some event that once happened in the North End. The opening of the port or the groundbreaking of a factory. Again I research it, both in the library and in the paper's archives.

This paper has been printed for over one hundred and fifty years.

I also write about the meeting, twice a month, of a commission who has responsibility for this area. The city government was disbanded, the area unincorporated nearly ten years ago. But we still fall in a county. The commission has so far been unable to let go of their responsibility for the North End, although they've tried to do so many times. The commission members meet in an old community center near the last overpass across the highway. They come in cars. They park close to the building. They talk for exactly an hour, spending very little of that time discussing what should be done for the North End.

Nothing that they talk about is ever acted on.

I'm not sure who owns this paper. Maybe the same family has owned it since it was first founded. There's no explanation in the paper. No owner who is listed.

For the most part, though, it seems this paper is like most everything in the North End—it is no longer owned by anyone.

And yet the newspaper is picked up and read by people who live here. I watch people take a paper from one of our old and beat-up racks or boxes. I see people outside our office, watching them through the dim and yellowed glass along the front of the building, taking a minute to read the front page of the paper they've picked up, then slowly walking away. There are three more boxes I can see from up in my hotel room and I've many times watched people take papers from each of those boxes too.

Always when people pick up a copy of the paper, they pause, standing still as they skim the front page for a moment. Every time.

It's as if they are looking for a specific thing. Maybe looking for some answer that, every week, the paper doesn't have. Or a next step they and everyone should take. A step that I have no idea how to find, articulate, or define.

• • •

From my room I stand watching the scavenging of buildings and homes and factories along the southern edges of the North End. Very slowly and methodically, the buildings and homes are being stripped of everything by the scavengers. Pipes are pulled from the basements. Aluminum gutters are pulled from the sides of buildings and homes. Copper wire is pulled from inside the walls.

As the North End began its final collapse—after the city government dissolved and services like schools and the police and the fire department were officially ended—heavy equipment was moved out of some factories, furniture was put on moving trucks, fire engines and police cars were, for the most part, driven away from their stations.

But, in the end, so much was left behind. People leaving their homes took only what they could afford to move. Some had the money to hire full moving services who could pack up and transport their things. But many could afford only to move what they could fit in their own car.

The scavengers, they don't come from other places. They live here. They are us.

17

We are slowly dismantling the remnants of our city.

The scavengers pile up what they find in the streets where they are working. Men and women arrive, driving beat-up panel vans and offering money for what has been scavenged. Some days there are two trucks, some days five or six. These brokers for the items sell these things to junkyards and other buyers in the South End. The brokers, all of them, also still live here in the north.

The scavenging is terrible and hard, slow work, and the people who do it—some days fifty of them, some days a hundred or two hundred—they are covered in filth when they leave these structures, hair and faces and shoulders turned gray from the dust, their hands blackened and bloodied even through their gloves.

Every few weeks, I go and watch them. Making notes for an article I will write for the paper. Taking pictures of the scavengers as they enter and leave a home or office or factory.

They look like miners emerging from a coal mine. Or firefighters leaving a burned-out home.

From the windows in my room, I can see where the scavengers have been. They've disrupted the landscape along the southwestern corner of this place, turning the edges of houses a barren white where the gutters have been pulled away. Leaving square, white spaces on the roofs of stores where the heating and air conditioning units have been pulled from their mounts.

They've scavenged whole neighborhoods. Entire factories and warehouses. A square mile or more and still they slowly move forward and how far they will go and what direction they'll take next is not clear.

There is, though, no longer any scavenging from the various abandoned stores throughout the North End. There was looting once. In the early days. But now, in the stores, people only take what they know they need.

I suppose there was a time when someone might have said that the things we take are not ours. But no one thinks that way anymore.

What we take we've clearly earned.

• • •

I type quickly on the typewriter, the sounds loud and steady, and sometimes as I sit here alone in this office finishing my stories, for a moment I'll think it is the sound of the typewriter that I'm creating, not the words in the stories themselves.

• • •

There aren't many ways to earn money here besides scavenging. It's hard for anyone to make or sell anything that the rest of us can't get for free.

But there are people who sell cooked food from a table set up near the corner store. Restaurants, in a way, without anywhere to sit.

None of it is very good.

People sell liquor, mostly liquor they seem to have found, a stray assortment of half-filled bottles, though a couple people sell harsh, homemade liquor from a still. The same with cigarettes, sold mostly in small bundles of three or five or ten, no thought given to the consistency of brands. They sell coffee, half-filled bags and cans they've found, sometimes sold as is, other times mixed together and sold in brown lunch sacks taped tightly into small and heavy blocks.

The vendors sell these things from their tables on the sidewalks near the corner store.

I can remember walking through cities many years ago, and always there was some man or woman on a street selling their paintings, their necklaces, drawings or bracelets they'd made. But here there is none of that.

Periodically, people set up a table of items of some distinction, items from homes but items that you wouldn't easily find. Books and music they've gathered. Fine cloth and containers of beads.

Not much of it sells. And the few valuables that the scavengers do find, electronics or tools or silver, are sold to the brokers in their panel vans.

Often, though, the scavengers seem to keep the jewelry they find. They wear many rings and bracelets and necklaces, so much jewelry that no one item is distinguishable from the rest.

19

The spoils of their work.

The vendors who sell things near the corner store only do so intermittently. They sell for a few days a week or a few days a month. Then they take what they make at their table and go to the corner store or to another table and spend that money on something else.

The small economy of the last survivors.

Many people, though, it's unclear how they make money. Maybe they simply have savings from when there was a city here. I've heard that some people regularly cross the overpass to the South End. They could get money from a bank there and return. It does not take much money to live here now. It would not take much in savings to survive in this place forever.

These are, also, the things I write about for the paper. The progress of the scavenging. The offerings of the vaguely functioning economy on the streets near the corner store. I let people know what food is for sale. I let people know what's being sold at the tables.

I never cross over to the South End.

• • •

I come upon the missing woman because, as is often the case, I can't manage to get warm.

Often, at night, I find myself wanting another blanket near my feet, a second pair of gloves on my bare hands. I am looking for blankets today. Searching through apartments in a building a few blocks from mine.

I wander down the long hallway, shoes kicking up dust from the wooden floors. There is trash in the hallway, a few broken chairs.

When I go looking for things in the apartments or houses, I have to make sure I'm not taking from someone who still lives here. It can be hard to know for sure, as most people live in such a bare and minimal way. An inhabited home can look like a home abandoned a decade or more ago. And so I have learned to look for simple signs. Food is the most obvious. Cleanliness another. An ordered space, a tidy room. A lack of dust and random debris. The few times I've accidentally gone into a house or apartment that was still being used, I saw some sign immediately. Two chairs pulled up to a clean table, the table cleared of everything except for a stack of napkins, a salt and pepper shaker, all arranged neatly together. A few books stacked carefully on a side table near a fireplace. The windows on the outside wiped clear of the gray and oily grime that otherwise coats this place.

These are the smallest signs of order, surprising in this place of forgotten chaos and disrepair. But these signs of some human need stand out, the base instinct to make sense of our surroundings, to create order in the devolving world in which we live.

Never have I walked in on anyone. Sometimes I think I know, can sense, when someone is actually near me. When they are behind a gate or door.

Probably, though, it's just the odds. There are enough homes and rooms here for the million people who once lived in this city. The chance of walking in on any of the few people left is very, very small.

I am trying doorknobs as I walk through this apartment building. Most are locked. But the doors that are open, most are for apartments that have already been gone through, years ago it seems, the apartment strewn with boxes and a broken picture and glass shattered across a living room floor. But all of it is covered in dust.

Whoever damaged this place, they did it back in time.

The hallway comes to a turn. In the corner, I see water, dripping down from the molding along the ceiling, clear water following a long-stained brown path. It rained hard last night. This is the tenth of fifteen floors. The rainwater, even hours later, still finds its way through the cracks and seams of this old structure. The buildings here bleed water when it rains, perforated as they are by cracks and breaks and holes, the water coming down from the roofs, in some places rushing, in some places dripping, the water for days after the heavy rain still making its way through ceilings and stairwells and the walls themselves.

I reach out toward the wall, lightly touching the water with the very tips of my pale fingers.

"Hello," a voice says, and I jerk in place, step back. Turn my head.

She says again to me, "Hello."

She's twenty feet away, standing in the hallway on which I was about to turn.

I nod. In my mind, I answer her. Then I realize I haven't spoken. I say, "I'm just looking for a blanket."

The voice, mine, is once again unfamiliar.

She nods. "I think I have one." She has brown hair and her eyes in the dim light seem black, colorless, and the way she moves I think she is probably very strong. "Yes," she says. "Sure. I can bring you a blanket."

I stare at her. It's a moment and I shake my head. "No, not like that. I can find one. Somewhere else."

I take a step backward, toward the hallway I was on.

It takes me another moment to realize this is the woman the police are looking for.

She still stands in her hallway, in the middle. Arms at her side. She wears a heavy, black wool coat. Boots. Her brown hair is pulled off her face. As she talks, there are thin wisps of mist.

For a moment, I'm struck by the fact that it is cold for her here too.

Again I realize I've said something only in my mind. "Thanks," I say now. "For the blanket. The offer."

She nods.

I say to her, "Do you read the newspaper?"

She stares. Confused. "What?"

"Do you read the newspaper?"

She glances down, then looks over her shoulder. She says, "Not lately."

Down the hall, behind her, I see a child stick his face out from a doorway. Once more, I step backward.

"My son," she says. She's walking to him, glancing at me over her shoulder. Nervous, protecting. Instinct here, safety. Let nothing bad now happen.

"There is a newspaper here," I say. "You should find it. The paper. One from a month ago. It'll be in the library."

She waves her son back into the apartment. But he doesn't move. The woman turns to me and nods. "Okay."

We're quiet a moment. I'm thinking very slowly. No grounding in what I might say. "They're looking for you," I tell her. "Here. In the North End."

She seems to gnaw her lip.

We're thirty feet apart now. She is standing near the opening to the apartment.

"The paper is in the library," I say again. "It doesn't include much detail. Just says that the police think you are missing."

She nods. Gnawing her lip, I think. I hear the water from the molding, behind me, dripping from the ceiling to the floor.

The boy, maybe eight years old, he stares straight at me. He's a portrait to me, of a boy staring plainly forward.

I still can't seem to think right. Thoughts come to me slowly, shapes turning into words, forming sentences in my mind. I think to shake my head, visibly, so she'll see me do it. "The police," I say. "The article. None of it mentioned a child."

I step back again, accidentally pressing myself against the wall. The water is already soaking through to my hip and the back of my thigh.

"I don't need to have seen you here," I say, awkwardly. I have to pause. "I'm just looking for a blanket."

I turn and leave, walk down the hall.

I touch the rainwater that still spreads across my leg.

There are no children in the North End. I've never seen a child on the street. I've never once seen a sign that one might be here.

I think to myself that I like this.

Seeing children would make the emptiness only that much more apparent.

• • •

The best way to burn down a house is to light on fire the steps leading up from a darkened basement. It does not take much effort. Usually there's a gas can or paint thinner in a shed out back or in the basement itself. The basements are often filled with forgotten boxes of books, plastic toys that were never discarded, old wooden cribs covered in dust and basement grime.

Pile these on top of each other, or just push them close together, and they will burn very easily. The fire will grow steadily in the shallow windows of the basement, soon spreading up the wooden basement stairs, now cutting holes in the floor of the living room and kitchen.

And once the furniture is burning, the fire will move fast throughout the first and second floors.

I always check the houses to make sure they do not have natural gas coming into them. Gas like that, when it's lit, it can go off like a bomb.

And I don't want to light off a bomb. I wouldn't like the suddenness. The anxious waiting for the explosion.

I don't like loud noises at all.

Instead, I want for the fire to, very slowly, build.

• • •

There are days when I sleep so much it's as if I'm very sick, waking every few hours like an ill man with a fever. Turning, shifting on my couch, thinking I will get up. Thinking that I should.

But I fall back asleep before I'm able to stand. The cold air from the open windows in my living room blows across the thick socks on my feet and I know that I could tuck them under this heavy, rough blanket or that I could stand, pushing my feet and legs free from the couch where I am lying. But again I find myself asleep. The rain falls and some of it sprays on the windowsill, even the table near the wall. I see this through half-open eyes, face pressed heavily against a thick pillow, and the water will sometimes seem to reach as far as me, a stray drop hitting my cheek or my hand as I hold the blanket. Then I'll realize a drop could not travel that far, or maybe it can and I wonder what will happen in this room if everything gets wet, and again I'll be asleep, lost in a heavy and circular dream that makes sense only for a moment, when, hours later, I finally wake up, dulled and heavy and confused.

I wonder for a moment why that woman and the boy came to the North End. But I know that people sometimes pass through here on the way to somewhere else. They have for years. I assume the woman and boy will too.

Somewhere in the building, a phone is ringing.

I lie there, listening to it. Ten times, maybe twenty, and then it stops. A wrong number. Or the call of someone who has not been in touch for many, many years.

. . .

There is, of course, the question of why it is I choose to stay here. Why I chose to come back to this place at all.

I can say that I find comfort in the isolation.

I can say that I find comfort in my removal from the world.

I can say that I have no idea how long I will stay.

I can say that I wish none of this, none of what brought me here, I wish none of it had ever happened.

I can say there was a family, mine, and all of them are gone.

CHAPTER 2

When someone dies in the North End, there is a funeral. Many people attend. It is our only communal act. There are really no other reasons to gather in a crowd.

There is a church downtown that still has a minister, an older man who I see sometimes near the corner store or near the church itself, where he sweeps the wide steps leading up to the church's entrance. The minister holds services each Sunday and from my windows I can always see a few people making their way to the church in the morning.

When there is going to be a funeral, the minister brings a notice to the paper, which I print on the front page. A short announcement listing the name of the person who has died and the time of the funeral service.

Often, a few hundred people attend, far more than ever go to a Sunday service. Far more than the dead person could have possibly known here.

There are bibles and hymnals in the long wooden pews of the church, but the minister doesn't have us open them. He is a small, thick man who stands at the front of the vast sanctuary, the dead body before him enclosed in a very simple casket on the wide altar, the minister reading from notes he himself has written. This is a Catholic church, but he is not a Catholic. His notes, they come from many religions. Christian and Muslim and Jewish and Hindu. He'll mention Buddha. He'll mention the Greek gods. Roman.

The group always sings a hymn we all know from childhood.

The group always stands at the end of the service, spread out among the pews, silent for a full minute.

Even here, there is something strange in the unexpected depth of the silence of a crowd.

The group always follows as the casket is carried out of the large sanctuary. The crowd stands on the steps of the church, watching as the casket is slid into an old hearse, the minister saying a last thought, a prayer of sorts, not specific, speaking toward all of us on the steps. Then he gets in the hearse and drives the body away.

What he's said is not important. He emphasizes this. What matters, he says, is the process. The gathering. The continuation of a ritual.

The group watches the car drive off. It is very quiet. Not silent, people do talk. But not many, and not loudly.

And then everyone walks away, leaving in many different directions. Returning to their homes or to their scavenging or to the corner store to get that week's food. A few hundred adults, some very old, some younger than me, half men, half women, white or black or Hispanic or Middle Eastern or Asian. We wander off. Few say good-bye.

It's hard not to do the math, to realize that every funeral marks a diminishing of our numbers. Enough of these deaths and, finally, no one will live here at all.

• • •

The network of canals and levees that stretches from the bay to the center of the city was world-renowned when it was built many decades ago.

Now those same levees are slowly collapsing, the water they release steadily pushing toward downtown.

To build them, city leaders brought in engineers from countries an ocean away to lay out a plan that would allow the North End to grow. Many square miles were reclaimed from the water. The industrial zone expanded massively as barges were now able to unload raw materials directly at the factories where they would be used, manufactured products immediately loaded onto other barges along the docks.

I write about this, again, for the paper.

Along the canals, apartments were built. Wooden houseboats gathered in long rows, soon forming tightly knit communities. Bridges were constructed, each more ornate than the next, stone and steel, and some include tall stanchions that still stretch upward in sweeping and unnecessarily grand arches, bridges that were celebrated upon completion for their beauty more than their utility.

Yet as the city expanded into the suburbs in the South End and began, more and more, to neglect the north, these same bridges and the canals they crossed and the series of levees that made most of the North End possible, all of them began to crumble and decay.

Ultimately, the repairs to these structures were deemed too expensive to undertake.

Ultimately, the repairs were part of what drove the last of the city's leaders to encourage even faster growth in the South End over any commitment to the north.

That most of the North End was built below sea level did not seem to enter into this decision.

That those same decaying levees hold back water that could flood many square miles of homes and buildings and factories was, for the most part, entirely ignored.

The water in all the canals looks very still. But if you get close, leaning down, you see that it moves steadily, circulating through the canals, moving from here near my hotel to the bay far to the north.

At night now, from my room, I can sometimes hear a levee north of me give way. There is a grinding crash, the rushing sound of water, all of it echoing up into the dark night sky, reaching me where I stand some long seconds later, the millions of gallons of water already having covered fifty more acres of the North End.

Homes, maybe, or just streets. Maybe a long-abandoned park.

The newly released water flows unbound until it reaches the next levee, caught there, stopped. The system was built to compensate for storms and rising water and emergency disasters.

But even as the echoing sound of that newly broken levee dissipates into the night around me, the water that has just been released is already putting greater pressure on the next levee in the system, this levee too some decades past its last round of maintenance or repair.

Someday, every levee around us could give way. Each collapse of one levee builds pressure on the others, so while the breaks now happen only every few months, they are inevitably becoming more frequent, so that the whole North End could finally be flooded, neighborhoods and roads and stores submerged, only the utility poles and streetlights and tall office buildings rising out of the water, structures that, ultimately, might also be washed away, eroded and knocked down and drowned one by one, until finally this city would only be a footnote to the bay, waves running endlessly across this place where we all lived.

· · ·

Alone in the vast city library, I often find myself asleep. There are long leather couches in the main reading room, an old, high-ceilinged atrium with tall windows looking out at the downtown buildings nearby. The ceiling arches upward, three or four stories high, covered in tile and gilded molding and paintings of the stars and the gods their patterns form, all of it spread across the apex of that high, domed ceiling.

It's cold here. A year ago I finally brought a few blankets from my hotel, which I store in a drawer in a desk near the periodicals. Most days, I need to have the blankets over me even to sit at one of the long tables and take notes from the history texts and bound books of public records.

Eventually, I find myself lying on the couch in the main reading room, staring up at that high ceiling, wrapped heavily in the wool blankets, using my jacket as a pillow and finally covering my head with my arms as I fall asleep.

A few sections of the library were trashed at some point. The books pulled off the shelves, cards dumped out of the old card catalog. The kids' section is the worst of it, books thrown everywhere, graffiti on the murals of farm scenes and fairy princesses and castles with dragons and knights.

Most of that sort of damage here in the North End happened in the final months before everything collapsed, when people staged a last and unorganized fight against an end we now know to be inevitable. When there were still a few police cars, a city mayor that claimed to be in control, residents angry at the loss of their jobs and their schools and any shred of value in the homes they had long owned. When this place still had the pretense of being governed, then there was something against which to rebel. That's when a few storefronts were broken, when some looting occurred, when teenagers ran wild through schools and the library, throwing books and desks against the walls.

But when the city government collapsed, when everyone finally walked away from responsibility, then the destruction and rebelling all soon came to an end. The angry people loaded up and quickly moved away. The few who did remain, they simply closed their doors in silence. Like animals in the forest going limp in the jaws of a predator. Freeing themselves from a certain death. Wounded maybe. Lame. But alive.

I wake up on the couch in the library.

It's a few more minutes before I push the blankets off me.

The water still runs in the bathrooms here, and I drink long from the cold, fresh stream that pours brightly into the heavy porcelain sink, thinking again about the chemical plants and factories that I write about each week, the mountains of toxins that were knowingly, openly released over so many decades. Wondering, again, which of those elements might have invaded the water supply. Which might be seeping into it right now.

I rinse my face with the icy water, trying to wake up. I wet my head to the scalp, pushing the hair away from my face and eyes.

I look at myself for more than a moment. Maybe because I still feel half asleep. My hair is almost to my shoulders, brown, although there is also gray now, and the lines near the corners of my mouth and the lines under my eyes have all gotten deeper.

I tell myself I should shave soon.

Another hour at the desk in the main reading room and I have all the research I need for my article on an herbicide and pesticide plant. Dates of the ground-breaking, statistics on the volume of material produced during peak production. I use my camera to take pictures of a few old photos from the 1930s, portraits of men and women and small children among the piles of dry, dusty chemicals being loaded into railcars and onto barges along the docks on the forgotten bay that borders the far edge of the North End. There are a very few articles about the potential dangers of the chemicals used and produced at the plant. Articles based on the complaints by then neighbors of harsh migraines and constant flu, of kids with asthma, of senior citizens with a dry and endless cough.

Those articles are from the 1970s. The plant stayed open for another thirty years.

Before I leave, I go to the stacks of newspapers near the table where I work and place a copy of the most recent newspaper on the shelf. I do so every week. This paper has been published for one hundred and fifty years. Every copy has gone into the archives of this library. Microfilm and digital versions were also saved here before the library closed, and old printed papers are filed away in the vaults deep down in the basement.

The recent papers I bring here, I stack them up, organizing each one by date.

Even now, I need some sense of continuity. A sense of purpose greater than what I've done today or yesterday. It's a human need, I think now. One that even I have not been able to leave completely in the past.

• • •

Trash is picked up every other week. One man, in a large garbage truck, still makes his way through the North End. I leave money in an envelope that's taped to the side of the trash can I put out in front of my hotel. The pressman, he does the same with the trash can from the newspaper. Direct taxation, at a rate undefined but apparently deemed fair. The trash collector has never complained. When I see him driving his truck along the street, he nods toward me. Raises his hand to wave.

• • •

In a place that should be overrun with rats and roaches, with stray dogs and feral cats, there are none. I walk along the avenue leading from downtown to the industrial zone wondering what has killed or driven off all animals from the North End.

Trees, thirty feet tall and black now, are planted in strict order along the avenues and main boulevards leading into and out of downtown. None of them bloom or grow anymore and some have fallen over, tumbling part way, leaning to the side, their massive roots exposed, black now too, and as I walk I touch my hand against each tree. The trunks are smooth, almost slick, as if they've been varnished and preserved.

It's a vision of a quiet Armageddon, or an emptied wasteland following a chemical attack.

But this is only the wasteland of abuse and inattention.

Ahead of me I can see the vast and rusted warehouses and factories of the industrial zone. I'm headed for the plant that once made herbicides and pesticides, the largest of its kind until it closed. The last of the factories to shut down.

It's the plant I'm writing about in this week's paper.

Some days, when the wind blows hard enough, the dust of old chemicals rises up into the air, thin clouds of it spreading carefully across the buildings and streets and homes of the North End.

But this is not one of those days.

I carry my notebook and my old camera and an extra roll of film in my jacket pocket. The old factories, the empty buildings and skyscrapers downtown, the vast neighborhoods of houses built as many as one hundred and fifty years ago, these form some interest for me. I am not entirely sure why.

Maybe I hope to find some answer in these now emptied places, a solution to the question of how this city, the few people left, me one of them, how is it that we all ended up like this. How it is that we all chose to live here nonetheless.

Maybe it simply gives me something on which to focus.

It's another two miles to the chemical plant. But I can see its faded smokestack, red once but now more gray than colored against the clouds in the sky. I'll take a few pictures. I'll write notes about what I see. I'll head back to the library where I can research more about the factory. I'll find more articles that were written, these about the costs to clean up the decades of damage the chemicals did to the site itself. Costs that ultimately led the owner to shut that factory down, to bankrupt the company before, in just a few days' time, he deserted the wreckage he and his family had spent so long creating.

• • •

Near my hotel, a flatbed truck drives slowly, eight or ten scavengers riding on the smooth, heavy timbers that line the truck's open bed. Some sit with their feet dangling over the sides of the wooden platform, others are pushed up against the back of the cab. Their faces are pale white from gypsum dust, their hair streaked with paint of too many colors. The scavengers stare at me, one nodding as they pass, another now standing, leaning her head back and stretching her arms out to the side as she stares straight up into the sky, stretching or praying or asking for help or for forgiveness, no one explains which it is.

• • •

I can hear the boy in the library. The noise of children is unmistakable. Even when they are trying to be quiet. Maybe even more so.

I wake up on the couch in the atrium. It takes a moment to get out from under the blankets, to wake up and focus on the sound of the boy. I walk toward the children's section of the library.

It's very cold today, though not as cold as it was in the morning. Midday now and light comes in through high windows all along the halls and rooms of the building and even though it is not sunny, the light makes the air less harsh and biting.

The boy is running through the bookshelves in the children's section. He makes sounds as he runs, quiet explosions and muffled gunshots. He has brown hair like his mother, but his is dense and curly.

The woman stands up, quickly, her back straight.

I say to her, "It's okay." In a moment, I say, "Sorry."

I'm not sure why I'm sorry. My voice sounds very foreign. Maybe a week since I've last spoken. Since the minister brought a notice to the paper.

Yes, leave it there.

The boy circles around some chairs, coming up next to his mother. He has her eyes, colorless, almost black. He's watching me.

It seems like he is less nervous than she is.

She says, "You mentioned the library." She pauses. "A couple weeks ago."

I nod. "Did you find the paper?" I ask.

"No."

I turn partway. "It's over here."

I realized I have paused. Then I start to walk. It's another moment before I hear them follow. I glance back. They are both carrying backpacks, his a small one, bright blue and red with a pair of gloves attached to one of the straps and a water bottle tied to the other. The boy wears jeans and small boots like a hiker would wear and a black fleece jacket that is zipped up to below his chin. He moves to the left and right of his mother as we walk, crossing easily underneath tables and looping once or twice around sets of shelves.

The hallway is relatively free of trash. There is the layer of dust, though, and with the light coming through the high windows, I can see dust in the air, a million brilliant sparkling fragments, each briefly frozen still in the air around us and, for a moment, I forget to breathe.

"Here," I say, stopping at the shelves holding the newspapers.

The woman's brown hair is pulled off her face, and she wears clothes similar to the boy's, jeans and boots but with a black wool jacket buttoned up to her chin, and it's impossible for me to know if she's distinct looking or attractive or somehow different, because here, in a place so lifeless and cold, the people have all grown nondescript in the always fading light.

She is scanning the stacks of newspapers.

"It's there," I say, pointing to a lower shelf. "In the middle."

She picks it up, the sound of paper rattling, sheets rubbing together as she holds up the newspaper. I move to the other side of a table.

"Inside," I say. "Third page."

She glances at me.

"I wrote the story for the paper," I say. "I write all the stories."

She blinks and it seems to me that it's the first time I've seen her blink.

"I guess it could seem strange," I think to say out loud, "that I'd know this much about an article. An article about you."

I look around for my table and walk to it. I take a drink of water, then another. The boy is watching me from a table near his mother. He sits down in a chair, his backpack on the floor next to him.

The article is very short and says very little. Just what the police had told me. That there is a woman missing. That she might have come to the North End.

In the picture, she looks quite different. Her hair surrounds her face, long and sticking out from her head, and she looks like she has just woken up or is sick or is on drugs. A mug shot, almost, but it's not.

In the picture, she is crying.

She spends a lot of time reading the article. I wonder for a moment if she doesn't read well. But then I figure that she's just thinking. About what it means that they are looking for her. About what she might decide to tell me.

"I don't need any information," I say, awkwardly. "I mean, you don't have to tell me anything."

She nods, even though she's still looking at the paper in her hands. She starts to fold it up again.

"I thought we would be safe here," she says, quietly, staring toward the boy.

I can't help but glance at the boy when she's said this. He seems unchanged. He knows, it seems, about whatever it is that might make them unsafe. I would have thought she wouldn't talk this way in front of him.

But I realize, of course, that it is obvious to him they are in danger. Of course it is.

"You can be safe here," I say to her. "This is a place where it is very easy to hide."

She is looking at me.

"I'm sorry I put that article in the paper," I say. "But I had to. The paper," I start and can't quite find a way to say it right. "The paper has to do those things. It has to cover what is happening."

She glances toward the table where I had been working. "We shouldn't be bothering you," she says. "You're busy. We'll go."

"And," I say, "I think I wanted to put the article there as a warning."

She watches me as I move along my table, then lean back against the edge. In a moment, she blinks again. "Thank you," she says. "We should go. Let you work."

I shake my head, now responding to what she said before. "It's not my library," I say. "It's still here for everyone."

She glances toward the boy and he gathers his backpack, swings it over his shoulder.

"Thank you," she says again and they are gone.

I wait, staring toward the hallway they went down, the light once more catching the million flecks of dust held in the air around me, this time the dust all moving, slightly, a wind I can't feel, so slowly moving the dust in one direction.

Then I go over to the shelf of newspapers and move the paper she'd been reading back to its proper pile.

• • •

I shower in cold water, in the high-ceilinged bathroom in my hotel. The room is dimly lit, with only a small lamp on the floor near the sink. It's often like showering in the dark, the cold water sourceless, just a spray, wet and nearly icy all around me.

I wash myself, every part of my body. My thick hair is tangled some, and it takes effort to wash it, effort to shave off whatever thin beard has grown across my face.

I don't feel cleaner after showering, though. I feel only like I've done something I'm supposed to do.

I dry off and dress in clothes I wash in a washer that works in a utility room down the hall.

It can take me hours to get warm after showering. I will often have to get under the blankets on my couch, fully dressed, under layers of heavy bedding, head covered, hands tucked between my legs, shivering and breathing hard.

And still I can't get warm.

• • •

Two weeks have gone by and it is time for the commission to meet at the community center near the highway. It takes half an hour to walk there, but still I get there early, taking one of the hard wooden seats in the back of the big room, notebook and pencil in my hands.

Only seven of the thirteen members of the commission show up. Most of the seven mention more than once how they are under a court order to hold this meeting. It's another reference to their clear desire not to be here. Not to have this responsibility. Not to want to deal with this doomed area separate from the South End, where they all now live.

Men and women, black and white and brown, yet they all look the same. Interchangeable public figures making vaguely circular, clearly noncommittal statements. They sit at a long table on a stage at the front of the room. I have to follow the conversation very carefully just to take accurate notes on who says which empty words.

Fewer than ten people who actually live here are sitting in the audience. Each sitting alone, spread across the two hundred or more chairs. They don't say anything. There's a sense of acceptance among the people living here. A resignation to our fate or an embracing of our circumstances, I don't know for sure.

In the years since I came back, I've heard few people here complain.

But there was a time when people fought with this commission and with the city council before that. A time when citizens wrote letters and filed lawsuits and held protests at government buildings and yelled from the audience during massive public meetings.

Asking what would be done. Saying their neighborhoods were being destroyed. Screaming that they were losing everything they had.

But nothing changed. The end still came.

Now, no one speaks from the audience. It is, after all, not like we can't leave. These people on the stage, they have not forced us into staying.

"I'm sorry, but if we finally convinced the courts to let us turn off the power and the gas and all of the utilities," says one of the commissioners on the stage at the front of the room, "I'm sure that everyone would then, finally, vacate this area."

Another commissioner shakes his head. "I don't think it will work to turn off the utilities," he says. He stares out at the people in the seats, looking at us as if we don't know he's there. As if he watches us on a video screen or sits behind a one-way mirror. "I don't think they'll ever leave," he says.

The few people in the audience stare blankly at him. Listening.

Still I'm not sure why.

But we do in fact fear that the power will be turned off. No one pays for what they use. Only court orders from many years ago keep the power on. And court orders can be changed.

And we do also know that the power comes from heavy lines that span the highway, towers that could one day simply crumble and fall over.

Maybe that is why people listen.

I take notes for another half an hour. The discussion ranges from the debts the North End incurred to the cost of removing the final overpass to the success the commissioners claim they've had in shutting down failed neighborhoods in the South End.

But there is no money, the commissioners all eventually admit. Even to cut off what does remain.

There is one commissioner who has not spoken. Her dark hair is pulled back tightly and she wears a gray jacket and white blouse, the nondescript aura of a business executive. "It's not just that there is no money," she says now. "There is, among us sitting on the stage and among the people in the South End who have forgotten about this place and among even the people living here, including the few of them sitting in this room, there is not just an absence of money. There is an absence of will. Desire. Need. And without those things," she says, sitting forward, "this place will not ever change. Accept that. Because without it, this is how life here will always be."

• • •

Sometimes I'll see beyond the curtained window of a house the bright and shifting glow of a television screen. I'll see antennas and small dishes on the roofs of homes I walk past.

It's strange to me that people here would watch television. Or listen to the radio stations that it's also possible to pick up. I can't imagine wanting to be reminded that there is a world outside this place.

If you wanted to be part of the world, why would you be here?

Some old phones work, landlines that I hear ringing in a house along a street or in a room somewhere in my building. I hear the sound of alarm clocks too. Randomly going off, a loud and steady beeping emanating out from a darkened home.

I find the ringing quite disturbing. Abrasive in how it intrudes on the isolation of this place. I hate the silence of the North End greatly, but the ringing, I hate that more.

It's like the sound of the smoke detectors, a faint and intermittent beep from a house I pass or from a room somewhere in my building. The warning sound of a battery that has finally started to die.

• • •

I've stopped in front of an old brick hospital after leaving the newspaper's office, a massive structure just four stories high but covering two city blocks. I don't enter. I just stand. The hospital was looted heavily when it was closed, addicts and criminals and kids of all ages searching every crevice of every room for any sort of drugs.

But I don't enter, don't go looking at the scene of chaos and destruction. I trust what I've been told.

It is the hospital where they all were born. Where I was born. Where she was too.

I don't enter the double doors.

I don't move from where I stand.

I don't shiver in the wind that blows or the rain that falls across me.

I just stand as, overhead, near the bottom of the thick blanket of clouds, a large jet flies slowly, silently above me. Visible but too far away to possibly be heard.

• • •

Most nights, I allow myself one drink. Late, in the darkness of my hotel room, the living room lit if at all by the distant light of the South End reflecting off the layer of clouds. When the clouds are low enough, it's as if I live in the sky itself, suspended here, miles above the surface of the world.

The air blows through the room, windows pulled open from the top and bottom of the frames. I stand at the window with a blanket wrapped around my shoulders, knuckles tucked tight under the edges of the wool.

I see shapes in the clouds. Houses and ships and flowers. Never once the same shape, but each time I look, I see them.

I sip my way slowly through my drink. Some sort of liquor I've bought from one of the vendors near the corner store.

It would be easy to drink too much here. It would be tempting to drink any time of day. It's not a struggle to resist this. But it is something about which I do remind myself. That I could lose myself completely. Not just to drinking. I could lose myself to this place. I do not have to work and I do not have to leave this room and I could lie down on this couch with a drink, all day, drink easily, drink steadily, and let myself think of nothing.

Let yourself forget.

I don't, though. I haven't yet.

Instead I stare out at the sky, at the layered and rippling clouds barely lit by the few lights below me and the clouds so slowly shifting in their shape and distant colors, moving south, rolling steadily to the south.

I take a sip. Stare.

I think only about how much they would have loved this part of being here.

. . .

In the morning, I find a dead man.

There is a playground along the base of my building. In the daytime, I can see it, from above, if I lean out my open window, face into the wind, feeling very much like I am about to fall. From that view it looks like merely the schematic of a playground, the swing set and monkey bars and a winding brick path circling through the structures, the path lined intermittently by black park benches and a stone water fountain.

The boy is down there playing, his mother sitting on the ground nearby.

Even from this twentieth floor, I can see that the trees and bushes are all dead. Branches black and shiny, a few dry leaves still clinging to spindly twigs. The grass on the ground is brown and dry and frozen in place. From above it only looks like the drawings of a plan, the intention of greenery within a representation of a park.

The boy swings, doubling his body over to swing back, kicking his legs out to push forward, again and again until finally he jumps off, floating, spinning his arms for balance, landing and he's already at a run, heading to the monkey bars where he climbs to the very top, standing, balancing, still, and now he slides down the iron pole to the ground and then to the seesaw where his mother waits.

Then he does it all once more.

With my binoculars I can see that she is barely smiling. Watching the boy. Never taking her eyes off of him.

There's a brick wall around much of the playground. I assume that the wind does not blow so much in there. That it is almost warm.

It's now that I see the body. On the ground. Outside the walled playground. Not far from where the boy is playing. A man, sprawled forward, one hand reaching out, face pressed down into the pale ground.

It's as if he died trying to reach the playground just thirty feet away.

There are sometimes dead people in the houses here in the North End. But not dead people in the streets. Not dead people on the ground.

The boy still plays, the woman watching him, both of them on the other side of the brick wall. If I close my eyes, I can hear the boy as he screams, laughing, the steel hinges of the swing a creaking squeal that lifts upward even through the wind.

I will go down when they have left. I will find the minister and get him to help me with the body. I will write an article in the paper. I will write that there has been a death. I will take a picture of his face.

I will document everything I see.

But for now I only know that I find myself watching that boy play. How he runs and jumps from slide to swing, how he crawls across the ground and leaps up onto the seesaw with his mother, screaming as he laughs and it's impossible for me to look away. Or to even move.

• • •

I am standing near the playground, looking down at the dead man at my feet.

Only after the woman and the boy left, the two of them walking out the entrance on the other side from where the body lies, in a minute disappearing from my view, only then did I go downstairs.

The body lies on its chest on what used to be a grassy field. It's dry, pale dirt now, and looking close the dirt seems almost to move, grains of dust and tiny pebbles rattling in the cold wind that blows steadily across everything near me.

There are small pebbles driven into the dead man's hands from when he fell. Blood, almost black now, is spread across the side of his head and ear, the pale dirt turned purple in a wide circle where the blood has soaked into the ground. It looks like he hit his head when he fell.

I stand over him, staring down. The silence of the North End can be total.

I know I will have to touch him.

This is what you do. You make sure the body's dead.

But instead I am thinking about them.

There were the six of us. Our own ruckus, we would say. Our own party wherever we were.

Four children, eight, nine, nine, and ten years old. Two boys, two girls, and I hear them now, in my mind. I hear them playing, each sound of them bouncing toys off the walls, and the sound of a board game being spread across a large wooden table, and the sound of laser beams and gunfire as they chase each other out the door. I hear each step across the upstairs floor. Each roar as they come inside from the backyard.

I hear each of their separate voices. The way they say their words. The way one pauses after each sentence, how another races as she speaks.

And I hear the sound of smoke detectors, all of them at once, as if the fire was nowhere and then everywhere in just a second.

In truth that fire spread. Even though we didn't hear it. Didn't know it till it was everywhere.

Of course that fire spread. Of course it took some time.

We just didn't know it.

We managed to fail to realize.

I managed. I failed. I only realized when the fire was already everywhere.

Because from the couch, where I had fallen asleep, I knew suddenly that the rest of the house was completely wrapped in flames.

I close my eyes again. Still standing over that dead body.

The dust on the ground blows lightly, rattling in place.

I am haunted by the echoes of violence, a constant sense that there is a nearby place where everyone, right now, is screaming.

I open my eyes. Lean down. Press my hand against the back of this man's body.

It's hard and still. Dead.

I'll burn down a house tonight. I know that this must happen. And as I watch that house begin to burn, I will as always find myself counting slowly.

The seconds the fire takes to spread from room to room.

The seconds it would take to get out of there and not die.

CHAPTER 3

A smell like sulfur blows through the windows of my room. It's been blowing since yesterday, the smell having risen as I walked from the newspaper to the library, and a full day later it hasn't dissipated at all.

It's a week since I found the body.

The funeral is today. The article in the paper came out a few days ago. *A dead man was found near the center of the North End.*

The picture of his bloated, misshapen face runs three inches by four inches on the cover.

His eyes, in black and white, stare vacantly upward and away.

It is the minister who tells me that the cause of death is not clear.

"Heart attack," he says, almost to himself. "Tripped and hit his head. Maybe someone pushed him down," he says, glancing at me with a slight, strange smile. "Who knows?"

We are standing in the basement of the church. The body lies on a wooden table, a white sheet pulled over it.

"Sometimes," the minister says, "I can figure out the cause of death for certain."

I ask him in a moment, "How?"

The minister glances at me. He has a density to him, the minister. The thickness of his chest, his slightly shortened arms and legs. I realize for the first time that he's Hispanic. That he is roughly my age. I'd thought he was much older.

He is looking down at the body. "I was a mortician," he says. In a moment he says, "I still am."

The fluorescent light overhead reflects pale, cold blue off the sheet covering the body. The minister's profile is pale as well, his skin turned almost green. He keeps his black hair cut close to his head, wears a black sweater and black pants.

"You're not a minister," I think to say.

He shakes his head. Smiles slightly. "Not by training."

The two of us are quite sure the dead man is not from the North End. The minister knows many people here. Knows the scavengers and brokers and vendors near the corner store. He comes to most commission meetings and he gets around the North End.

"Making myself available," he says, still looking down at the body. "That's what I do. And I've never seen this man."

I realize the minister acts like he knows me, yet we've only spoken when he's dropped a notice of a service at the paper. But, I guess, this is just his way.

Now, on the steps of the church, a crowd has gathered quietly for the funeral. Two hundred or more. Most of them have come alone, though there are some people who arrive together. There are a few couples, older people, who help each other up the steps. Some of the crowd is fresh from scavenging, twenty men and women with their clothes and hands and faces turned chalky white from the work they've been doing that morning and the previous day. Their eyes all shine, wet, their lips a bright and unnatural red, shining too, and a few have jewelry they've scavenged tight around their wrists and forearms and throats. Nomadic or warlike or cannibals or saints, they stand together to witness the funeral rites.

I see a man next to me has a folded newspaper in one hand, tucked carefully under his arm. He glances at me. "That's quite a picture," he says quietly.

I put my cold hands in my jacket pockets, rubbing the fingers slowly against the wool, warming them.

"Yes," I think to say.

He pats my shoulder. Walks away.

The minister begins the service as he always does, singing, alone, a hymn that I don't recognize. He doesn't hold a book or a sheet of paper. He knows the song by heart.

. . .

I am walking to my hotel after the funeral. I pause at the low hill where I found the body, where the ground was scuffed and disrupted. But already the wind has spread dirt and dust over the tracks of my shoes, the minister's boots, the thin ruts from the dead man's heels that were formed as we dragged the body to the church, so that now there's no sign anyone had ever been here.

The woman and the boy are behind the brick wall, the boy squealing as he swings in the playground. For a second I can see his feet above the wall, his head then popping up with each back swing. His eyes are closed and his feet are high and he leans farther back with every swing, pumping himself even higher.

Then he sees me and he's quiet. He only watches me with each swing above the wall.

But still he keeps swinging higher.

When I walk into the playground, the woman is already slowing him down, quickly, grabbing at his shoes and the chains of the swing. She turns to see me and though she is still slowing down his swinging, I can see that her shoulders lower. Relaxing some.

"Hello," I say. I'm standing at the edge of the playground. Safe distance.

She stands very straight. Ready, it seems, and again I think that she does not blink. "Hello," she says.

The wind is not as strong inside the playground and it's warmer than outside the walls, so that for a moment it almost feels like there is sunlight shining.

"They found a dead body near here," I say. "They found it a few days ago."

The boy is off the swing now, ready to run to the monkey bars, but the woman reaches for his hand. He stands in place.

I say, "I thought that you should know this."

She's forty feet away from me on the other side of the playground, but I can see how very focused she is.

47

"Do you know who he was?" she asks.

I shake my head. "No one knows."

She nods slowly. Looks down at the boy. He stands still, staring over at me. I think that if she lets go of his hand, he'll simply go back to swinging, unfazed completely by the conversation about a dead man.

Unfazed completely by the desolate landscape where he plays.

"There's a photo of the man," I say. "In the paper."

She nods, letting go of the boy's small hand.

"You took the photo?" she asks.

I find that I'm biting my lip. "Yes," I say.

"Thank you for letting me know," she says.

I nod.

"We should go," the woman says. To me, I guess, but also to the boy.

"We should go," she says again, head turned slightly, speaking now to the boy alone.

But he can't hear her. He's already swinging again.

• • •

The smell of sulfur stays with us for weeks. This happens. Sulfur or chlorine or a rotten egg scent that blows across the North End for hours or even days. Most times, it's impossible to see the source of the smell. The wind inevitably finds a source of chemicals in the industrial zone—a door to a shed broken open in a storm, a rusting valve on a huge tank finally splitting along a weld. Sometimes I can even see the source of the smell from my windows, a haze of dust or gas that rises up from the rows of sinking factories.

I write about the sulfur smell and its possible sources in the paper.

The North End was not sealed up and left carefully preserved. Its many parts, its buildings and factories and roads and neighborhoods, were neglected, forgotten, and finally abandoned. A succession of deferred or unidentified blame, each act of desertion setting the stage for the next failure and departure.

I type alone in the office.

48

Everywhere, I can still smell whatever chemical has broken free of its source. And for the first time, I realize the scent must reach the South End. Must leave people there thinking that this place and anyone who would live here are all as diseased and decrepit as the smell that drifts, day after day, through the gray, cold sky above us.

· · ·

After a few minutes of staring at the shiny metal sheet spread across the ground, I realize I've lost track of time. I'm in a vast series of warehouses and factory buildings, wood and iron beams, tall broken windows reaching four and five stories high. Once, engines were built in the acre after acre of manufacturing space that I've been walking through and somewhere in my mind I am confused by how such a space, such an assimilation of facilities and equipment, could be devoted only to one component of a vehicle that would be completed in yet another set of buildings, the engines shipped from here to there via rail lines and roads and canals throughout the industrial zone.

The sheet of metal across the ground is oddly shaped, round and elongated, a hundred feet across. I throw a rock at the slick metal surface and immediately it sinks, a surprising and hallucinogenic experience that for a moment leaves me thinking that all of this is an extended dream, a sleeping memory of throwing rocks through impossible sheets of silver, the metal warping sickly as it slowly absorbs my throw.

But I realize that the sheet on the ground isn't hard metal. It's mercury. A pool of shiny liquid of unknown origin and depth, collected here on accident or on purpose, the unwanted by-product of one process of the creation of car engines over so many years.

I look around for a stick. I find an old broom handle and step closer to the pool. I put the handle into the liquid to see how deep the pool is. The handle sinks till my hand nearly touches the surface, five feet at least, and I let loose the handle. It sinks and soon it's gone, the surface wrapping around it, consuming it, and I can't help but wonder what else is inside that mercury.

49

I take a few pictures of the pool. Light reflects off the long, far edge for just a moment as I take the picture. I find a long two-by-four piece of lumber to slide carefully into the slick substance, nine or ten feet it goes and does not touch a bottom and I tie the top end of the heavy piece of wood to a rusted beam nearby. The end of the two-by-four sticks up a foot or so, as if frozen in concrete or molten steel, and I take a picture of that as well.

One more story for the paper. One more history of economic boom and eventual decline. The decline of a company that made engines for which there was no longer any demand. The decline of people who could not manage the wasted by-products of industrial success. A pool of mercury. Vats of a tan and creamy substance frozen in thick swirls. Abandoned engine blocks too many for me to count, ten by ten by ten is a thousand and the piles I find far exceed any quick measurement I can make. Roads and rail lines and canals all leading not just to the factory, not just through these vast and interconnected buildings, but that once linked this place to the farthest reaches of the world.

This place, this industrial quadrant of the massive North End now dead, fed products of every type to a world that has forgotten their source. That remembers this place only as a distant symbol of a fall from grace. The grace of wealth and progress and mass production, bringing jobs and growth and security to a once booming population.

I finish my notes. Sitting still alongside the pool of mercury.

I'll type it all up as I've sketched it out. Add facts and figures and the history.

People seem to read what I write. They take the paper from the racks. They sometimes even seem to nod toward me when I see them on the streets.

I leave the warehouse, heading out between two massive buildings, a narrow space, dirt between the huge metal walls. The path lets out onto a canal. The water is still and in another city it'd be murky with algae and other unidentifiable substances. But not in the North End. Even in their decrepit state, these canals are part of a system that circulates in new water from the bay to the north, keeping the water here from stagnating but taking with it unknown quantities and types of chemicals and pollution, toxins seeping down from the limitless factories around me.

Why do I stay?

I stand on the edge of the wooden wall that borders the canal.

The same answer comes to me, the one I always have.

I don't have anywhere else I want to be.

It's some time later before I leave.

At dusk that night, staring out from my hotel room windows into the wind and the cloudy, gray sky, I still find myself thinking about that canal at the engine factory. One of so many canals I pass by and cross over each day. But now I'm wondering if I could find a boat that works. That would take me from the factory to the north, through the denser and denser series of canals and levees and bridges that were built up there, passing houseboats and old businesses and many neighborhoods until finally I reach the bay.

What I'd do there I don't know.

But I keep picturing it, imagining this, until I've fallen asleep.

• • •

Police come to the newspaper office, some weeks after the body was found. It is the same pair of officers who came to the North End about the missing woman.

They walk through the front door with a great deal of noise. Their belts rattle with gear, an array of guns and flashlights and clubs. The radios on their belts are connected by wires to handsets that are attached to their shoulders. The officers seem bigger than anyone who lives here. It's not just the heavy vests under their blue shirts. Even their hands, the features of their faces, their height, it all seems larger and, now, unnatural.

The office manager is already gone when they arrive.

I don't stand when the police enter. But I wonder, a few minutes later, if I should have.

They ask questions about the body I found. One holds a copy of the article I wrote. The other holds a copy of the picture I took.

"Why didn't you call the police?" the male officer asks.

It takes me a moment to find an answer. "I think I assumed you wouldn't respond."

The woman nods. "I didn't want to," she says.

The other says, "But we would have. It's a dead person. That still matters. It's a dead person. Whose death is unexplained."

I find myself looking from one of them to the other. Waiting.

The female officer says, "You're the guy we talked to about that missing woman."

I try to think of something to say. But I can only nod.

"Did you give us this name?" she asks, pointing at my name in the newspaper.

I nod again, even though that's a lie. I'd given them a fake name.

"Where's the body?" the man asks, now taking notes.

"I helped take it to the church," I say. "The minister. He held a funeral. Then took the body away."

They both look up from their notes. Staring at me.

"It's how we respond to a death here," I say.

Still listening, the woman lets her head fall slightly to the side.

Disbelief.

I say in a moment, "I'm sure the minister will tell you where he took the body. There's nothing anyone is trying to hide."

Again they both are making notes in their small pads of paper. The pads make their hands look even bigger than they are, oversized, almost grotesque.

I ask, "And did anyone ever find that woman?"

The male officer shakes his head. "She's still missing."

"What's her story?" I hear myself ask.

"She's just missing," he says. "The family reported it."

"Parents?" I ask. "A husband?"

The man says, "Family. Just some family."

But the woman speaks up now. "A friend called us, actually. Some man. As far as we know, she has no family."

I am blinking. Not sure what else to do.

"Has anyone seen her?" she asks. "You ran her picture in this paper, right?"

I blink again. I push my hand across my face. "I ran it," I say. Standing now. Beginning to turn away. "But there was no response."

• • •

As I walk along the dark streets at night, only every few weeks do I see an old car drive past me. There simply aren't very many cars that drive here. Those that do always seem to have a very weak and tired engine, the miscolored wheels rolling slowly, the doors rusted and the trunk tied shut with rope, the face of the person in the driver's seat lost completely to the shadows on the windows.

• • •

Storms come like hurricanes, but they are shorter, more sudden, lasting only half an hour or less, with wind blowing rain sideways so hard that the drops hurt your face, and thunder bursts come frantically, and bright lightning strikes so close you can smell the ozone burn of the explosion.

I watch these storms from my building. Standing as close to the open windows of the hotel as I can. The wooden floor and windowsills have bubbled up from so much water spraying on them.

Small tornadoes spawn within the storms and I see them touching down, to the north, black cones inverted and now bending, lifting water from the canals and levees, water spraying out and water lifting upward, funneling and spraying into the air, and eventually the rain is so thick and blowing so hard that I won't be able to see more than twenty feet out my windows.

And the sound is like a jet engine.

And the building sways beneath me.

And I wonder if the walls around me might begin to crack, to crumble, to fall away into the storm.

The rain thins and I see another small tornado, this one over the industrial zone, floating above the warehouses and old factories, throwing water outward from the cone but not touching anything on the ground. Moving slowly, bending, twisting thinly, thinner, seeming ready to spin itself to nothing before suddenly it shifts, stabbing downward, growing thick again, and now the destruction will begin. Long pieces of wood and wide sheets of metal and it's impossible to understand the size of the area being damaged until you see an old pickup truck being thrown upward, out, like a child's toy flicked away, and the roofs of factories are split open, bursting upward, a ceaseless hammering, a relentless cutting through the guts of an already dead and disintegrating zone.

And then the tornado disappears. Sixty seconds and it's gone, dissipating in the rain that has already weakened, as the wind now blows without violence or intent, and in ten minutes the storm has passed, low and darkened clouds moving toward the horizon, clouds still black and purple and the deepest blue, shedding rain in wide streaks of silver, flashing with silent lightning strikes, moving fast, and now gone.

The tornadoes do the worst damage.

Releasing unknown and unmeasured chemicals from factories and large warehouses.

Ripping houses off the ground.

Crumbling the stone walls of the oldest canals.

Blowing down the power lines.

Weakening and breaking the levees.

Yet there are so few people here that no one has ever been hurt or killed. The math in that sense simply doesn't work. There are two hundred thousand empty homes here. The tornadoes are not likely to find one of the few that is still occupied.

This would not be the case if the North End had not died.

And it's in that moment that I remember what I've long forgotten, that these storms aren't just hitting here. They hit the South End, they hit east of here and west. They hit everywhere, everyone.

It's been this way for years.

• • •

A massive train emerges from the fog, the headlight on the engine pointing directly at me. I blink. Take a breath. But I know already that this train isn't moving. The fog has simply drifted away, revealing a locomotive I hadn't seen.

I stand on the second floor of a small building in the industrial zone. The fog came in as I walked and soon I was lost and so an hour ago I climbed up to the second floor of this building, laid down on a hard, vinyl couch, and slept.

The fog is breaking now, like smoke dissipating, and I see so many trains, a rail yard, lines of boxcars and tank cars and more locomotives facing me.

On the wall a calendar says *January 1981*.

I turn back to the lines of boxcars strung together, one after another now once again disappearing into the thick and dense fog that has only broken temporarily, that now is covering the train cars and train tracks and locomotives, all of it, everything I can see outside this small room.

So I lie back down and sleep.

• • •

I watch the woman and the boy roam the playground below my windows. They've been playing for almost half an hour before the woman sits down in one of the swings. She is still, though. Not moving. I think she's watching the boy as he runs to the monkey bars and starts to climb. But I realize she is not. I can see she's staring down. Toward her feet in the dirt below the swing. And she stays that way for some time. Fifteen minutes. Now it's twenty.

The boy keeps circling, climbing, running quickly, then swinging again.

He watches his mother, looks her way very often, but he never goes to where she's sitting.

Now I realize that she's crying. That she's been crying since she sat down. The way her shoulders move. The way she holds her face.

I can see now that she wipes her eyes.

"I could ask her," I say very quietly to myself, and I hadn't meant to speak out loud.

I could ask her.

It seems like it would be very hard to ask. I wonder how the boy would respond, wonder what he might say or do.

And I'm not sure why I'd ask. Why I even had the thought.

I watch the woman as she stares toward the dead vines along the ground. She's been down there for more than an hour.

She reaches forward. She touches the dry, brown leaves of some shrub that once grew there.

"Nice," I say, quietly, into the wind that blows against me from outside the building. "You'd be doing something nice."

I watch the woman as she kneels down. She touches the low rows of dead plants, the leaves gray and white and brown. Even from this distance, I can see each dead leaf she touches, each leaf disintegrating in her hands, the plant turned to dust, blowing away, and soon the boy crouches down beside his mother, reaches out, and now he is also touching those same dead leaves.

• • •

If they turned the power off, it would change our lives completely. Turning our narrow, spare existence into something more difficult and barren. The power gives us the lights. It keeps the water pumping. It keeps the streets from falling into utter darkness, a darkness that might be lost to crime and fear and violence. Because we wonder if it is the power that keeps this place from turning bad. Are there people living here who, without light and heat and water, might finally go insane?

I write this all up for the paper.

For many people, the power is what keeps them connected to the rest of the world. The flickering blue scenes I see through dark and curtained windows. The shadows of people sitting in front of their TVs.

My own choice is to stay completely unaware, disconnected entirely from anything outside this place. But other people who live here, they have made a different choice. They stay here for different reasons.

I have to remind myself of that. Because it seems sometimes that we live here as if we've chosen to be together. A tired, silent mass of survivors and the forgotten. But in truth we are more disparate. Varied forms of living, discrete choices for why we stay.

Not everyone here sleeps with their tall windows open to the wet and freezing night.

Not everyone here sleeps in their clothes, sprawled out on a heavy couch right near those same tall windows.

Not everyone here denies themselves all connection to the outside world.

Not everyone here stays so silent and alone.

I stand at my windows, thinking about this, freezing in the wind.

I sip from my one drink. I pull the blanket closer.

It doesn't ever get warm here. That ended too, like the city itself. Near the time when the city was already inevitably going to be abandoned, the weather never turned warm in the spring. There were days warmer than winter. But summer did not come.

That didn't happen only here. All kinds of places no longer have a summer. And other places, now, they no longer have a winter.

A change evolutionary in scope, played out in a very few years. Gradually, then suddenly.

When it rains here, I wonder what could be in those drops. What sort of chemicals are falling all across this city, across my building, across my hands as I stretch them out into this cold and constant rain?

• • •

I type my stories on an old typewriter. Then I put them in a tray on the office manager's green desk. She retypes my stories into the old Linotype machine, which lets her print them out on waxy paper that I glue to the wooden paste-up boards. The old boards are twenty inches wide by forty inches tall and have worn blue grids printed on them. I paste onto the boards the waxy paper articles and the just as waxy headlines and the black and white photos I have taken then developed in the old darkroom in the basement. The pressman turns the boards into metal plates he attaches to the press.

Everything is black and white. The print quality is very good. This was once a new and magnificent way to create a paper. It's not as if the process changed. All that changed was people found newer, faster ways to make a newspaper.

• • •

In the gutter along a street, I see the pages of a newspaper, twisted and damp and peeling apart. I walk toward the pages, to pick them up and throw them away.

The North End has very little trash and litter. Seeing even a newspaper in the gutter is a disruption of the landscape, the North End having been washed down by the years of rain and storms. Whatever trash was left in the streets during the final, dying years of this city was long ago blown away.

Yet there is a sense that, actually, the weather that has cleaned this place is managing to, very carefully, strip the city down, eating away at its buildings and homes and structures, methodically reclaiming the skyline, the streets, the land.

The paper I've found in the gutter isn't a copy of our newspaper. I've just realized this. The paper is from the South End. I see the year and month. It's only a few days old. I think to drop it. Want to leave it here. But already I've seen the headlines, scanned them, absorbed them for what they are.

City Budget in the Red.

A Horrific Murder in the Night.

Further Doubts on whether This Change in Climate Is For Real.

Rain drips down my forehead. The paper is soaked through. I've stopped reading. Folding the paper on itself, again and then again, as small as I can make it.

The news as it has been for years and years and years. No change in the world outside this place. No reason to learn more about anywhere but here.

I'll carry the paper home. Throw it away in my small kitchen.

Or burn it. Use it. In the basement of a home I'll once more light on fire.

CHAPTER 4

Office lights flicker on. Whole floors of tall buildings suddenly lit up through-out the night, triggered by timers whose schedule is long out of sync with any purpose at all.

There is a mural covering the first five floors of the building in front of me. Painted figures of Greek gods, naked or bearded or weeping or aflame, all at the crest of a wave of water and cloud.

Lights shine bright on the mural, these lights too connected to the timer that just now lit the floors of the building above me.

Granite chimeras reach out from the corners of the building, unidenti-fiable beasts standing guard on every floor, one after another reaching to the chrome spire some twenty stories in the sky.

A bank building. Next to an insurance headquarters. Next to tall edifices built to house the management of car companies, shipping conglomerates, oil companies, a stock exchange, more banks.

Twenty buildings. Now empty.

So much effort. So much work. The money and time and desire to build great structures, to create grand environments in which to work and live.

The timer triggers again. In the silence of the North End, I hear the click, loud, echoing into the night, and the building and the mural and my hands stretched out at my sides and the breath from my mouth blowing white into the air, all once again go dark.

. . .

I walk to the newspaper's office. I walk the old neighborhoods to the south. I walk the industrial zone to the west. I make my way through buildings near the hotel where I live.

I wander through the tenth floor of a building near downtown, crossing through the long abandoned offices of a company I can't identify.

I make my way to the industrial zone, through factory floors still lined with the machinery of mass production, heavy tools and automated arms and the means of making such sophisticated items, parts and pieces and accessories that I again cannot decipher until I've researched them in the library.

I make my way to my office, where I write a story for the paper.

I make my way to an empty neighborhood, where I light a house on fire.

I make my way to my hotel room, where I lie down in the dark, alone up here in the coldest air, blowing steadily tonight. Pushing hard against my arms and hands and face. Heat rises from any gaps I allow into my heavy covers, escaping near my feet, escaping from the smallest space near my hand and chin and face, and I have to shift now, slowly, carefully twisting the covers tight to seal off the loss of heat.

I see my breath blow white.

And with my fingers numb and my face cold I've been asleep and now awake, all night, waking up, then asleep, waking every hour, like I do every night, the way it's been since I came back here. Asleep then waking up.

Asleep, then waking up.

I might think of the woman and the boy when I do wake up. Might think about the commission or the paper or an article I will write.

I will inevitably think about those things.

But those things are still like dreams. Distant memories I can't define, lacking shape or definition. Someone else's story. Someone else's pain.

All that's real when I wake up is everything I remember about the people I have lost.

Mostly, I wake up crying.

An air-raid siren wails from a horn atop a building across from mine. In a moment, a siren in the industrial zone joins the wailing too, then another from the neighborhoods stretching south, then more than I can manage to follow.

This happens roughly once a week. Preprogrammed civil defense tests that have continued automatically for so many years.

The sound is very loud. Rising then falling then rising to nearly a scream.

I picture people in the South End, hearing these sirens spinning up to their horrific pitch. The warning cries from a deadened place, an empty place, an area of waste and abandonment and danger.

The sirens seem always to get louder. Each fall in the sound followed by a rising wail even louder than the one I remember from a moment ago.

And so I can only stand still at my open window. Hands over both my ears. Pressing hard now, harder, closing my eyes, whispering to myself, *It's almost over. Soon. It is almost over.*

• • •

A scavenger hangs from the rafters of a house, the sides of the home already stripped away, another scavenger scaling the boom of a crane as, below him, scavengers move from the roof of one house to the roof of another, crossing a series of narrow boards they've stretched from chimney to chimney, the boards bouncing heavily as the scavengers make their way through the air.

Tightrope walkers in the sky.

Meanwhile, I take pictures. I make notes.

Loud music plays from a flatbed truck nearby, tall speakers set up on the back of the open, wooden bed of a big truck. Nearby stand huge barrels of water and pallets stacked with meat and cheese and bread. Blocks of each. The scavengers carefully cut off slices for themselves.

The music grinds, loudly, no words at all.

It's been so long since I've heard music.

The scavengers are stripping down homes in the last neighborhood built in the North End. Thin, cheap homes built on the vast remnants of a park that was flattened after being cut in half by the highway trench.

A precursor, this neighborhood, to the vast and faceless subdivisions that would sprawl across the South End.

When the North End started to collapse, these, the new homes, were the first to be abandoned.

As they work, scavengers nod in my direction. But none speak to me. And I don't speak to them.

Men and women and brown and white, they are one age it seems. I can't tell. As marked up as they are by the work they do, stained and scratched and cut. Dirty, maybe filthy, but now it's a choice they've clearly made, the outer sign to the rest of us, bleeding manifestations of the purpose they have found.

• • •

In the morning, I stand at my windows with my binoculars, trying to find the canal I saw in the industrial zone a week ago. I can see the engine plant that I'd been inside. But the buildings hide the canal.

I will need to do research at the library. Need to check the maps. Read the histories of the development of the port to the north and the waterways connecting the port to the industrial zone and all the neighborhoods in between.

I don't know why, but I want to use the canal to find my way from the industrial zone to the bay.

Maybe it's one of those things you only understand when it's done.

I picture myself as a child, when I went to the park along that bay, a small amusement park and a very small zoo and a place for picnics and a beach where people swam. All those places are now gone. Replaced some twenty years ago by a port that was meant to ship goods around the world. But in truth those goods were hardly wanted by the time the port was finally finished. The tall cranes and shiny rail lines were barely ever used.

Before then, I rode a roller coaster there. I learned to dive. I ate cotton candy and walked along the cages where elephants and giraffes wandered among hay and rocks and the halfhearted efforts at making a lifelike habitat for them. I didn't think that then, of course.

I just thought the animals always seemed so tired.

I only took my own kids to the zoo once. The new zoo, built after they were born. The one down in the South End, with realistic landscapes and much more space in which the animals could roam. They went, the kids did, with their school and with their friends and they went with their mother. But I only took them to the zoo one time. I found it much too hard to look at all the captive animals. Trapped in those friendly, unreal habitats. Staring blankly into space. Looking no less tired and worn and fearful than the broken beasts I'd seen so many years ago, when I was a kid myself.

• • •

I hear a car drive past me, but I'm staring forward, walking toward the corner store.

I hear the car drive past me again. I turn and a very old, very large car painted yellow and green has stopped. A woman, in the passenger seat, is pointing forward, then backward.

I stare.

She seems to argue with the driver, a man, then in a moment she just slightly opens her window.

"How?" I hear her say, but her other words are lost.

I shake my head. *I don't understand.*

She lowers the window another inch. "How, sir, how do we get out of here?"

They have surely been lost for hours. Here in the center of the North End. But they are only two turns and one mile from the overpass they mistakenly crossed. It's the middle of the day. The signs pointing to the South End are all still displayed along these roads. But in the confusion born of their fear of this place, these people couldn't see the signs. Or didn't believe that the signs could ever be right.

I tell this woman where to go, what street will take them home.

The man guns the engine. The woman stares ahead, pointing frantically forward with both her hands.

The people of the South End fear us. I'm not entirely sure why. But they do.

Even the commissioners, their disdain for us, it too comes from fear.

Fear of the unknown. Fear of our choices. Fear of how we live.

• • •

I see the woman and her boy at the playground, where they sit on the ground near one of the walls.

They are eating. Her backpack is spread out in front of them and I can see a few opened cans of food, a bottle of water that they share. A small towel she uses as a napkin.

She turns herself toward me when she sees me. I raise my hand slightly, begin to turn away.

"You don't have to go," she says.

In a moment, I sit down near them, on the end of the slide. The boy still eats, sitting now so that he faces me. The woman is putting away her food.

I have always found it hard to watch people as they eat. I don't know why. It seems so very personal, a private and visceral necessity, to be taken care of quickly and alone.

I look around the playground. Dead shrubs, yellow grass. Two small trees so thin and dry they don't even move in the wind.

The woman sits with her knees up. Leans her chin on her hands. Her hair falls forward but she doesn't move it from her face.

"Go play," the woman says quietly to her boy. He doesn't move. She leans back, hair falling from her face and she stares at him, says to him this time, "Go play right now."

And he does.

Still watching him, she says, "I should go find that newspaper."

I'm not sure what she means. In a moment, I say, "Which one?"

"The one with the picture," she says. "The picture of the dead man."

I shake my head. "It doesn't matter."

I feel the fog of tiredness come over me. The weight of conversation, of navigating her words and mine, it takes all the energy I have.

I close my eyes. When I open them, she's watching me.

"It's so lifeless here," she says, turning away. "I'm still not used to it."

My hands move slowly toward my face. I rub my eyes, think I should shave soon. I say to her, "I'm not sure I'm used to it here yet either."

She sits cross-legged now. "Maybe," she says, staring down at a dry leaf in her hands, pulling lightly on its edges, small tears along the veins of its delicate, small structure. "Maybe I know that man."

Again I shake my head. "He's dead now," I say. "That's all."

She turns to watch her boy on the swing, still absently pulling the leaf apart. Her fingers move slowly, carefully, across the leaf. She glances at me. Then nods.

I realize I find it easier to talk when I'm looking at the boy swing, steadily, forward then back. There's a clarity that comes to me. I see my words quite simply. I talk without the fog or exhaustion weighing on me.

Moments pass. She stares toward her boy. She shakes her head. "Maybe," she says. "Yes."

Then she stands, walks to her boy. She nods back toward me, a slight wave, as she leaves.

• • •

As I do every week, I take the paste-up boards down to the basement and put them in a worn old wooden tray.

The pressman nods.

The press is made up of five tall printing units, each twelve feet high, with a large roll of paper underneath every one of them. The paper is strung from unit to unit, through rollers and metal drums, precise steel cylinders lined with metal plates, each one holding an impression of the words I wrote and the photos I took. The old pressman only uses two of the units in a given week. This creates eight pages, wide broadsheet pages folded neatly as they come off the end of the press. Each week, the pressman alternates the units he uses, so that no one unit wears out faster than the others. As the units start up, the pressman moves quickly, to the folding apparatus at the end of the line, to the finished papers steadily stacking on a small conveyor belt at the end of the press. The pressman twists small dials to adjust the ink, to lay more black on the page where there are photos, to cut the ink back where there is just text. He moves quickly, staring sometimes through the bottoms of his bifocal glasses, hopping up onto the side of a unit, reaching far into the rolling wheels, where his fingers, his hand, could easily be crushed.

He bounces lightly from one unit to another.

It's a skill, not a job. A craft, not a repetition.

When I first came back to the North End, I sometimes noticed these newspapers in the racks. It was months before I realized that the racks would sometimes be empty, then full again. I'd assumed the racks were unused and abandoned. Filled one last time before the city and the newspaper were abandoned. But soon I picked up a copy of the paper. And it was only a few days old.

The paper listed the location of the office.

A few weeks later, I went to the address. The office manager was there, along with a very old man who was the paper's only reporter and editor. The editor and the office manager both stared blankly up at me. In a moment, I said to them, "I can write." They both continued to stare. "I mean, I can write for a newspaper."

The office manager turned back to her big typewriter.

I thought this was her way of telling me to go away.

But the editor said to me, "Okay. Come back next week with a story."

I did, every week. The editor and I, we didn't talk much. I just handed him a story, typed on a typewriter I'd found and hauled to the same hotel room where I still live. After a few months, I went to the office and he'd left a letter on his desk. It was addressed to me. "I am going away now," he wrote.

"I hope you'll keep the paper going." Then he listed, on the next page, what needed to be done every week to produce the paper.

There was also a tan envelope containing a small amount of money, the same amount the office manager still brings to me.

A few months later, I asked the office manager where the editor had gone.

She stared at me a moment. With a look of something like surprise. She said, "He went off to die."

It takes just twenty minutes to run the seven hundred newspapers we put out every week. I sit on the basement steps. Watching the pressman work. He stacks the papers into bundles of twenty-five and fifty as they come off the end of the line. Then he uses a heavy steel cart to roll them toward the far end of the basement, where there's a large wooden elevator that lifts them up to ground level. The pressman will load the papers in his old truck then, and leave to stock the racks still left out around the North End.

He cuts the power to the press. He lifts the lever to open the doors to the elevator. Glances back at me.

I raise my hand. *Thanks.*

Every week. The paper has been published many thousands of times. We keep this going. We don't know what would happen if ever we had to stop.

· · ·

The rain turns heavy before I realize what is happening. The noise of it, of the rain turned steady and solid and so thick I can barely see, it covers the sound of the thunder and the wind and the roar of small tornadoes forming just behind us.

We are not near a place that can possibly be safe.

We're on the edge of the industrial zone, along the bank of a canal, the woman and the boy and me, and the storm has come upon us impossibly fast.

I don't know why the woman and the boy were out this way. I hadn't gotten a chance to ask. We had only said hello. Only barely nodded to each other when the boy pointed to the sky behind me.

We turn, the woman and me, see the black clouds pushing toward us, a thick and monstrous mass so tall it seems to reach too far into the air, blinking with lightning and swirling down to the ground not far from us.

The three of us are running. It's not clear where. But we run.

There are tall warehouses everywhere ahead of us, wooden and flimsy and with the wind already reaching us, the walls of the warehouses have begun to shake and bend.

I lead us right, running fast with the woman and boy next to me, yelling, "I know, I know where to go."

At the end of the warehouse, there is another canal and leading out to the canal is an old, heavy dock.

"Underneath," I yell, although the wind is so hard now that I can barely hear myself. "Get underneath," I yell.

The woman and boy scramble down on their knees and then their stomachs and they crawl underneath the dock. I follow them, sliding along the dirt and scraping my leg against one of the heavy support beams.

We sit now, in the dirt, the two of them huddled together across from me. The boards above us are thick and the crossbeams a foot or more wide, the whole structure bolted to thick wooden pilings that have been driven into the ground.

The sound of the storm is everything now, screaming so loud that it's all I can hear.

Sticks and dirt blow under the side of the dock and large objects begin to slam into the top of the dock, unidentified objects that hit so hard that the structure shakes even harder and the sound is even louder.

The boy has crawled into his mother's lap and she leans over him, holding him, face pressed against his neck, covering as much of him as she can.

There is movement in the noise now, a horrifying motion as even under the dock we can feel the wind shift and the air change and now there is a tornado, right on us, and it is louder now, painful, and the dock shakes harder than could ever seem possible.

I see the boy is screaming. I see the mother screaming. But all I hear is the noise of that wind swirling so fast on top of us and beginning to lift the water from the canal, the surface of the water bending upward as if the domed head of a monster were emerging just ten feet away and still that water lifts, bending upward until it breaks, spraying up into the air lit bright by constant lightning.

The boards above us disappear now, pulled away as if they had never been attached, and I watch the woman and her boy flying upward, together, the boy still digging into his mother's lap and the mother still covering him with all her body and both of them with mouths wide and open, screaming, silently, into the roar.

• • •

I walk the industrial zone, looking for the woman and her boy. I've been searching for a few hours.

The damage from the storm is immense. Buildings cut in half. Tall smoke-stacks knocked to the ground. A massive knife, more than one it seems, cut through this place, opening fissures through the densely gray and abandoned landscape. Dark brick walls are turned bright red where sections cracked and fell into large piles. Wooden walls knocked down to reveal brightly blue containers. A yellow car, old but polished clean and shiny, rests atop the edge of a very tall, brown building.

The car is left there, gently it seems, so that anyone passing by can see it.

It rains lightly, intermittent drops on my hands and face. The sky is bright now, white, the clouds one uninterrupted sheet so high up in the sky.

I really don't know where or how to look for the woman and her boy. I just keep walking through the refuse that's been created by the storm.

I turn a corner and see another warehouse that's been flattened. A massive building, wooden, only its distant ends to my left and right still stand, more than three or four blocks away. The rest is flat, steel beams crushed and twisted, wooden siding fragmented into shards. I feel small. All of the building is pressed down upon itself, except for a staircase still standing in the middle of the destruction.

It takes me a few minutes to climb over the debris and reach the stairs. They're built of steel beams and concrete steps and somehow they've survived, completely stable and intact. I climb slowly up the steps, four stories high. They don't shake or sway or move at all.

I can see far from here, able now to see the whole of the flattened path of destruction through the industrial zone. It's a path that ends, remarkably, at the edge of the oldest neighborhoods. The path is like a runway, the storm lifting up at the last moment, avoiding the old neighborhoods where many of the few people in the North End still live.

And now I can also see the storm, directly south of here, a wide black blot on the near horizon, purple in places, almost blue, but in its center it is black and flashing white and if I stare I can see it moving, can see how the very surface of it swirls and speeds and shakes with the rain falling from it and the wind blowing through it and with the debris it still lifts from the ground.

The tornadoes, surely, are still deep inside those clouds.

Here, though, it's silent. The rain is light enough that it makes no noise.

And so I can hear, from the South End, very far away, the faint sounds of the air-raid sirens, an echoing, distant wailing that rises and falls and rises, again, once more.

I touch my ear with my hand.

It's been hours since the storm hit the North End, and the storm hit here at speed, on us and gone in twenty minutes or less.

But it seems to have stopped moving when it reached the South End. As if settling into place.

I look away from the storm. I'm still standing atop this staircase.

Along the far side of this flattened building, I see a trench has been cut, twenty feet wide and a hundred feet long, tapering down into the earth. The hard-packed ground of the industrial zone, the lifeless gray surface I have walked along so many days over these past years, it's been cut open, deeply, and the earth below is red and brown and orange.

The woman and her boy lie down inside the trench.

They are a quarter mile from where they were lifted off the ground.

I climb down the stairs quickly, then make my way across the debris. The trench is deeper than I'd thought, ten feet or more, and the dirt down here is soft and damp. Not slick, though, or muddy. The dirt here is light and somehow fluffy, so much so that I am conscious of how it feels as I slide down the side of the trench.

The woman is on her back. Her eyes are closed.

The boy is next to her. The side of his small body is pressed against her. His eyes are open. He stares at me, unblinking and not moving. His face is bleeding from his nose. His mouth and forehead are covered in dirt.

I can't move.

"Please," he says quietly. "Help."

• • •

More than five thousand people are killed by the storm. All in the South End.

The minister tells me this. Little news about the South End is usually discussed here in the north. The people who do watch TV, they don't talk about what they see.

But this is something different.

I'm here at the church with the woman and her boy. The boy, though bloodied across the face, is fine. The woman has a broken arm. A concussion. Many bruises and cuts. But she is conscious now.

"She should probably go to a hospital in the South End," the minister says.

We're outside the small room where the mother and her boy are lying on two small beds. Priests' quarters, I assume. Very spare but functional, with two beds and two dressers and two wooden chairs near a stained-glass window.

It takes me a moment to form an answer for the minister. I say to him, "I don't think she'd want to."

"I figured that," he says. "But I thought I should say it anyway."

"And probably she'd just be stuck in a hallway in some hospital," I say. "Given what you said happened. They've got a lot worse to deal with down there."

73

I replay what I've said to him and the words seem correct, seems clearly to be an accurate and practical thing to say. But it seems like someone else must have said this. Or that it's something I've been told to say.

Like everyone here, when the minister is not moving, he is so very still.

It's nighttime, half a day since the storm hit. The woman was able to walk from the industrial zone, leaning on my arm, limping some, and it was slow going, a long walk, where she did not once speak.

The boy walked ahead of us, only sometimes looking back. I told him we needed to get to the church downtown. He nodded and didn't speak again.

"She's from the paper," the minister says to me now. We're standing in the hallway. "Right? The one the police are looking for?"

It's a moment before I say, "Yes."

He crosses his arms high across his chest. "She knows they're looking for her?" he asks quietly.

"Yes," I say again.

He nods. "Okay," he says. Nods again. In a minute, he says, "The article didn't mention a boy."

"No," I say. "The police never mentioned her boy."

"None of that's my issue," the minister says. He leans to his left, looks into the room. He turns back to me. "I think they're sleeping now. You can stay here too if you want."

It takes me a long moment to think about what he's said.

He says, "There's another room. A few of them. Just pick one."

I say quietly, "Oh." I rub my hands on my jacket. "No. No, thank you." I am looking at my hands, filthy and covered in blood in some places. "Am I bleeding?" I ask the minister.

He tilts his head back slightly, looking my face up and down. "Not anymore," he says.

I nod.

"Five thousand people," the minister says.

"I'll come back in the morning," I say. "You know. Check on them."

"Think of it," the minister says. "Think of all those people."

But I'm already down the hall.

· · ·

I document the destruction from the storm in an article for the paper. I try to be as thorough as I can, identifying not just the areas in the North End that were hit, but the buildings and structures that were destroyed. I find addresses, I find the names of companies that once occupied the buildings. I include more photos than I usually do. Five of them across two pages. The flattened buildings. The still standing staircase in the wreckage of that warehouse. The shiny car sitting on top of the corner of that brick building. A view of the storm as it dominated the horizon to the south.

The article and pictures take up most of the eight pages of that week's paper.

After the paper has gone to press, I realize I didn't mention that the storm moved on to kill some five thousand people in the South End. To do major damage there as well.

But I then remember that they have their own newspapers down there and it seems to me that's for them to report.

The woman and her boy had already left the church when I went to check on them the morning after the storm. The minister said that she thanked him and offered him money. He declined. "And that boy," the minister said to me. "He's an odd one. I don't think he ever said a word. But he never once stopped watching me."

· · ·

Rainwater still drips through the walls and ceilings of the buildings, days since the storm passed through here.

Inside, some buildings bulge inward, the plaster walls swelling as if bruised, wide swaths of ceiling tiles bending downward, dripping at the corners, and ceilings have collapsed in an explosion of tile and wooden beams and soft plaster and rotted wire.

As if a bomb was dropped inside here. But still this is only rain.

From the outside, the walls at the base of tall apartment buildings and massive churches bow outward, soaked through with the weight of so many years of this rain, the buildings seem to be sinking in upon themselves, the first floors absorbing the water and weight and the slowly descending flow of matter from the floors above still soaked with all that rain, the buildings left to melt, steadily, down upon themselves, until someday each structure will finally begin to burst.

. . .

I stand in the bell tower of an old church along the avenue leading through the oldest neighborhoods in the North End. There's a frozen beauty to these ancient neighborhoods. The brick homes lit red even in this pale and color-less sunrise. The outlines of once ornate and elaborate gardens just discern-ible in the patterns of the dry, dead branches and the tall black tree trunks, trees that, even from this tower, shine slightly in their slick and atrophied state.

I hold my hands over my ears. The air-raid sirens spin once more to their peaking and horrific volume.

One of them was long ago installed atop this old, stone tower.

There was a beauty here.

I close my eyes. My chest shakes with the noise and there's a feeling that I can't breathe and I think that if I move, if I run away, the siren scream will only grow.

It was beautiful.

. . .

I am making my way through houses not far from my hotel when I knock an old phone off the receiver.

They'd never heard that sound. Their world, the kids', was one of cell phones and touch screens, bright and shiny objects not attached to plaster walls. The dial tone was a mysterious sound emanating from the old red phone mounted to the kitchen wall when we moved into our house in the North End.

But they loved that house. The wide hallways and the heavy staircase and the deeply cracked wooden floors and the yard itself was an adventure, with so many places to hide and so many places to run and so many trees on which to build a swing.

They would, each of them, periodically pick up that wall phone. To hear the dial tone. They would listen to it, together, all four of them leaning close, and the simple sound of it made them giggle and shake their heads and laugh.

I blink.

I reach out to the phone receiver that I've knocked from its metal cradle.

But I can't touch it.

I can only walk away.

Can only set the fire.

Still hearing that distant dial tone, in my mind, as I watch the house now burn.

• • •

I hear the woman and the boy.

I've woken up on the couch in the library. Staring into the high atrium. Light from the tall windows spreads down across the room. It feels like sunlight here, for a moment, as I'm still waking up. But there's no warmth to the light, gray and pale, and I can see my breath as I exhale.

It's really the boy I hear, the speed of his steps. The stops and starts. The soundtrack to his movement.

Small explosions, a jet pack or a rocket ship, the artificial pop of a laser beam or gun.

I sit up. Fold the blankets. Put them in their cabinet.

The boy comes around a corner, backpack on, hurling himself onto the ground, then somersaulting into a crouched, hidden position behind a massive set of shelves.

He sees me now and stands straight up. Staring and quiet.

I say in a moment, "How are you?"

He has his mother's black eyes and the ability not to seem to ever blink.

In a moment, the woman comes around the corner, quickly, looking for the boy.

She sees me and the fear leaves her face. "Sorry," she says.

"It's the absence of sound," I say. "When you hear the child, then the sound disappears."

She mouths a word, *Yes,* I think, but I can't be sure.

Her hair is not pulled back, is instead pushed behind her ears and she isn't wearing her heavy jacket. There's a person in there, I think, an observation without wonder or surprise or any form of curiosity.

"I should thank you," she says. "For saving me. For saving both of us in that storm."

I shake my head lightly. I'm not sure what I should say. In a moment, I say, "I thought that dock would protect us. I'm sorry that it didn't."

She shakes her head. "There was nowhere better to go."

I find myself nodding. "I suppose," I say.

"The minister too," she says. "Your friend, he was very nice to us."

I say, "I'm not sure that he's my friend."

She glances at me. "Okay."

I shake my head, again, lightly. "It doesn't matter."

The air in the atrium is very still. Shadows float across the tables, variations in the gray sky above us moving, layers of clouds pushed, slowly, to the south.

She says, "I was never a person who feared the worst." She looks toward the ground. "But that changed."

"And yet you've come here," I say.

"Everyone here says there is no crime. They say it's very safe."

She looks up toward the high ceiling. A moment of wonder, I think, unexpected, seeing the high atrium and the tall windows and the signs of the zodiac formed by hand-painted stars and she sees the way the light—even as cold and gray as the sky is—she sees the wonder in the way the light spills down across the walls, and shelves, and us.

I say, "But it can't feel very safe to you."

It's a moment before she looks back at me. "No," she says. "No, it doesn't."

The boy, he is still standing, looking at me.

"The police came again," I say to her. "Asking questions about the body."

She nods. She pushes hair from her face. "I wanted to find your article," she says, pointing toward the stacks of newspapers on the shelf. "About the body."

I tell her which stack the paper is on.

She stands still, though, only looking toward the papers. It's a full minute. Silence. Her not moving, and when she does finally go to the stacks of papers, bending down to the paper that shows the picture of the man, she doesn't stand. She stays crouched down. Her back to me and to the boy.

The boy looks at the paper she holds. Then looks back at me. I lean to the side, putting my hand against a shelf, and the boy's hand seems to lift then and he lowers his shoulder to let his bag slip down, just an inch or two, his other arm sliding up the side of the backpack to the zipper, and although he stops moving when I stop moving, there's still a fixation, on me, very deep inside his flat black eyes.

It's more than a fixation.

I say out loud, "I asked the police if they'd heard anything about that missing woman." I pause. "They said no."

"And they won't ever," the woman says, still crouching and turned away from me.

I watch the boy. The backpack now dangles from just one shoulder. The thing in his eyes grows sharper and more focused.

"Okay," I say. "That's okay with me."

"This was supposed to be a place where we could hide," the woman says. "Right? A place where we'd be safe?"

I say, "The police told me that the missing woman, she was reported to them by a boyfriend."

The boy stares at me.

I say, "But apparently that person lied."

The woman is standing now, staring up at the high atrium again.

"He wasn't a friend," I hear the woman say.

The thing in the boy's eyes, I'd thought maybe it was fear. I move my hand again. Testing. I lift my hand from the shelf, put it in my pocket, staring at the boy, staring at his eyes.

The woman is looking down. At the picture. Shaking her head. Seeming to whisper something.

The thing in the boy's eyes isn't fear.

"It's okay," I say.

The thing in his eyes is violence.

"For me," I say. "It's all okay."

I'm certain that if I move again the boy will try to hurt me.

"Yes," I hear the woman say. "It has to be."

I'm certain that if he tries to hurt me, he will definitely succeed.

"This can be a safe place for you," I say to her, though I'm still looking right at the boy.

"Yes," I hear her say now. "Yes it can. It can be very safe."

I don't move.

And in a moment, the boy turns away, to his mother, lifting the backpack onto both his shoulders. He walks to his mother and touches her arm. She turns to him. Takes his hand.

She blinks. Rubs her hand across her face. I think she says something to me, maybe she says *thank you*, but I can't really tell. I'm lost to staying still. Lost to my motionlessness.

The woman saw nothing the boy just did.

Even when they've gone, I stand there, very still.

I know that boy would have hurt me. Maybe killed me.

I know he'd have beaten me in the head with something in his backpack.

And I know the woman would not have had any way to stop him.

In a minute, I move my hand from my pocket. I lean back against a table behind me.

And as I look up at the daylight, staring at the cold, pale color of another endlessly dying day, I know one more thing.

The one thing is this.

I know I would not have wanted the boy to hurt me.

Which was not clear to me before this moment. Before I stood here in this light staring at a child who would have hurt me without hesitation.

The light from the windows is unbroken and relentless and I try to remember how many years it's been since I've seen the sun.

But what I know is something else. What I know is that I have realized that, truly, I do not want to die.

• • •

I find myself touching everything in my cold hotel room. Each object and every item. The couch and chairs and tables. The lamps and the bulbs within them. The blankets folded and stacked squarely on the shelves. My clothes stacked on the other shelves, pants and socks and shirts and shoes.

I've done this all before.

It starts when I am looking for something, for a pencil this time but it could have been anything. Not finding the pencil leads me to want to see what else I might have lost.

I touch the frying pan and the pot next to it and the lids for each and the fork and knife and spoon and plate.

I lift some items, feeling their weight and texture. Other items I only barely brush my fingers against, checking them off, noting their presence and existence.

There aren't many objects that I now own.

None of them are ever missing.

At some point I'll realize what I'm doing, tell myself that I should stop. But then I remember that it's not as if I have something else to do.

I touch each cushion on the couch. The pillows stacked on top of blankets. The album of photographs I never open. The small box of things I retrieved from the house in which we lived, one box, that's all I wanted.

I tell myself it's strange to touch these things this way, here alone in this hotel high above an empty city.

But then I remember that I've always done this. I've been this way since before they died.

• • •

The bright, cold light still shines on the outer wall of the otherwise darkened church. A small church, two hundred years old, and the light shines down on the small graveyard where I stand. Air-raid sirens sound, cycling up and down from their various points throughout the North End, at midnight this time, the sound echoing through the air for longer than ever before, twenty minutes now, and I wonder if maybe this time the sirens won't ever stop.

There are headstones here and small tombs raised above the ground.

The church is on a hill, one of the few high areas in the north or south, once an area of elevation above the bay, an overlook before the water was contained and these many square miles of land were created for the city.

The headstones and tombs are carved with family names and long gone dates and the oxidized faces of people now forgotten.

Along the road near the cemetery, I see the woman, running, and in front of her is her boy, running too.

The boy runs along the low, iron fence bordering the church grounds. I walk toward it and when I'm closer I see that he runs with his hands over his ears, pressing hard, his eyes half closed, and it seems that he is screaming. But it's a sound I can't hear in the wailing of the sirens.

The boy sees me and falls down, onto the dirt along the fence, and already he is curling into a ball.

The woman reaches him, drops to her knees, then lies down, curling up around him, legs tucked up against him, arms wrapped around his chest and around his arms and with one hand she tries to hold his forehead.

I stand watching them, just a few feet away.

The air-raid sirens cycle one last time.

And now it's quiet.

The mother and her boy still lie in the dirt.

It is many minutes later that she speaks. The boy still covers his ears. But I'm sure that he can hear her on the ground, her voice right next to his ear.

"The sound of sirens terrifies him," she says. "I think it's the volume, not the sirens themselves. This is one more reason we came here. The quiet. The absence of sudden noises."

She runs one hand along the boy's forehead, lightly. Gentle.

"He was not always like this," she says. "He used to talk. He used to sing."

The boy still covers his ears.

"They wanted us to leave our home," she says. "Our dying neighborhood in the South End. They shut off the power and they shut off the water and still we would not leave. Fifty people. Thirty homes. We still lived there. But they kept at us. Cutting the streetlights and the bus service and making clear that the fire and police would no longer respond. But still we all stayed. We had jobs near our neighborhood and most of us owned those homes and even those that didn't, they felt like they owned their homes too."

She stops. I hear my hand touch the rail on top of the fence. I hear her breathing. I hear the boy breathing too.

"So they condemned our homes. And when they'd condemned our homes they could declare us, me, everyone, they could declare us all unfit. Unfit to stay. Unfit to live there. And unfit to be a parent. And I came home and they'd taken him. Away. To a foster parent. A protector. Because I was unfit. That's what they said. 'You are unfit. Look at where you live. Now the boy will be safe.'" She looks at me from the ground. "The abuse started within days. Abuse of every kind." She speaks without moving. Only stares. "What happened to that man, it was entirely deserved." She leans down, kissing her boy's head where he still presses it into the ground. "That man deserved to die. And all of them, every one of them who took my boy and my home from me, all of them deserve the same."

• • •

In the morning, the woman and her boy are gone.

She has left me a handwritten note, sealed in an envelope she's slid underneath my office door.

The woman killed that man. On that hill near my playground. She hit him once in the head. She did not think that he would die. But she left him there to bleed.

I will leave now, she writes. *With my boy.*

Thank you, she writes. *For how you've helped us both.*

And for me, in the morning, there is always a reason to cry.

PART II

CHAPTER 5

The lack of crime in the North End has not completely erased a sense of wariness. A lifetime's expectation, even teaching, that, left on their own, some people will turn to violence. That some people will inevitably, maybe necessarily, manifest the worst that humans are capable of doing.

It has not happened here. It's as if there is no motivation for such a descent into darkness. No items worth stealing that aren't easily available to possess. No places of importance to defend or protect. No market for drugs or sex or some activity over which people would be willing to fight.

We live the uneasy peace of the tired and resigned.

I write this up for the paper.

Yet the next day, while walking back downtown from a commission meeting, a red car playing loud music passes me, slows half a block ahead, then reverses. The kids, white and brown, look out at me, the music still thumping in the car.

Of course I am wary. These people aren't from here.

"What have you got?" one of the kids asks.

It's clear they've wandered across the overpass. It happens a few times a year. Wannabe gang members or rich kids killing their boredom. I'm not sure which these ones are.

"What have you got?" someone asks again.

"Nothing," I say.

"Where can we find something going on here?" another asks. "Where's the party here?"

I shake my head. "There isn't one."

They are laughing. I'm an unshaven older man in a heavy, black blazer, carrying a camera and a notebook.

"What about that camera?" one of them asks.

I can't say that I am nervous. I know that I'm not scared. I am just very aware of what might happen.

"Let me see that camera," one says.

I say to him, "No."

"I said, 'Let me see that camera.'"

"No."

We're in a dark area, a few square blocks where all light has been shut off. The only streetlights are a few blocks away.

"One more time," says the kid in the passenger seat. "Let me see the camera."

I turn and run. I cut between two houses, through a back gate, into the alley, and I can hear their voices somewhere behind me. Not close yet, but moving.

I turn right, down the dark alley, staying close to the fences and garages, running fast. Faster than I'd thought I could run. Wind blowing past me with force. My legs and arms and chest pushing forward.

A block and a half away, I hop a fence, then slip into a garage. It's hard to see because it's so dark, but my eyes are adjusting to the limited light.

I hear their voices in the alley, right outside the garage. I can see the outlines of their bodies through the dirty, cracked windows.

Once they pass, I find what I am looking for, gasoline in a metal can high up on an old shelf. I also find a screwdriver on the floor and put it in my jacket pocket.

I hear the kids still walking down the alley. They are talking to one another, bouncing their hands along fences and garage doors. Not trying to be quiet as they look for me. But also there's the reality that there is no other noise. In the North End, at night, there is a nearly total lack of sound. These four kids, they have no idea how loud they are. And so I hear it all, every step they take, every fence they touch, every breath they inhale then exhale as they walk.

"Where'd he go?" one asks.

I listen for a minute and make sure I hear four voices. All four of them left the car.

I slide out of the garage door, then head into the dark, abandoned house in front of the garage. It's a small house that only takes a few minutes to get started. I leave through the front door. I'm two blocks from their car. I cross the street in darkness, standing behind a low shed, watching the house begin to burn. In another few minutes, the kids all show up, staring at the burning house, standing near it at first, but then having to step back as the fire grows. They are laughing as they watch it, one jumping in place, another beginning to do some bad Native American dance, a bad impersonation of a warrior around a campfire.

Boys always like fire.

I turn away from them, moving behind a house, then finding the alley and running again. A few blocks away, I go back into the street.

I can see the glow from the fire. The boys still stand there, the four of them now still, watching the flames, staring up, mouths slightly open, rooted in place in the street before the blaze.

They have forgotten all about me.

And the sound of the fire is loud. Consuming every other noise the kids might otherwise hear.

I'm standing next to their car. I take the screwdriver and break the valves on both front tires, the air now escaping with a high and steady hiss. Through the open window on the passenger side, I pour the last of the gasoline on the seat and light it, the fabric catching quickly, already spreading up the insides of the car's upholstery.

I look back to where the kids are, but they don't even turn. They are staring at the house on fire. I'm sure they'll watch it for some time.

I lift my camera. Take a picture.

Then I walk toward the nearest fence and slip through the gate. The car burning brightly now. But I only cross the black backyard, then enter the alley.

It's another twenty minutes till I reach my hotel.

There was a time when those kids would have scared me. A time when I would have quickly handed the camera to them. But I'm past that time. I'm not that person.

And although it's unclear to me who I have become, I know I'm not a person that I would have ever known.

• • •

It's months since the woman and boy left here.

Moments that fade. Conversations I can't quite remember.

Because much of my memory is, of course, taken up with the things that happened.

So much of my memory. My thoughts.

My time.

• • •

At night, even covered by the many blankets on my couch, I hear a crash, thick and deep and distant, as another levee collapses to the north, the hiss of water rushing southward, the sound in the air echoing heavily, the water from the bay moving another few blocks toward me.

• • •

I have been walking for a few hours along a very old section of downtown when I notice something out of place in the rows of old, two-story brick buildings. I see the difference only because I'm across the street, where I can see past the top edge of the rooflines.

There is ivy. Bright green ivy, growing along the top edge of three of the buildings.

And there is a tree. A tall, leafy tree, only its top visible as it grows inside one of the buildings.

It's the first green tree, the ivy the first living plant, that I've seen in many years.

I cross the empty street, wind blowing hard against my right side. There are windows on the fronts of the three buildings, but heavy shutters have been pulled tightly closed. The doors are all locked. Two doors have metal gates on them but the wooden door to the left does not. There is a burned-out car half a block away and I sort through the mess in the car before finding a tire iron.

After a minute of prying on the building's door, I get it to open.

On the other side of the door, there is green. A courtyard, or small park. The three buildings have no roofs, no interior walls or floors. The front brick walls are braced with large timbers leaning at angles against them, the timbers also green, with ivy and flowering vines twisted all around them.

I am not far from my hotel. But I had no idea such a place existed. There is no green in the North End, no trees or flowers or shrubs of any kind.

Here, though, are shrubs and flowers and a tall tree in the middle of the space. It's a young tree even as tall as it has grown, the branches covering a narrow space, the trunk itself not much thicker than my hand.

There's something astonishing in this. An awe that renders me not quite able to speak or think or move.

The entire area is a hundred feet wide and two hundred feet deep, bordered on the front by the facades of the buildings, bordered on the sides and back by the tall brick walls of the neighboring structures. The ground floors of the three buildings have mostly been removed. But in some places concrete and brick remain, creating pathways between the plants, leading to a small stone fountain attached to a wall, to a table and chairs near another wall.

The only sounds are the running water from the fountain and the wind blowing across the open door I came through.

"The tree took quite a bit of effort," a voice says and I flinch, startled by the sound. I turn to see a man sitting in a low chair near a table. "I'd prefer if you did not cut it down for firewood."

"Of course not," I say. "I'm sorry. I'll go."

91

He stands up slowly. He is middle-aged, semi-bearded, a black man wearing old corduroys and a heavy sweater under his thick blazer.

"You don't need to," he says. "But close the door if you would."

I close the door, then turn back to him. With the door closed, it's nearly silent here, no sound of wind. Just water running. I see that the water flows from the fountain to a stone pond on one side of the courtyard.

The man has a book sitting on the low table next to him. There are blankets on his chair. It is not too cold in here, though, as the wind doesn't blow.

The stillness, the quiet, are deeper than anything I can remember.

"I'm sorry I broke your door," I say.

He shakes his head. "Don't worry. It's fine for it to be unlocked. I don't come or go that way. But maybe now I will."

I look around to see how else he might get in and out of here. On the far back wall, there is a doorway, open, that leads into one of the buildings.

"This is what I do here," he says. "I garden." He looks around. "I guess everyone here has some kind of purpose. This is mine."

I put my hands in my jacket pockets. An affirmation, I think, a sign that I am listening.

"For years I worked with the scavengers," he says. "But eventually I focused just on this."

I have a question but can't figure out how to ask it. We're quiet for a while.

"Nothing grows here," I finally say. "Nothing grows at all."

He looks around. "It's not that nothing can grow," the man says, pausing. "The old plants, the vegetation that existed, obviously that's all been wiped out. It will no longer grow. But that doesn't mean other plants can't survive."

He begins to walk along one of the brick paths, slowly, and in a moment I follow him.

"You brought the plants in from the South End?" I ask.

"I trade with the scavengers. They then trade with the brokers, who can find me every type of plant I want. It comes with their mentality. Traders and barterers. There seems to be no plant too exotic that they cannot eventually find."

We're silent again.

"I was a professor," he says. He moves very slowly and his arms and hands and even his fingers seem very long, his brown skin in this light made flat and colorless. "I grew up here. I left a long time ago." He pauses. "Then I came back a few years ago."

He sits down at the table with the two chairs. In a moment, I sit in the other chair.

My wariness is sourceless but ingrained. A way of life for so many years. Wary of people and what they might say. Wary of strangers and what they might ask. Wary of my ability to interact, to talk, to even for a moment connect.

I ask him, "Why come back?"

"I came back to try to help," he says. He leans an elbow on the table, but is sitting facing slightly away from me.

"Quite obviously," he says, "I got here much too late to help."

The garden he's created, it brings about some kind of calm. The place feels warmer, not just in the absence of the sharp wind, but in the aura of the branches and the vines along the walls and the long grasses planted in curving rows along the ground. I find myself touching a small flower that grows up the side of the wall. I hadn't meant to touch it. I only realize what I am doing as I notice he is watching me.

I take my hand away from the flower.

"Why are you here?" he asks.

I think of him as being much older than me, but as I look at him I eventually realize that we are about the same age.

In another moment, I shake my head. I can't answer his question.

He leans back in his chair, again turned slightly away from me. Staring up at the tree in the center of the courtyard. He moves very slowly, as if some part of him is very much asleep. "That's fine," he says.

I find myself staring at the tree again, following the trunk where it meets the ground up to the branches spread out above us. Growing, right now.

"I should ask," he says, "what is your capacity for violence?"

I shake my head. Confused.

"The scavengers ask that of the new people," he says, smiling some. "'What is your capacity for violence?' People are honest among the scavengers. You work from dawn to dusk next to a group of strangers, doing work that is terrible, hard, involved. You want to know something about a person's nature. At what point do they become impatient, what makes them angry, are they frustrated by difficulty."

I run my fingers along the waxy leaves of ivy. The leaves are smooth and soft and spring back in place after I disturb them. I have a moment where I want to press my face against the leaves, but I blink then, and pull my hand away.

I say to him, "I don't think of this as a place where there is violence. Or danger. Not from one another."

He leans back farther in his chair, balancing on the rear legs of the chair, the back of his head touching the ivy. "It's a strange thing, isn't it? No roaming bands of violent men. No lawless acts of depravity."

"Maybe we're just too tired," I say to him.

"Maybe," he says. "But it's also a place of an unexpected abundance. There are no luxuries. But, at the same time, there are few basic needs that are not readily met."

I can't understand how he's gotten so much to grow here.

"And yet, none of that," he says, "speaks to a person's capacity for violence."

I don't understand how all this can be alive.

"I'm one of the people who believes," he says, turning to me, "that whatever poisons are in the air and dirt and water, I don't believe they're insurmountable. Don't believe that what is happening here can't eventually be stopped."

He tells me his name. I nod and tell him mine.

"I know who you are," he says. "Most everyone here, you see, they know who you are."

This makes me wince, though he's turned away and doesn't seem to notice.

He is pointing toward a table near the fountain. I can see my newspaper, three or four of them, stacked on the table's lower shelf.

94

"I enjoy what you write," he says.

I remember that, from years ago, before I came here. People enjoy what I write. They like me because of what I put in print.

I ask, "How do you know this can actually be stopped?"

He smiles some. Shakes his head slightly. "Good question." He leans to the side. His motions are remarkably slow, methodical. "Because we don't know for sure, do we?"

I'm staring at my hands for a moment. Seeing if they move as slowly as his. After a minute, I think to ask, "What do you trade with the scavengers? To get them to bring you these plants."

His hand reaches out to his armrest, grabs it as if he's going to stand. But he doesn't. "Gardens," he says. "I help them build gardens of their own."

I shake my head. In silent surprise. That there could be a garden like this. That this man can even help people create gardens of their own.

"They are really quite beautiful," he says.

His arms, I realize, his cheek and neck, are all scarred. Deeply. From his time as a scavenger.

I touch the tree trunk before I go. He watches me do it and it seems like a much too personal, even intimate act. But still I need to touch it. The bark is rough but slightly soft, water in the surface of the bark, the tree growing now, right in front of me.

"Come back some time," he says. "Any time."

And again I think I've spoken out loud, but in a moment I realize I haven't. "I will," I think I've said. But I'm already out the door.

• • •

I'm looking across acres of cars and trucks and buses and farm equipment, all spread out in the collected order of this junkyard in the industrial zone. The newer cars are parked farther away, I can see that with my binoculars, and the oldest vehicles are nearest me.

A half a mile by a half a mile, the junkyard is lower than the rest of the industrial zone. And the ground is covered in water. Six inches of it. From a levee that is leaking or has collapsed completely. It happened recently, the cars, the thousands of vehicles, all now looking like they are simply floating on the surface of a sea.

• • •

The scavengers are within a few blocks of where people here still live. They have reached one of the once grand boulevards that runs from downtown to a group of some of the North End's oldest neighborhoods. I can see this from my windows, the clean swath of buildings that have been scavenged already, leading toward the wide avenue, gray and still. Block after block of houses are in the scavengers' current path.

It's not clear which direction the scavengers will go when they reach the avenue. The decisions about direction, about which area will be scavenged next, have always seemed so fluid and unclear. No one person is in charge of the scavengers. Instead, the value of what they find has always seemed to define the direction in which they move, as they quickly survey a house or building, sometimes passing over it just by looking at it, sometimes exploring that building for minutes or an hour before deciding it is not worth the time.

The scavengers will not touch a property where someone lives. There is no mentality of the angry mob. They are guided instead by the barely spoken decisions of a few hundred different people, those choices drawing the brokers who buy the items, the vendors who sell them food and water, the scavenging concentrated as the group slowly edges forward.

But now, if they move across the avenue, they will be scavenging a neighborhood dotted with current residents. It would represent a major change, a disruption of the landscape where people have chosen to continue to live. A neighborhood would then be altered even more, making it even more uninhabitable.

"Scavenging an occupied neighborhood," the gardener says to me, "would confirm a fate that, now, goes unspoken. That the neighborhood will never come back to life."

I write about this in the paper.

Within a few days, people are leaving letters at the office. They have written to say that the scavengers should not come across the avenue. Six letters in total, each short, but all signed at the bottom. Most have street addresses in or near the neighborhood, but then others are from addresses far away from the scavenging. They are people who know that, someday, the scavengers could move toward them.

I print the letters in the paper. More letters follow the next week. All say the scavengers should turn away.

Within a few weeks I can see it, the swath of distorted cleanliness, it is turning, southward, away from the avenue and the neighborhood. Instead it moves along the highway wall.

Some of the scavengers probably live there, I realize, in the neighborhood they've avoided.

But also there is the fact that the scavengers are people who simply need and want to work. Who've found some purpose and sense of place.

Their point is not to destroy, they've now said. It's not to ruin. Or to even harm.

• • •

I'm in the office, the press running in the basement underneath me as I file my notes in pale yellow folders. My notes from that week's stories. I pull the pages out of my notebook, staple them together, put them in the file folder with my typed copy of the story about a house along one of the canals. I put the negatives from the photos in the folder too. Everything related to that story is in one place. That way my notes are easier to find. And there's the continuity. I have made something, even just a file, with facts and numbers and a history of a building, a house, a week in the life of the few people who now live in the North End.

The notes, the photos, the newspapers themselves, printed and distributed and archived here at the office and archived carefully at the library, I think of myself as leaving these things for someone else to someday find.

• • •

There is so little noise here. Mostly, when I walk the neighborhoods or the industrial zone or among the buildings near my hotel, I am the only sound I hear.

But in a neighborhood near downtown, I find a brick building taking up half the block. The building buzzes. It's a mechanical sound, I realize, as I get closer to it. A steady, arrhythmic drone.

WATER PUMP NO. 1.

A name is cut into the stone about the doors.

Inside, there are pumps, massive black pipes leading out of and then into the concrete floor.

"Hello."

An old woman, sixty, is standing up from a green desk near one of the pumps.

I shake my head. "Sorry."

She shakes her head. "It's okay."

I look around. "This brings water to the North End?"

She nods. "It comes up from the massive aquifer beneath us. For going on eighty years."

I take my notebook from my pocket. "Can I write this down?"

She points to her desk. A newspaper, an article of mine. "Yes."

No one pays her to still work here. Yet she's worked here for three decades. Lives in her family house just a few blocks away.

"I don't need very much," she says. "And really, the station, it runs itself."

"The water seems so clean," I say.

"I guess it is. I don't know." She smiles some. "I just make sure it's pumped up from the ground."

She lives alone. Her husband passed. No children. A sister left long ago.

She smiles again, more this time.

I take her picture.

"It's a good life, I think," she says. She looks around. "I read. I listen to music. At night, I sleep very well."

. . .

There is an abandoned airport here that I sometimes visit. It's far away, nearly eight miles from my building, on the outer edge of the oldest parts of the industrial zone. I ride my bike there, a simple black bike that I found years ago and that I don't often use.

Most days, I would rather walk.

Most days, I do not go very far.

Most days, the speed of traveling even by bike is unnecessary and almost upsetting. A reminder, in the wind pressing at my face and whipping past my ears, of the pace of a life I used to live. Driving fast through neighborhoods, seeming to run from my car to my office door, from a grocery store to the parking lot to the driveway to the kitchen, crashing into the house, the rest of them crashing in there too, all of us in constant motion, bouncing off each other as we hugged and said hello and pushed one another lightly but with purpose toward the next event of another day, homework and dinner and baths and sports, the rapid dance of the well-meaning and disconnected, beyond conscious, beyond aware, simply moving forward still, keep on moving forward, toward your next task and your next activity.

The wind, on the bike, is cold across my face and eyes.

I've decided that this week I'll write about the airport.

I ride up the long ramp leading to what was once the departure area. Signs for Terminal A and Terminal B, directions for parking, commands to stop or not to stop, the brand names of airlines now faded and peeling from metal signs stretched above the road.

There are doors missing near the center of Terminal B and I ride through them into the building. It's a vast and empty place. Blue counters where passengers once checked in, black conveyor belts where luggage once disappeared into the bowels of this facility, rope lines still cordoning off an impending rush of passengers, ready to corral them into simple mazes.

Enter Here.

This airport was closed a decade before the North End was itself abandoned. A bigger, brighter airport was built in the South End, justified through so many promises of new uses for the old airport.

Nothing happened.

The airport has been partially stripped of items. Most of this was done when the airport was first closed. The TV monitors were removed. The stores and restaurants were emptied of goods and cash registers and kitchen equipment. Since then, not much else has changed. There are chairs and tables in the empty food court. Rows of seats at each gate.

I ride toward the security checkpoint, passing through a dusty metal detector. The floors of the airport seem to have been formed from the densest bedrock, as if the airport had been built on stone that has always been here, that was simply buffed and polished into a floor.

The children once ran along concourses like this. Late for a flight or excited to have arrived. Six of us, our own tour group we joked, with six suitcases and six backpacks and a multitude of soft and special items, a favorite blanket or a favorite bear, brought along on this trip for comfort, a necessity, a mobile connection between some new destination and our home.

I glide now, coasting on the bike.

We always loved to travel.

A security guard walks along the end of the concourse, in blue and black uniform, a hat, black shoes, a gun and flashlight on his belt.

I have seen him here before. Have spoken to him one time, for an article in the paper. "I have worked at this airport for many decades. I worked here when this place was new. Worked here when the city built the new airport to the south. Worked here when this airport was shut down but still a crew of twenty watched over and maintained the place. Worked here when, one day, no one else showed up. When the power no longer came on. When the street on which I live saw its last neighbor pack up and leave in his small car. I have always worked here in this airport. I have decided that I always will."

He raises a hand in my direction now, but makes no motion to come toward me. He turns to a door along the concourse, pushes it, disappears out of my view.

EMPLOYEES ONLY.

I ride to the very end of the concourse, where the walls push out into a circle and the ceiling rises even higher, vaulting upward, like a church or concert hall. I circle the room, slowly, staring up at the tall and unnecessary space. A grand reflection of our want to travel, an epic celebration of routine departure and arrival.

I circle again. Circle once more.

After a few minutes, I stop my bike along the wall, push open a door, carry my bike down a flight of stairs to ground level. On the tarmac outside, I start riding again. The smoothest concrete.

The airport was in near perfect condition when it was closed. There were complaints of an outdated baggage system, of a need for updates to the lighting. But these were really just excuses, thin justifications for the fundamental desire to have a new airport, one closer to the South End. To save twenty minutes in a car. To prevent people from having to drive through the rapid decay in the north.

This happened many times here. The central train station was demolished then replaced with a massive parking lot. Retail was abandoned downtown for a vast mall on the edge of the South End, a mall that was left vacant just a few decades later as a newer mall was built even farther to the south. The trolleys were torn up with funding from automakers who wanted more room for their ever larger cars. The roads themselves built wider, separating neighborhoods as crosswalks were removed to help the traffic move even faster, the roads getting so wide that the cost to maintain and repair them grew beyond anyone's expectation or ability. Parks removed to make way for strip malls and highway on-ramps, the biggest of the parks cut through with the highway and the overpass near the community center, the south side of the park turned into strip centers, the north littered with thin, cheap houses of one size. Neighborhoods dominated by brick buildings and corner stores and baseball in the street were wiped away and replaced by vast and anonymous apartments. Grand homes torn down to make way for low duplexes with few windows and no porches. Schools left half empty as more and more people moved away, willing to spend tax money only on the new schools that they built, not the once-great schools they left behind. The wealth of a whole city drawn south, where billions could be spent on the new as the old was left to survive on a fraction of those dollars. And the city government that allowed all this to happen, that made decisions that drove more and more people away, some members of that government ended up in jail for their corruption. But most people in the government simply moved south with the masses, their abuse and their ineptitude never acknowledged or documented.

As I ride, I am in my mind writing this all up for the paper.

It's not a story I've written before. Even though all of us here know it to be true.

I near the airport's tall control tower, fifteen stories high, a concrete cylinder topped by a white circular structure, like a 1950s UFO with antennae and dishes atop it. I climb the stairs to the top room in the control tower, looking out over the whole airport. The spider web extensions of the terminal and its concourses. The accordion draped tunnels used to empty passengers from the planes. The massive hangars where aircraft were once maintained and repaired.

Like all of the North End, the airport was built on land claimed many decades ago from the bay, the land made available by a massive extension of the levees and canals. I find binoculars in a cabinet. I look out from the tower to the north and can see the far edge of Runway 1.

There is water, spread out, covering half of Runway 1. And covering all of Runway 2.

And beyond the runways, there is only water.

This is new. This is recent. Another few square miles have been reclaimed. The failure of the levees spreads. The destruction, it moves south.

But really, I'm still only thinking about how we always loved to travel.

CHAPTER 6

The commission meets. Empty talk of fixing things. Fixing this. Making the North End right.

Empty talk of leveling things. Destroying things. Flattening this city to the ground.

Fifteen people sit in the audience, silent, listening to the words.

"Why are we even here?" one of the commissioners asks. He is getting angry, animated. It is cartoonish for him to do that here, in a place where people live in a self-imposed quiet and calm. He shakes his head repeatedly. He throws his hands up in the air. I wonder if he will stand, throw a fit, angrily march off the low stage.

I try to describe his actions in my notebook.

"Why don't we shut down the places where these people still live?" this commissioner asks. "Cut the power and water, as we did in the bad neighborhoods in the South End?"

I find that I am angry. At first I don't even know what the feeling is. A weight on my chest and a desire to stand. A need to move. To yell. To say something to these commissioners.

"That," he continues, "that, we know now, was the smartest thing we did in the south. Now let's do it here."

And then I picture the woman and her boy. I remember her story. And I know that what I feel is anger.

The commissioner wags a thick finger at the crowd. He shakes his bald head from side to side.

The people in the crowd all stare.

I find I want to yell at him. But I only take my notes. Different notes than usual. Where I write down every single word. Wanting suddenly to be sure I put each of his words into the newspaper. So that everyone can read each word he says.

"Can I speak for a moment?" one of the commissioners says to the animated man. She is leaning back in her chair, staring at him. Again she's in a suit, again with her hair pulled tight to her scalp, once again the nondescript vision of a business executive. It's unclear to me how old she is. She could be fifty. She could be thirty.

The first commissioner throws his hands up, lurches back in his chair. "Fine. We've obviously got all night."

"We are here," she says, and I see her tap a finger on the table, "because the court has ruled that this is our place to oversee. That, quite clearly, is the reason you are here, albeit against your will. And against your wishes." She pauses, staring at him. "And because you are forced to do this, because you haven't chosen it, you speak at every meeting about destruction. Tearing down what's left here. Driving off the few residents who remain. You speak of this not for any reason other than this: you want your responsibility to go away."

He stares down at the table. There's a moment where it seems like he will argue with her. He looks out at the room. At the few straggling people who sit and watch the commission talk.

In a moment, he only nods.

There is no one here he needs to impress. No one here he needs to deceive. Even he must see this now. He leans back in his chair. He sighs and closes his eyes.

"And so," the woman says, "I think what you need is to be quiet. Because there is no money, none, to do these things you talk about. Tearing down buildings, cutting power and water and gas lines. Even putting up a for sale sign to sell off every parcel in the North End. Even if we wanted to do these things, and I do not, even then there is no money to pay for these things to happen."

Eventually, he nods his head again.

"Two thousand people live here," she says. "Maybe there is something we can do to help them. Because that is the other reason we should be here— maybe, possibly, we can help."

Still I want to yell. To stand and yell. But I am only sitting, writing in my notebook as quickly as I can.

Why this commissioner thinks his effort to clear people of their homes will help is unclear. Instead, all evidence is that the commission has, for decades now, failed and failed and failed.

There is a newspaper rack near the door to the community center. As they leave at the end of the meeting, only one of the commissioners picks up a paper. The woman. She holds the paper in her hands, skims the front page, then turns to where I am still sitting, finishing my notes. She walks over.

She puts her hand out and introduces herself. I stand slowly, then shake her hand. It is smooth and warm. So rare for me to be near anyone, let alone touch someone in any way.

"Obviously," she says, "I'm new to this commission."

I hadn't noticed that she is new, even though I've come to every meeting for years. How many of these people are new? How often have old commissioners dropped away? They are interchangeable to me. There has never been a difference between them.

I nod, though. As if acknowledging what she's said.

"Do you have time to talk about this place?" she asks me.

I stare for a moment. The normalcy of interaction is almost unknown to me. She doesn't understand this.

"Time," I say. "When?" I ask.

"Now?" she asks.

She seems taller than me, though I know she isn't. But she stands on high-heeled shoes and her hair is pulled tightly up and away from her face.

I look down at my notebook. I notice my camera on a chair and pick it up.

"Another time," I say. "Yes. I can talk."

"Okay," she says. "When?"

I put my notebook in my pocket. It takes a moment for me to speak. "When," I repeat.

"Do you have a phone number or email?" she asks. "A way to get in touch."

I look around the room. It takes a moment.

"It'd be best," I say, "for us to meet."

She gets her phone from her purse. "Where?" she asks.

I say, "At the paper. At the offices of the paper."

"I will be there tomorrow morning," she says and puts her hand out to me again.

I take it, warm fingers, the oddity of this convention, touching to say hello and to say good-bye, the strange but accepted intimacy of a glancing, routine connection.

"In the afternoon," I say.

She nods. "Thank you," she says and turns to leave.

And I am suddenly exhausted, foggy with a need to sleep, unsure that I can even walk, walk all the way to my hotel. But I go outside and the air is cold and the wind blows sharply in the night and as I walk I stay awake, even with the fog all across my mind. Too much talking, too much touching. So many questions from another person, a strain on my mind and voice and my ability to respond as if this all were normal. As if this place were normal.

As if I were normal too.

It's a full hour of walking before I'm able to escape the circling exhaustion. To emerge from the hazy, fading warmth and now begin to focus on the house, the basement, the fire I now start, burning down this home again.

• • •

The commissioner comes to the office on time. I'm alone and the door is propped open, letting cold air pour into the room, sometimes rattling the papers on my desk.

She looks around the dimly lit office. Ten empty desks where reporters and editors and salespeople once sat. Framed covers of old papers on the walls. Dark, metal file cabinets lining the room, one holding my story notes, the many others filled with old story files, accounting records, ancient advertising orders.

The office manager is already gone. The press does not run today. And so we're here alone.

The commissioner sits in a wooden chair across from my desk and begins to ask me questions. She speaks quickly and, for this place, almost loudly. She operates at a much different speed than anyone I've dealt with in years and it's hard for me to keep up with her. For the most part, she is interested in facts about the North End. How we live. How we eat. What people do with their time. She has a vague understanding of these things, it seems. But the details aren't clear at all.

"How do you have money?" she asks.

"Many people work as scavengers," I say. "Brokers buy the things they gather. Vendors sell food and other items from tables set up downtown."

"And you," she says. "How do you make money?"

"I'm paid to run the paper," I say.

"By whom?"

I am sliding my finger along the edge of my desk, absently, thinking about my answer. "By whoever owns this paper."

This slows her down a moment and she pauses, looking around the room. She turns back to me. "Why do you live here?" she asks.

"I grew up here," I say.

"That's not an answer," she says.

"I know," I say.

She moves her head, maybe in agreement, I'm not sure. Her fingernails shine in the dim light.

"What would you like to see happen here?" she asks me.

I have to think about what she's asking. "I'm not really sure," I finally say. "It's not something that I think about."

"But you write about this place every week."

"I write about how things are. How things were. I guess people find that interesting."

She moves her head again, not nodding, not disagreeing. Her hair is black, uniform in color and in the way it is pressed against her scalp.

"If I could bring one thing to this place," she asks, "what would you want that thing to be?"

It's a very confusing question for me and I find myself having to break apart her phrases, each word, before I can answer. "I don't want anything," I say. "I don't need anything."

"What would other people want? The other people living here."

I shake my head. "I don't know."

Her face changes, her eyes getting smaller, and I realize that I'm frustrating her.

"I'm not trying to be difficult," I say.

"I guess that your choice to continue to live here, to live this way, it's just something too personal to discuss."

I find that I'm biting my upper lip. I tap my hand on the table, a sign of agreement, I think. I'm not sure that I agree with her. But I think that I should give her that impression.

She presses her hands against her knees. It seems like she's about to leave. I don't like that I have frustrated her.

"I think," I say, pausing, "I think that what most people here would like are very basic things."

She leans back in her chair. "Like what?"

"Like better food. Different food. I think they'd like the streetlights to work wherever people live. I think they'd like for outsiders to stay away."

She smiles slightly and it seems strange to me. I didn't think she is a person who smiles. "I'll be sure to remember that," she says.

I shake my head. "No, not you. By outsiders I mean bad people. Sometimes, bad people come through here. Teenagers. Gangs. People looking for trouble. That's what I mean, what anyone here means by an outsider."

The words, the thoughts, the effort to answer her questions, it wears me out. My eyes feel heavy with sleep.

But she keeps on asking. And I keep trying to answer. We talk about electricity. We talk more about the food. We talk again about how people make money and where they spend it. We talk about the overpass staying open and about how little the commission has done.

"Truly," I hear myself say, "they have done absolutely nothing."

It's dark outside by the time we've finished talking. My eyes feel like they are half-closed and I want very much to put my head down. I have not answered so many questions, have not talked for so long, in many, many years.

"Thank you," she says, standing.

From the open door, I can hear the rain falling onto the street and side-walk, quietly. There's no wind in the cold air tonight, so it's as if I can hear every drop around me.

I remember one more thing to tell her. "And the levees are breaking to the north," I say. "People want the levees fixed. Or else we'll all be under-water."

She stares at me. Silent. She says finally, "What do you mean?"

"If enough levees break," I say, "then the North End will be flooded."

She looks down at her notes, then back at me. "I didn't know that."

"Only so many levees can break," I say, "before all the rest will give way too."

"How many is too many?"

"I don't know," I say to her. "But each one that breaks puts more pressure on the rest."

She stares at me. "An hour we've spent talking about how people live here, how small improvements might be made in their lives, and only now do you tell me that the entire North End could be washed away."

I can't tell if she is angry at me or just surprised. I've lost that sort of ability to read people's tone and their expressions. I say to her, "Most days, even people here don't think about the levees. They think only about the day before them."

Soon she stands in the doorway to the street, looking out into the dark. I sit at my desk, watching her. The air blows into the office, colder now and rattling the papers in the rack near the door.

She turns back toward me. I'm slow to realize that she is nervous about going outside.

I get up and go to the door, standing next to her and looking out at the street.

"I know I shouldn't be afraid," she says quietly. "Everyone here says there is no crime. But in the South End, they tell you this place is more dangerous than anywhere in the world."

In a moment, she adds, "I parked around the corner. I didn't quite know where I was going."

I say to her, "I'll walk with you."

I close the door behind me, then walk next to her. We turn a corner and she points toward her black car parked halfway down the block. I hear noise, though, and turn to look down the street. A white car is moving slowly, music thumping, the underside of the car lit up neon blue.

"There isn't crime here," I say to her, watching the white car slow at the intersection, then gun its engine as it makes a U-turn. "But those people," I say, "they aren't from here."

Two kids, in layers of T-shirts and their arms tattooed and faces pierced across their noses and mouths and eyes, they pull up in front of us. The kid in the passenger's seat is closest to us. He says, "Where are you two going?"

I say to him, "Nowhere."

The kid has his hand on the car door, as if ready to open it at any moment. "No, really," he says. "Where are you two going?"

The other kid, the driver, he is laughing.

"Nowhere," I say, staring at them.

Their car is pointed away from the office. I push the commissioner, suddenly, and she is moving as I pull her arm. I hear the car's engine behind us and hope that they've pulled forward, to turn around, hope that no one has gotten out of the car. We turn the corner, running, crashing against the office door, now inside, slamming the door shut and locking it. Turning off all the lights.

I can see through the dingy window the car turning onto this street, driving slowly. But it doesn't stop in front of the building.

In a moment, though, I can see the shadow of one of the kids getting out of the car.

He keeps walking. Along the street toward the office.

I don't want him to find us, but I also keep thinking that I don't want him to know about this office. To know where to find me when this is done.

"Follow me," I say to the commissioner, and we make our way through the office, to the stairway leading down to the pressroom. There's only one light on in the pressroom.

We stand for a minute.

She presses her hands together, hard, so that her fingers bend. "I hate to be afraid," she says.

"We'll leave through the alley," I say. "Give them a minute to move on."

She still presses her hands together. I see her teeth are pressed tightly together. She is trying to get rid of her fear.

We can hear one of the kids, maybe both, banging on the front door upstairs, the glass rattling. They move on, though, and I can hear them banging on the doors of buildings next to us, soon breaking windows as they move down the street.

"I hate to be afraid," she says again. "It seems so weak. Unnecessary."

The noise upstairs, from outside, has stopped. I am breathing hard. Then I realize this. Hear myself breathing. And so I close my eyes. One more breath. Calm.

I say to her, "It doesn't seem unnecessary."

From a closet near the tool chest, I pull out a broken axe handle, heavy and smooth, like an old baseball bat. "We leave now," I say.

She is looking at the handle. She moves in place, oddly, and I realize she is stepping out of her high-heeled shoes.

We head up the back staircase to the small loading dock. There is a small door at the end of the big garage. I listen at the door, then open it and we go out into the very dark alley. The door locks behind us.

We get to the end of the alley, a dark street, with streetlights all out. We walk close to the buildings, turning right, then right again to come out on the street where the commissioner's car is parked. The teenagers and their white car are gone.

We move quickly, not quite a run. She gets her keys out as we reach her car.

The white car pulls around the corner.

"Go," I say to her.

"Get in," she says, as she slides into the front seat.

I shake my head, turn away. "Go," I say. I push her door closed. I am yelling now, a voice so unfamiliar and loud and coming from a place I no longer know or recognize. "Go now."

Along the building next to me there are loose cinder blocks in a pile. I walk to them and pick one up, heavy, the surface so rough that it feels like it will cut my hand.

The commissioner's car has started but she's hesitating to leave.

As the white car comes down the road, I begin walking toward it, the cinder block heavy but I step faster, turning slightly, building momentum as I move into the street in front of the white car, hurling the cinder block upward, less throwing it at the white car than just lifting the block up into the air so that the car drives right into it.

It crashes through the windshield.

The car stops, the driver screaming, the passenger screaming too, both covered in tiny shards of glass. I have the broken axe handle in my other hand. I bust out the driver's side window, move to the back of the car and bust out the rear window too.

The kids are screaming at me, screaming, "Stop," but I am on the passenger side, swinging at another window, breaking it in an explosion of tiny shards of glass.

I see, for a moment, the commissioner in her black car across the street, still not driving away. Staring at me from her seat.

But I turn back to the white car.

The passenger is writhing in place. The driver is holding his arm. I can see the cinder block next to the gear shift. The passenger keeps writhing and then I see it, silver, a gun in the passenger's hand, and I shove the heavy handle straight at the side of the passenger's head, the blunt end smashing against his ear. He grabs his head, dropping the gun, and I lean my head into the car, the driver moaning and the passenger gagging like he might vomit and I pick up the gun.

It's heavy. It feels like it will fall over.

I don't know if the gun's safety is on so I just pull the trigger, aiming at the dashboard. The shot is loud, ringing, a flash of light and the gun jerks back, far enough to hit the roof. I almost drop the gun. My head is still in the car and I'm not far from the passenger. Both of them have turned their heads away, bending over, the passenger covering his head with both his hands. The driver is holding one hand over his head, the other hand still pointing down, lame and bleeding, broken by the cinder block I threw at the car.

"Go away," I say to them, loudly I think, but my ears are ringing so it's hard to know.

They are both still bent over, away from me, not looking.

"Throw your gun out the window," I say to the driver, and he does, quickly. "And now go away. Like I said. Go away."

I pull my head out of the car. The passenger is still leaning over. The driver takes a moment before he allows himself to look my way, briefly, then he turns, to the steering wheel, realizing the car is still running. He starts to drive, the car moving slowly down the street, turning at the corner.

The commissioner is still in her car. Staring at me.

I walk over to the other gun, pick it up. I don't know much about guns, so it takes me a moment to find the safety on both of them. I look around and see a sewer drain along the curb. I drop both guns in the drain, hearing them rattle as they fall down into that sewer.

The commissioner is still staring. Her window is open. She is saying something, but it's quiet because of the ringing in my ears or because of her car's engine or because she's not speaking loud enough.

I walk closer to her.

"They'll come back," she is saying.

I shake my head. "No, they won't."

"They'll come back," she says.

"No," I say again and I put my hand on her door frame and she stares at it. She slowly leans away from me. And there it is, me causing her to be afraid. But I'm able to say to her, "People fear this place. That's why the commissioners barely step inside. That's why kids come here looking for trouble.

Because everyone believes this place," I say, "they believe it will somehow kill you."

I find myself needing to breathe. My left hand is shaking but I realize this and think about it and, in a moment, I make it stop.

"What I've done," I say to her, "is made them fear the North End even more. So that they'll stay away."

I start to talk again, but I can see that she doesn't hear me. Doesn't hear a word. She knows nothing but her fear. She knows nothing but the memory of a scene she can't imagine. Nothing but to stare at my hand still pressed against her door.

• • •

I remember the woman and her boy in the playground below my building. Air against my face as I look out my hotel window.

I think that I should ask the gardener what could be planted to make the playground grow.

It would be nice to have some things that grow.

"I would like to plant some things," I say to him a few days later.

The gardener is sitting in his chair in his courtyard. He has a blanket across his lap, draped down across his legs and feet. His motions are so slow and in the pale light his brown skin looks like clay and I remember that when I first met him I thought he was older than me. But he's not.

He smiles some. "What sort of things?"

I'm sitting too and I also have a blanket across my lap.

"There's a playground," I say. "Near my building. Whatever would work there."

He nods and from his table picks up a pencil and notepad. He writes a few things down.

"It'll take a few weeks," he says. "But when they get here, I'll show you what to do."

I thank him.

"Do you have anything living in your home?" he asks.

"What do you mean?" I answer.

"Just that," he says. "Within your house or your apartment, wherever it is you live, is there anything alive?"

It takes a moment before I say, "No. Nothing at all."

He carefully pulls the blanket from his lap, lays it across the table next to him. He stands and walks across the courtyard. I focus on the sound of the water in the fountain. When he returns, he's carrying a small plant in a red clay pot.

He holds it out to me. Two of his fingers are cut off at the knuckle, the scars of the stitches still rough and red. Scavenging.

I shake my head. "You don't," I start to say, fumbling somewhat. "Really. It's fine."

"Take this," he says. "Water it only weekly. Someday soon, it will bloom. And even the green, just the green leaves, trust me. We want this. Need it. Our desire to find life, to base some part of our experience in the natural world," he says, now turning his eyes to look up at the sky, "that desire runs very deep, as we seek to find even fleeting, small experiences of the living."

And so I take it.

• • •

I stand outside the community center near the overpass, finishing my notes after a commission meeting.

The commissioner who met with me has missed the last two meetings. I assume this is her reaction to the incident with the teenagers. The gardener once asked me, *What is your capacity for violence?* By her absence, it seems, the commissioner is saying her capacity has been breached.

I don't fault her for this. Maybe it says something good about her, that seeing such a thing compels her to stay away.

The commission meetings are shorter when she's gone, I realize. Without the group's conscience in attendance, the commission is left to rapidly dismiss the problems they are charged with solving.

I write this in my notes.

Later, when I am typing up my article for the paper, I pause, thinking for a moment about whether to include the comment about the commissioner.

After a minute, I decide I will.

The group has always dismissed the South End's problems, I write. *But the commissioner,* I write, *she forced them to admit their collective weakness and futility.*

· · ·

There are worms in the soil and for a moment I am overwhelmed by a sudden and silent revulsion that makes me pull away. Reddish brown and in places almost purple, the worms writhe in the dirt, twisting themselves away from the surface I expose.

I'm in the playground below my building, digging up the dead plants along the brick wall. I've started with an area thirty feet wide. The plants and trees are slick and hard, but when I put a shovel under them, push down, the dead roots prove weak and shallow.

In just an hour I've already torn most of the old, dead shrubs and trees from the ground. I drag them to a pile outside the walled playground. Then I begin to dig in the middle of the now-cleared bed. I am planting with whatever the gardener has gotten for me. In this first delivery there are two trees just four feet tall that haven't yet managed to bloom, mere sticks, and a few low shrubs that are full and green, plus a whole pallet of low vines, ivy of a sort, green and white, and some leaves are deeply red.

I found the shovel and a rake and a few small hand spades, and a wheelbarrow that was in a shed behind a house just a quarter mile from here.

I'm on my knees, digging with one of the small hand tools, when I turn the gray dirt over and find the worms.

I lean back, lifting my knees, now squatting on my feet, still wincing some at the sight of the worms, five or more of them, entangled in sticks and one another just below the surface and I squint to think of all the worms beneath me, everywhere, if they're here they must be everywhere.

I wipe my hands on my jeans. I reach for a bottle I've filled with water. I watch as the worms dig down, twisting themselves into the dirt.

They're gone.

I have to remember that worms are good. That they are necessary. That there was a time when this world was filled with living things.

I drink water again.

Then I stick my shovel back into the dirt, digging my hole, and after a few minutes I've planted the first of the trees.

As I dig and clear the old shrubs, I find a stone fountain that has been knocked over. I find a small pond that is filled with dirt and matted leaves. Brick benches connected to the wall. A pathway that leads from benches to the swing set and the monkey bars. All of it had been covered with dead plants and matted leaves and the dirt that has spread everywhere.

The playground is quite old, the toys all made of heavy steel frames, thick chains on the swing set and the heavy, smoothly worn steel of the monkey bars. The brick is just as old. I don't know why I know this. But I touch it, run my hand along the rough bricks and the rougher mortar that holds them all together and it's clear these brick walls are many decades old.

The way they're made. Something permanent in their texture and design. Something that conveys the care with which they were so long ago created.

In my mind I have a rough idea of where the new plants will go, where the trees should grow and how the shrubs and ivy should fill the spaces. I don't know what the gardener will send me next, what types of plants he knows will grow here. But whatever he sends me will be fine.

I dig again. Then again. After many hours of this I am too cold to continue. It's dusk and the light is almost brown in the sky, something that happens periodically, when the cloud cover is oddly thin and spare. A sunset through the clouds, it seems, without bright light and golden sun. But even brown is a change from the otherwise constant gray.

My jeans and shirt and sweater are wet through to the skin, covered in dirt, and my hands, which had been hurting from the cold, have gone mostly numb. I gather my shovels and tools and take them inside the building.

There's a closet there, just inside the door, with a mop and bucket in it, and I stack the tools neatly next to them.

In my hotel room, I heat water on the gas stove in the kitchenette, standing close to the heat that flows from the flame, warming my hands over the burner as the kettle begins to tick and rattle. I lean close to the stove so the heat that's rising passes my chest, my arms, finally glancing past my face and finally I close my eyes, breathing in warm air, for minutes this goes on, maybe longer.

Soon I start soup on another burner, the rising heat now doubling on my hands and on my face. I strip off my clothes, wet and stiff with dirt, and I pile them in the corner. It's odd to see them there, a mess, muddy, out of place in rooms I normally keep in order.

I want to sleep now. My eyes are blinking shut against my will even as I stand half naked over the heat rising from the stove. But I finish my food first, spooning it into my mouth from the pot, hot soup dripping some with my eyes closed over the burner. My hands sting with pain as they keep thawing and I haven't been hungry like this in many years and I'm tired, so tired I can barely stand. I finish my food, though, and turn off the burner and after I've found my way to the couch, I think to kick off my wet socks and underwear, pulling a blanket over me, now naked, covering my shoulders and legs and sides and I feel myself falling asleep already, falling, dark, and I sleep, still and dreamless and complete, and I sleep straight through till morning.

• • •

"Why will those plants grow here when everything else is dead?" I ask the gardener.

It's a few days since I started working in the playground. I spent the morning planting the last of the ivy and the vines and have now gone to the gardener's courtyard on the edge of downtown. We sit in two of his chairs.

"Whatever has killed all the plant life here," he says to me, "it doesn't affect certain species from other places. Those plants, the ones I got for you, most originated in the mountains of northern India. An area where miners have, for decades, dug for gold and other metals. Horrific chemicals are used to separate the gold from the rock. Those chemicals seeped into the mountainside and the groundwater and although originally most trees and shrubs were killed, eventually some life near those mines did find a way to survive."

I see him sip from his drink. He has offered me a drink but I've said no.

"And so is the point that life survives," I say. "It adapts, no matter what?"

It is very cold today, my breath faintly white and his white too. But as in the playground, the gardener's courtyard blocks the wind and so, here with a blanket across my lap, I feel almost warm.

"No," he says. "Clearly there's a point at which nothing will come back."

He presses back in his chair, stretching his legs out, then crossing them slowly.

"Had the factories kept pouring toxins on this place," he says, "then absolutely nothing, no one, would survive."

I think about this. Slowly, staring toward the vines climbing up the walls. "So, that the city died, the factories shutting down, in some way that stopped the damage before it got even worse?"

He stares forward. Rubs the raw tips of his shortened fingers against the arm of his chair.

"Yes," he says.

Always, there is the rain. Light. On my hands and face now.

"And keep in mind the change in weather," the gardener says. "The weather has changed dramatically. That is killing the plant life too. Some think that alone is what's killing everything."

I notice newspapers on his table where he normally sits to read. My paper is there, but there are papers from other places too. I realize the gardener stays in touch with the world beyond the North End. It doesn't surprise me, but I find myself now thinking that the gardener knows so many things about which I'm unaware. The countries that are at war. The politicians who are in charge. The teams that have won. The movies made. The books that have been written since the last time that I read.

I don't ask about any of this, though. I have no interest in knowing what's in those papers.

The gardener touches his hand to his head, slides his fingers slowly across his brow, barely damp from the light rain.

"What's it look like," I hear myself say, "to see a landscape that's alive?"

He says, "It's been years since I've seen a world not scarred in some way."

In a moment I ask him, "How long have you been here?"

He nods. "Just two years now," he says.

I think about what he's said, the timing, and it seems off. "But why years?" I ask. "Since you've seen a place not scarred like this?"

The gardener turns to me. He's thinking. Trying to understand something. I see him nod to himself. "Even in the South End," he says. "The areas near the highway are the worst. But it has stretched in some places for a few miles. Trees turned slick and black. Flowers turned brown and dry. The only animals are the cats and dogs kept trapped in homes by their owners but even those animals are restless, sometimes panicked, all wanting desperately to get away."

I try to picture what he's saying, but can't. It's hard for me to understand. "It started here and spread?" I ask.

The gardener looks up at the high, gray sky. He shakes his head. "Not at all."

I shake my head as well.

"Far south of here," he says, still staring up at the gray sky. "Or a thousand miles west. The trees in entire parks have stopped blooming in the spring," he says. "Grass will not turn green. The ivy-covered walls of schools and homes and buildings are covered now in a dead, brown tangle of drying leaves and stiffly atrophying vines."

I stare at him. I'm confused.

"Farmland gone white and dead," he continues, staring up. "Vast stretches of forests that have all turned brown," he is saying, staring calmly at me now. "The death of things, they call it. It's happening all over the world."

. . .

The trouble with kids from the South End continues to get worse. Someone is chased near the church, having to run up the stairs and into the sanctuary before the kids will leave. There is drag racing down one of the main avenues leading from the neighborhoods to downtown. People are robbed walking to the corner store where we buy our food, knocked to the ground as the kids take the few things they can find. One person has a broken arm. The others are bloodied across their hands and faces.

All of it seems to be a kind of aimless, menacing joke, bored kids from the South End increasingly making a game of roaming through the north.

People write letters to the paper. People show up at the commission meeting to raise their hands and quietly complain.

Four letters to the paper. Five people raising their hands to ask questions of the commission.

Small numbers. But in the North End, we are very few.

The commissioners, they talk in circles.

"Oh, I'm sorry," says one commissioner, looking out on the thirty people in the room. "But do you really think these kids are only causing trouble here? Pay taxes. Close your broken neighborhoods. Come back to the real world. Maybe then we can talk about help."

The commissioner who met with me, she still has not come back.

I document each incident of trouble in the paper. Writing a long account of the absence of a response from the commission.

"Why now would we think that the commission would decide to help us?" someone writes in a letter to the editor.

"When has the commission, or the city council before them, done us any good?" another letter reads.

"Let us just accept," someone writes, "that we are entirely alone."

I spend hours among the shrubs and trees now growing in the playground. The gardener has had more trees dropped off, along with another type of vine that already wants to grow up the mortared grooves in the old, brick walls. There are low shrubs with leaves like tiny diamonds. Low and leafy plants that will someday bloom and rise a foot or more.

I sit down, on the ground. Soft here, and slightly damp. It has rained recently.

I look up at the gray, cloudy sky. There is sunlight behind the clouds. Enough to make these plants grow.

The death of things, the gardener called it.

Of course it happens in other places, I think. I'd just never thought about it.

Near the corner store at dusk, with ten or fifteen people buying things from the small vendors nearby, a black car lit underneath with neon, it turns the corner, heads our way.

I think about the two guns I took from the other kids, then threw into a sewer. It's not a thought of wishing I had the guns with me. It's more a memory. A fact. A reminder of what this could involve.

There are four kids in the car. They look very young. The music thumps and thumps and thumps.

People turn from where they buy things from the vendors. Some go into the corner store.

The car moves very slowly toward us. It is lit with neon on the inside too, the kids all glowing, smoke coming from the open windows and I see bottles being passed.

I can't quite say what it is I feel. But what I know is that these kids are a disruption to the order that the people in the North End have created. It is quiet here. There is space. How we live, what we do, it is simple. These kids, all of them, are to me becoming a faceless, nameless threat to the North End.

I can't say it makes me angry.

I can't say that I'm upset.

But I know I want the threat to stop.

I walk over to a vendor table. I buy a large glass bottle filled with liquid.

There are four vendors at their tables. Other people move closer to the corner store. An old man, an old woman, they turn and go into a vacant building.

The car has stopped in the street. The kid in the passenger seat opens his door. Smiling. Thinking he will stand.

I turn, holding the bottle by the neck and as I turn I release the bottle, letting it fly the fifteen feet toward the car, through the driver's open window, hitting the driver in the head, the bottle exploding in the car, glass and liquid spraying across the kids in the back seat.

I walk around to the passenger side, to the kid who has only now begun to stand, still smiling, but in a way that is not so happy, his confusion taking all joy from the expression he'd painted on his face.

I hit him in the mouth and he falls back against the car. I hit him in the chest, in the neck, in the ear. I hit him three times in the ear, his head thudding against the side of the glowing neon car.

The driver has slumped over, blood all across his ear and neck. His mouth moves like he is screaming. But he's silent.

The kids in the backseat are still sitting, almost motionless, only wiping slowly at the glass and liquid and the blood from their friend, all of it sprayed across their faces.

So far I haven't seen a gun.

The kid outside the car has fallen to the ground. I lean over him. "Why do you come here?" I ask him.

He is holding his neck. Gagging.

I hit him, very hard, directly in his nose. It breaks and there's blood pouring over his wet and open mouth.

"Why do you come here?" I ask again.

One of the kids from the backseat pushes open his door. I slam it closed, hard, catching his hand in the frame. He screams. I slam the door on it again.

I have decided there won't be a gun.

I kneel down, leaning over the kid on the ground. I ask him one more time, "Why do you come here?"

He's trying to talk. He spits blood.

"Because," he says, gagging on the words and blood and gagging because of whatever I have done to his neck and throat, "because there's nothing else to do."

Even now, we are subject to the failings of the South End. First their combined decision to give up on this place where we still choose to live. Then their collective effort to forget us. And now the weakness of the community they've built as a replacement to the North End leaves these kids with no purpose and no value, pushing them across the overpass not to explore but to cause trouble. To finally wreak havoc on anyone they find.

123

I hit the kid with the side of my fist, swinging down like I hold a hammer, hitting him in the eye, hitting him as hard as I think I can.

"Aimless," I say. "Lost."

He's writhing on the ground, holding his hands across his very bloody face, screaming into his palm.

I stand up and kick him in the side, very hard, the point of my shoe driving into the soft part under his ribs.

It's not that I have ever been taught how to fight. It's not that I have trained for this. It's not that I am very strong.

I simply have a willingness to hurt this person who's done something wrong.

I have simply lost the ability to experience anything that feels like fear.

The kid has turned onto his stomach. He's trying to crawl away. I kick him very hard in his ribs again, high, near his armpit, and he can't crawl now. He just curls up, on his side, barely covering his face with one of his arms.

I see the kid's friends in the backseat, leaning away. Not trying to get out of the car. Not moving at all where they sit.

I see the gardener across the street, standing close to the doorway of a building.

I see the minister next to him.

I see the driver sitting up in his seat, blood all across his face. He turns to me, sees me kick his friend again. But I'm staring at the driver.

What will he do?

I pull his friend from the ground, lean him into the passenger seat. Push him in. He grabs at the seat.

I watch the driver. But now his hands only move toward the wheel.

The music, it's still thumping.

The neon lights are still glowing.

The car, it is still running.

Around me, people staring.

The driver, eyes outlined in blood, his head already swelling, he is staring right at me.

That is fear.

I shove the heavy car door closed.

That is fear.

The car moves forward, slowly, then faster, and then it turns away from here.

That is fear.

· · ·

Three scavengers in a large, old pickup truck deliver plants to me at the playground. I stand and watch as their truck stops.

There are two men and a woman. Thin, wiry people who carry whole pallets of plants in their long arms, and the scavengers are so thin you'd think they'd topple over with the weight. Yet they lift the pallets with little effort.

They nod to me, each one of them, and I nod too, pointing toward the playground where I'd like the plants to be dropped.

Two of them are deeply scarred, one across the neck, the other across her cheek and nose. Scavenging is brutal work, men and women climbing on their hands and knees into attics and crawl spaces, narrow places where they are forced to slither forward, all the while pulling free the copper wiring, copper pipes, tin plating, aluminum linings along the hidden joists and beams and stanchions of the infrastructure of a home or building. Urban miners in dark spaces, wrenching free these precious metals for reuse, the value calculated on the weight of what is found, not the effort put forth to find it. Cut up and covered in their filth, bruised and sweating and exhausted, scavengers emerge from the structures they strip down, take a drink of water, then head into the next abandoned home on the street.

"Thank you," I say to the scavengers. The woman among them has put the last of the large trees just inside the tall brick wall.

"You're the writer," says the tallest of the scavengers. He's smoking a cigarette now and the others light up too.

I think to nod.

We're standing on the dusty slope outside the playground. A few feet from where, long ago it seems, I found that body. Their truck isn't running

125

and the wind is hardly blowing today and so it's silent here when no one speaks.

"You've got quite a capacity for violence, I hear," says the woman. "I hear I should stay a step removed from you."

She isn't smiling, but she isn't at all bothered either. There's no taunt, no awe, I'm not sure there's even respect. She's making what she thinks is a simple statement of fact.

"I don't know," I say.

"These kids who are coming over," one of the men says, pausing to drink water from a large and filthy plastic bottle, "it's not okay. They should be stopped."

His hands are gray and dry and scuffed, like old concrete from a broken sidewalk.

I don't know how to respond to him.

The three of them stand staring at me, the only motion their mouths and lungs slowly working on the cigarettes. Their faces are pale and nearly gray, their hair covered in streaks of paint and plaster, and their clothes are as colorless as the landscape that surrounds us. Their eyes seem wetter than is possible, but it's only the contrast with the pallor of their faces.

The jewelry they all wear, that I've seen on these scavengers so many times all these years, I realize now as I stand so close to them, they wear the jewelry of found objects, brass pipe fittings on their wrists and old coins bent to grasp the lobes of their ears.

The three scavengers are all fifteen feet apart and they've not spoken to one another since they arrived. Yet their appearance, the way they stand and stare, I think for a moment that I'm watching a family portrait, a snapshot moment of these three siblings taking a break from their day and life of work.

"Do I owe you money for this?" I think to ask.

The woman shakes her head. "The gardener handles that."

Still I'm standing, watching them. It seems like they'll say more.

"The brokers will take anything we scavenge," the woman now says in her monotone voice. "I've sold them a box of lighters. I've sold them stacks of bright white dresses. I've sold them boxes full of books and paper. They set a value for anything we bring. Because they know someone who will buy it. People like that, with that gift, they know where to sell anything. And so they know where to buy anything as well."

She takes a long drag off her cigarette, squatting down as she sucks the cigarette to the filter, then pressing the nearly dead ember against the ground. She stands, then reaches into the back of the pickup, dropping the cigarette butt in a bucket. The two men will do the same in a moment.

I realize these people won't litter on this dead field.

"If you need help," the woman says, "we'll help you."

"I can get all this planted," I say. "But thank you."

One of the men shakes his head very slightly. "No. With the kids. We mean with the kids. If we can help you, you just ask."

And for another long minute, we four stand there, two minutes now, maybe more, the three of them still staring straight at me.

• • •

To live here has always seemed to be a choice to exist among the dry and dead plants around me. That I can make another choice, that the gardener has done so and that he has even helped others make gardens themselves, it's an idea so foreign and unknown. Even more impossible than the choice people make to read newspapers from outside of here, to watch television or hear the radio, to even cross the overpass and then return.

The gardener's plant stands on a low table near the couch, the leaves at eye level as I lie here every night. In another minute, I reach out from under the blanket and I lightly touch the leaves. They are smooth. I touch the stems, oddly soft, covered in the faintest hairs. All of it wet in its way. Filled with water. The plant is living. The gardener said we desire this, seek out life and he is right, I think, he is right, I think, although I've already fallen asleep.

CHAPTER 7

I am making my way through the basement of an old theater when I realize I am lost. It's completely dark, no windows or lights, and even when I turn on my flashlight, I can't figure out which of the many doors will lead me out of here.

This doesn't worry me. I only think of it as a fact. *You're lost.*

As I flash the beam along the wall, I see a water fountain and a tall machine that once sold canned drinks and a cigarette vending machine, its front door broken open.

There's an ATM too, the front door also broken and all the money removed. But when I touch the ATM's screen, it lights up.

WELCOME.

In a minute, I pull out my wallet. Filled still with my driver's license and a health insurance card and a debit card.

The plastic remnants of my modern life.

I put the debit card in the ATM. Push buttons by memory, the rote maneuverings of a thousand days past. The machine manages to connect. It finds my account. It shows me my balance.

I stare.

A number that once had meaning for me. A number I watched and tended to and worried about and lamented.

And it's a number that reminds me there is another life I could lead. There is another life I once had.

That life still waits.

I push the cancel button and soon the screen goes dark and, once more, I try to find the right way out of here.

• • •

We are sitting in chairs facing the garden I have planted. The gardener comes by now, periodically, to see how I am doing. I found these iron chairs and a small table behind an old restaurant not far from here.

"I'm pretty good at all this," the gardener says. "Plants, trees." He smiles slightly. "Sorry. But I am. I am really pretty good at this."

"Yes," I say.

We sit. I've found heavy, wool blankets that I keep in the closet just inside the door to the building and we both have them draped over our laps and knees.

He asks me, "You didn't know about the death of things, did you?"

I shake my head.

"It is so bad here," he says, "so decayed and ruined, that it's hard to think of anywhere else. Hard to imagine that somewhere else could be dying too."

I watch the leaves on the vines shake slightly. Wind. All the plants, the branches, they move just barely and for a moment it's almost dizzying, unbalanced, to see so much movement in the world around me. My life, what I see, is normally so very still.

I close my eyes. "I pictured other cities dying," I say, and when I open my eyes I'm not dizzy anymore. "But not the trees. Not the animals. I just pictured the cities themselves."

I notice in a moment that he's nodding. "Does it make you wonder why you're here?" he asks. "Does it change things in any way?"

I'm not sure what he means. I'm looking at him.

"To know the death of things happens elsewhere," he says. "To know storms like the ones we have also kill thousands all over the world. Does it affect your reasons for being here?"

I think about this for a long time. Staring into the leaves and small branches and the vines already growing into the creases and cracks of the brick wall. I think about the gardener's question, repeat it to myself. It seems important. It is important.

Does it make you wonder why you're here?

And even as I repeat that question, again, repeated in the silence of the two of us sitting outside here, I can't think of an answer. I can't think about what that question means. I can't think about what he's asked.

I just know the question is important.

I turn to him. I shake my head. My shoulders rise. I start to say something but I'm not sure what.

The gardener is pointing toward a cluster of low, nearly purple shrubs. He tells me their name and where they are from and how at some point tall flowers, white and pink, will rise on thin and golden stems. "Quite beautiful," he says.

We sit that way for some time. He tells me about the things I've planted. He's brought coffee in a container and we drink it, hot, it scalds my mouth, but I feel the warmth in my chest and then my stomach.

The gardener is quiet awhile. The sky is dimmer and it's late in the day.

I turn to him. Steam from my mouth as I think to ask the words, "Why are you here?"

"I came to help," he says, which he has said to me before. "But it was too late."

I shake my head. "What I mean is, why do you stay?"

He nods, slowly. Looks toward the plantings all along the wall. "The trees will eventually offer shade," he says. He smiles slightly. "Not that there's any sun."

"Why do you stay?" I ask again.

He leans forward in his chair, elbows on his knees. "Because there's nothing left for me back there."

I picture us in our chairs, two men, unshaven, both in heavy blazers over sweaters, one with a scarf, one with gloves, sitting near the only patch of green as far as the eye can see, and are they thirty years old or fifty, no one would be able to tell.

"They died?" I hear myself ask.

131

His forehead sinks to his hands. It's a minute before he responds. Before he even moves. He shakes his head just slightly, still holding it in his hands. "She did."

• • •

I finally find a small boat in the industrial zone. It's suspended in the air, a set of pulleys holding it a few feet above the ground, the ropes attached to steel tracks overhead. The boat is just ten feet long, but there's a small outboard motor on the back of it.

The tracks overhead lead thirty feet to a set of large doors at the back of the warehouse. The large latch on the doors is rusted and I have to kick the doors a few times to shake loose the handle and pin. The doors swing open onto a canal.

Still water, dark, the banks lined with rotting beams that surely once seemed heavy and impenetrable and permanent.

It takes me a few minutes to figure out how to work the ropes and pulleys holding the boat in the air. But I'm finally able to slide the pulleys along the track, positioning the boat at the edge of the canal. I carefully pull another line loose and the boat slowly angles down, stern first, into the water.

The water is silent, heavy as it spreads, ripples escaping as the boat gently enters the canal.

I reach down and pick up the five-gallon gas tank attached to the outboard. It's empty. But there are eight big drums of gasoline lined up along the wall. All seem full. One has a pump and hose and spigot attached to it. I fill the red tank, then put it back in the boat.

I step down from the top of the canal wall into the boat. The movement of the boat is slow, side to side, I take a moment. Breathe and close my eyes, and soon the boat is still.

Under one of the seats, there is a compartment with plastic containers of oil in it. I pour one into the red gas tank, shake it slowly to mix the oil and gas, then connect the fuel line to the engine. In another minute, I prime the engine, then pull on the starter. The engine does not respond at first, but I keep working at it, pulling the cord another ten times, then five more, then five more, then ten. I give the motor a break periodically. Prime it again.

Finally, smoke begins to puff out with each pull, and then the motor starts up, more smoke, blowing almost steadily, and the noise is a loud, rattling bang, over and over and over.

I sit back, adjusting the choke and the throttle. I'm breathing hard from the effort, my breath just visible as it blows out in front of me.

After a few minutes the engine settles down, the smoke subsiding and the sound quieting. I put the engine in gear and move forward, slowly, pushing the handle to turn the boat, pointing it up the canal.

The canal is sixty feet wide here and lined by buildings, warehouses mostly, but also the walls of old factories and steel shipping containers stacked two and three high. But in some places there is nothing lining the canal, so I can see the tops of the buildings downtown. I see my building eventually, the hotel coming in and out of view as I make my way along the canal.

I come to a place where the canal splits. I slow the boat, look back at my building, getting my bearings. Then I turn left.

I'm going north. Wanting to see how many of the levees have broken.

In places the canal is nearly blocked by debris. A sunken truck, trees that have fallen partway into the water, utility poles that have fallen from one side to the other and that I have to duck underneath to get past.

Some of this damage looks new, probably a result of the most recent storm. The way the blond wood juts out in the broken beams along the canal walls. The way the paint of a large container shines brightly from where it now lies awkwardly on its side.

But most of the damage is clearly very old. Accumulated over the course of storms and many years or decades of inattention.

There are offshoots from the canal. But I stay on what I think is the main route north. I can look over my shoulder and, usually, see the top of my hotel. Even my room, at the corner.

The sound of the motor echoes in on me in the canal. I leave some wake and move at what might be five miles an hour. I'm not in a hurry.

It's about twenty minutes before I come upon a broken levee, an earthen wall with a missing section thirty feet across. The water on the other side of the levee is as still as the water in the canal.

I cross through the break in the levee. I'm not sure what this water covers. A park, maybe. A school. All lost to the water.

I'm sure that I've been here. Before it was flooded.

In a few minutes of moving north, I find another break in a levee, cross through it, and enter another canal. I take the boat out of gear, floating forward only slowly as I pause to take note of where I left the canal, of the markings on the side of a warehouse, of a clump of three tall, dead trees. The series of canals and levees in this area is complicated, I know, and only more so now that the levees have failed.

A bridge behind me crosses the canal, its heavy stanchions topped by stone lions' heads, large pedestals at each end topped by full-sized stone lions. Guards, it seems. Architectural excesses in a land that no longer asks for ornaments or protection.

I cross through breaks in the levees every few minutes. The water is still and flat and I can't tell how deep it is. There are more buildings now. Brick. Stores and offices and low apartments built along the edge of the water and I realize that probably the buildings were once along the edge of a canal, but the water from the levee flooded the area, breaking down one side of the canal, so that now the buildings seem to be built alongside of a small lake.

Looking back, I can no longer see my hotel, so I take out my compass to make sure that I'm still moving north.

I come around the side of a brick warehouse then and see a neighborhood. The top end at least. Roofs of houses and the tops of trees and utility poles with power lines strung out, all sitting in the still water, a mile of this or more.

It's an image I've seen before. Video footage of flood-ravaged areas. Images I would see so many times over so many years, back when I watched TV. The flooding of distant places. Rising tides along populated foothills. Unexpected deluges in nations long racked by drought.

News of massive damage and life-changing relocations that I watched, at most, from the corner of my eye.

Here, though, there is no sense that the flood will ever recede.

The water reaches halfway up the second story of the homes, leaving the neighborhood frozen at its base. Black, slick oaks stick up from the water too, branches reaching out and up forty feet or more. These were tree-lined streets, shaded by oaks and maples in summer, turned red and gold and orange in the fall. There were flowers in the yards beneath this water, bursting white and pink and red throughout the spring. There were long avenues marked by these once grand houses and yards. There were narrow side streets with small bungalows built more than a hundred years ago.

The water does not move. Even the wind doesn't seem to touch it.

Those floods on the TV seemed very far away.

This, though, is a neighborhood I know. From childhood. Where I had family, cousins, an aunt and uncle. I played here. I know the street names on green metal signs that hang from the tall utility poles at what were once busy intersections.

When I got in the boat, I had thoughts of going all the way to the bay. Now, though, here, I realize I can't go any farther.

Because this is where I grew up.

And this is where we later lived.

This is where they all died.

We moved back to the North End because we thought it was right. Schools and jobs were already in the south. But we moved back to an old and grand and beautiful house, worked on it, fixed it up. Stayed committed to a block, a neighborhood, to others who were like us. Fierce defenders of the North End.

The trees hadn't died yet. There were animals here still. Spiders in the windowsills. Ants moving in lines along the sidewalk.

I tell myself my family died because of where we lived. Because of the choice we made. To stay with this place, in this place, no matter what else happened. No matter the dangers others saw.

We knew the fire department was nearly absent. Knew the ambulances no longer had means to respond.

We stayed here anyway.

I lined their bodies up in the street in front of the house. Blackened, wrecked, and broken.

And still no one had come. Except the neighbors. All the neighbors. The people who believed in staying. Standing side by side. Staring at the fire, the bodies, me.

And still no one had come.

Even the news helicopter that circled the street, spotlight on me as they filmed the scene, it stayed for a very few minutes.

When they died, I left. To the South End. For almost a year. Tried to continue my life, but alone.

It didn't work.

I sometimes thought that it was just too loud there in the South End. If it hadn't been so loud, all the people, the cars, the televisions and the radios, if not for that I tell myself I could have made it. Started a new life. Recovered and moved on.

But that, I realize here, floating on this water, above my old neighborhood, that is a lie. I could not have made it in the South End. I could not have made it anywhere.

Instead, I came back to the North End. Where it's silent. And of course I have not moved on. Of course I am not recovered.

I float slowly forward, the boat pushing through the still, cold water.

When they died, within months, everyone on that block left. Everyone gave up. Everyone gave in to the deepest fears we always shared.

In the boat, I've found the street we lived on. It's not hard, even with the flooding. There are the tops of houses that I recognize. Church spires and school buildings that I've known since I was young.

The house stands like the others, submerged in the still water. Water inside the broken windows. Water inside the holes that burned through the second-story walls. The roofline is twisted upward, out, mangled still by the fire, and what shows above the waterline is black, all black, no color or shine.

136

I've turned off the engine. I float, motionless, above what must have been the street. Above what must have been the curb. Above what must have been the place where I last touched them after they had died.

• • •

Back near my hotel, in the darkness of a neighborhood very near my building, I burn down a house.

A house the same size as ours. Two stories, but not wide. Wooden siding and brick along the foundation.

I find paint thinner in the basement. Pour it into a metal bucket filled with stray pieces of wood—a broken handrail, a curtain rod, a broom handle, the remnants of a chair. In a moment, I can watch the firelight and shadows on the basement walls and the wooden beams above me. The fire is contained in the bucket. It seems for some minutes that it will not spread. That it will soon die out.

But it doesn't.

The bucket cracks open and the wood, just smoldering, tumbles onto the floor. In another minute it lights stray cardboard nearby. The flames soon reach the cabinets along the wall, curtains on the basement windows, napkins and books lining a set of shelves nearby.

It's hot now. Bright. I'm still counting the minutes, forty-five, since I first lit the fire in the bucket.

And as I sit across the street, in darkness except for the light of the fire growing, now it has been an hour and a half. That's how long it took. And I sit, and stare, and count once more to ninety, and it's quite some time now that I've been crying.

• • •

At the library the next day, I find maps of the canals and levees. I retrace the areas I went to in the boat. I mark the broken levees on the map. I measure the distance from the warehouse to the first of the broken levees that I found. I calculate the area of the neighborhoods now covered by all that water.

137

In history books about the growth of the city, I find pictures of my neighborhood from many decades ago. I take pictures of those photos with my camera. Then I sort through the photos I took from the boat as I made my way back downtown, trying to find ones that roughly match the view and perspective of the pictures in the history books.

A busy street packed with trolley cars and pedestrians and people pushing strollers along a tree-lined avenue. Now the slick branches of those same trees stick out from the still water.

A movie theater and surrounding crowd lit with the bright bulbs on the large marquee. Now that marquee slides at an angle into the water.

Before and after.

The next day I write this all up for the paper. I run ten photographs this time, the most I've ever printed. I also run two maps of flooded areas and, in my rough, bad handwriting, I carefully make notes on the big map, marking the distance between the floodwaters and downtown.

Two miles.

• • •

I'm watching the gardener and the minister pull a teenage kid from a jacked-up car. The gardener holds him down on the concrete, his knee in the kid's back. The minister goes to the other door. Reaches through the open window to grab the driver by the neck. He goes halfway through the window, both arms, his head and chest seemingly on top of the kid who had been driving. A kid who'd been speeding, doing burnouts, roaring back and forth along this central avenue near the corner store, the kid shooting a gun at trees and at buildings along the road.

I'm watching from the steps of the old church across the street. Other people, maybe ten of them, they are watching too.

I know I'll help the minister and gardener if they need me.

But it seems to be going fine for them.

The gardener stopped the car after it made its tenth or eleventh pass. He walked out into the street. Stood there. As the car came racing toward him.

The driver finally slammed on the brakes. Leaned out the window. Started yelling at the gardener who, still, only stood in the street. Staring at the car, the driver and passenger, here in the cold, slow rain of this day, as gray as it gets here, monotone in the daylight and silent throughout the North End, with only the sound of the kid's engine and his passenger yelling and the kid honking the horn at the gardener.

The minister then, that's when he goes after the passenger, pulling open the door, dragging him out and the gardener helping him and the driver, staring now, not saying anything, he only watches as the gardener pins down his friend, as the minister, in a black shirt, black pants, no collar but I think that kid probably knows he's a minister anyway, that's when the minister turns back to the car, the driver, and that's when the minister goes through the window.

Both kids are quite bloody by the time it's over. They drive away very slowly.

I think probably the minister made them promise.

I see the gardener drop a gun down a sewer drain.

You can hear the car's engine for another minute, long after the car has turned the corner. Long after the people here near the corner store have gone back to what they were doing. Silent mostly, a few nodding to the minister and the gardener.

Really, we just want our lives back. We want things to be how they once were.

• • •

We are not innately violent here. The violence fled with the last of the city's government and people and the structures that once defined how we should and should not live.

I write this up for the paper.

And where does this new violence come from? How is it that a gardener and a minister find such violence necessary? What makes us respond to these outsiders in such a terrible, dangerous way?

"I see this, feel it, and know it can't continue," I quote the gardener saying.

"I wonder about the cost in and to myself," I quote the minister saying.

What is it, though, that causes us to go to such ends to defend this place?

Is it just that we want our lives back? Is it just that we want things to be how they once had been?

• • •

The commissioner attends the next meeting. It's been at least three months. There are many people from the North End at this meeting. Sixty or more attend, ten or more ask questions.

What will be done about the violence?

The commission members sit silently through this. They look more irritated than they've ever been. Frustrated again that they must be part of this.

Sometimes they simply shake their heads. Sometimes they lean back and stare up at the ceiling. But mostly, for the hour they are required to be here, they only stare out at us.

After the meeting, the commissioner comes up to me. "I'm sorry I haven't been here for some time," she says, and my sense of her as a generic figure in a suit is different now. I've seen her scared.

It takes me a moment to respond. I say, "You don't have to apologize to me."

"I needed to rethink what I could do for the North End," she says. Then she is silent. She shakes her head. "And I was afraid."

I realize she's not as tall as she was. She's not wearing the high heels.

She taps her hand on her purse, nervous or impatient, I can't tell. In a moment, she says, "The problem is that you are not alone with this. On that point, the commissioners aren't exaggerating. It's a problem in the South End. And a growing one. That we have no idea how to solve."

"They have no purpose," I say. "Nothing to do."

"And they have guns," she says. "And cars. And each other. Which becomes their purpose. It becomes all they know and all that matters."

I look away from her, seeing people slowly leaving the community center. The only sound is the shuffling of their feet. No one speaks.

"I don't think I care about those kids," I say. "About their problems. Or the South End's." I turn back to her. "I know enough to realize that I should be a person who cares. But I'm not."

There's a moment where she looks at me very differently. Wary. Wondering what I might do. She's seen me beat a man till he was bloody.

"I was not always like this," I hear myself say, quietly I think, and I am wondering if I've actually said this aloud or if I only thought it in my mind.

"I know," she says now.

I am staring at her. Suit and hair and skin that all seem colorless, a hue or range I can't manage to identify. And yet I've seen her scared.

"I know," she says again.

I find myself nodding. Unexpectedly.

"I've read the stories," she says, almost silently, or maybe it's that I can barely hear anything at all. "About you," she says, and I think now that maybe I've only imagined that she's said this. "And about them," I hear her say and now I know I've heard those words. Know that she has said them. "Everyone knows your story," she says. "Yours is what everyone in the South End fears. That this place will kill them and their families and everyone they know and everything they have ever loved."

But still I am only nodding. Then moving away. Then walking out into the night.

CHAPTER 8

There is only one way from the South End to the north. Only one overpass linking the two parts of this place.

There is only one way for trouble to come to us, I write in the paper. *But if we take control of the overpass, we can end the trouble.*

The article I write is small, just three paragraphs, on the inside of the paper. There is no byline. The headline says only, Taking Control Of the Overpass.

The next week, someone runs a notice in the paper. It's not signed, only dropped through the mail slot at the office. A public meeting will be held, on the steps of the church downtown, to discuss taking over the overpass.

Nearly three hundred people attend. It is raining and blowing hard outside and so the minister invites everyone inside the church. The ceilings are vaulted, stone columns lifting upward to stone beams, the walls of the sanctuary lined with dark stained glass. The disciples gathered at the base of a tree, a god rising with the sunrise beyond a hill.

Murals on the altar shine with gold paint, silver, sunlight across so many outstretched hands.

It isn't warm here and the lights in the sanctuary don't work on the west side. And so we gather in the pews on the east side of the church.

There are scavengers and older couples and people whose names I do not know but who I see getting a newspaper from in front of the office every week.

More people arrive. There are nearly four hundred now.

I see the office manager. Sitting near the back of the room.

I see the pressman. Standing near the front.

I see brokers and vendors and the security guard from the airport.

I see the woman who works at the water pumping station.

I see the garbage man who picks up trash cans once a week.

I see scavengers, forty of them, together near the back of the sanctuary, all of them standing along the wall.

The sounds in the room are loud but muffled, indistinct talking and the scrape of shoes and boots on the stone floor. The rough slide of chairs being repositioned in the aisles near the pews.

It is not clear who is in charge of the meeting. Soon there are simply discussions, between various people in various groups, all over the room. Other people do not speak at all.

The minister finally says, his voice lifting loud from the front of the church, "How will we organize this?" He is standing on a pew. No one has gone up to the altar, where they could see the whole group and speak with more authority.

I see the gardener is sitting near the front. In a moment he stands up and takes a few steps up the altar so he can be seen.

"We need volunteers," he says, his hand moving absently to his neck. He presses the nubs of his missing fingers across his jaw. "A schedule. Rules for what to do when someone thinks that there is trouble."

There is discussion of this. Some people shake their heads. Other people nod. One man stands and says, "I want to be safe. But I don't want to die."

There is discussion of this. Heads shake. Others nod. But there's no yelling and no anger. People mostly talk among themselves. No one responds directly to the gardener.

"I think what we know," the gardener now says loudly, quieting the crowd, his hand slowly moving across the closely cut hair on his head, "is that to do this, to do it right, you have to understand your capacity for violence." He pauses. "You have to be willing to stand on that overpass and talk to the driver of every car that wants to enter the North End. You have to be willing to tell some people that they cannot pass." He pauses again. "And that means you have to be willing to enforce what you have said."

There is discussion of this.

I make notes. I've made notes all along.

"But if you're willing to enforce," the gardener starts now, a few minutes later, already pausing and waiting for the rest of the people to go silent, "then hopefully you'll never have to do it. Because it's disorder that these people want, the expectation of coming here and finding chaos."

"But it isn't chaos here," says a woman in the crowd.

The gardener nods. "That is what we have to show them," he says. "Right now, there is no sign of the order that, in fact, we live with." Again he pauses. No one speaks. He says, "A person on the overpass, a person very clearly willing to enforce order on anyone he or she encounters, I think we have to believe that will be enough."

A schedule is made. Volunteers stand in four separate lines. Sign their names on pieces of paper when they get to the front. They pick a time. Four-hour shifts, we decide. Four people at a time, standing guard at the overpass. Other volunteers will build a gate. Scavengers will position concrete barriers to slow cars down as they approach. Other volunteers will simply bring food and coffee to the guards.

As people stand in line in the church, ready to sign up, eventually I find the gardener near me. We're up against the west wall, on the dark side of the church. I'm still writing in my notebook.

He glances at me. "That was unexpected," he says.

I shake my head, slightly, not sure which part he means.

"Me," he says. "Talking to the crowd. I'm a botanist," he says, looking out at the crowd of people. "A gardener."

It takes me a moment to respond. "Did you ever teach?" I ask.

He nods. Says, "I suppose it's similar."

"Have you ever been in charge?" I ask.

He says, "Only students. Grad students. Research trips into the mountains. Searching for rare plant species in the Himalayas." He smiles slightly. "All quite different than this."

I think about what the commissioner said. That everyone knows my story. I realize the gardener knows. Of course he does. *I know who you are*, he said when I first met him. *Everyone does.*

145

I look around the room. These people, they know who I am.

I turn to my notes. It's hard to read my writing on this side of the church, with the lights out above me, and I think to myself I should have taken notes from the bright side of the sanctuary. "Everything," I say to the gardener, turning to him, "everything is different than this."

• • •

I stare at the high ceiling. The atrium in the library.

There are copies of the newspaper articles here, I realize. Articles about the deaths of four children and their mother. Transcripts, maybe even video, of the TV news reports.

The same stories the commissioner has seen. That, she says, everyone knows about.

Stories like that, they are widely read. Watched over and again. I know this. I always have.

I just don't think about it.

• • •

"Why did you think to take over the overpass?" the minister asks me.

We sit in my garden. He drinks and I do not.

"I woke up," I say. "And thought about the last time I hit one of those kids. And about the time you did. And the gardener. And I realized that moments like that could only lead to more attacks. Not just by them. But by us."

He sips. Rain dusts us lightly in a thin coat of mist or dew.

He says, "There's something about it that becomes appealing. The violence. Hitting someone. It's not the hurting. It's the power. The control you think you have."

I think for a minute about this. "Yes," I say.

"And a sense," he says, "that you will only push it further."

• • •

I make my way through the first floor of a building across the street from the paper. A three-story building, brick, some hundred years old. I've never been inside it.

I'm waiting for the paper to finish printing. With its account of the plans to take over the overpass. And I want, for the first time, to see how people will respond.

There are desks lined up in four perfect rows, green desks, forty of them, with a large typewriter on each.

The linoleum floor is covered in a very fine dust. Gray, almost black dust, and I look behind me and see my footsteps. The footprints of a long-ago explorer. The footprints of the first man on the moon.

It is so still here.

A calendar, on one of the desks near me, reads *February 1968.*

This building, this office I walk through, it was closed many decades before the North End was abandoned.

Foreshadowing, had anyone cared to notice, of the desolation that would come.

• • •

Within a few days we have established a regular rotation at the overpass. The scavengers have installed concrete barriers and two heavy steel bars to act as a gate. Brokers and known faces are waved through. Others are told to stop and answer questions. There are only a few every day.

But four guards are at the overpass all day and all night. Men and women, different ages. Scavengers bring a tent with walls, the guards create a fire pit. Other scavengers build a small, open guard house with a bench and windows.

Only a handful of kids looking for trouble come all the way to the guard-house. They pull up. They ask to be let through the gate. The guards ask

147

them why they want to cross. The kids are sarcastic, belligerent, sometimes threatening.

The guards just stand and listen, then they walk away. The gate stays closed. The kids scream insults, honk their horns, throw bottles from their car toward the gate.

Eventually, though, the kids back up. And pull away.

But most of the kids don't even approach the guards. They stop half a block away, watching the guards and fire pit and the gate and barriers. And then they move on.

They are not interested in the North End any more than they are the south. All they want is trouble. Wherever they can most easily find it.

• • •

The commissioners are furious that we've taken control of the overpass. They say they'll send police to arrest the guards. They say they'll send bulldozers to tear down the gate and barriers. One very old commissioner says he'll have us sued, all of us, each one of us, he will have us sued.

The gardener, not far from me, I see him smiling some, as the old commissioner lists off the basis for his lawsuit.

But otherwise everyone in the audience, the hundred and fifty people from the North End, they all sit quietly. Staring back at the commissioners.

All of the commissioners had to pass through the gate, first speaking to the guards, explaining who they are and why they needed to cross into the North End.

"I don't even want to be here!" one of the commissioners is now saying from the table, staring out at the crowd that's come to listen. "And now *you* are going to make *me* justify my being here? Who the hell do you people think you are?"

We all stare.

"None of this would be happening," he says, looking at the other commissioners now, many of whom begin to nod, agreeing, "if we had simply forced these people to move away."

Once more, I am angry. Picturing the woman and her boy. Thinking about her story. Of being forced from their home.

The commissioner has not spoken through all this. Finally, though, after twenty minutes of angry threats and accusations, she leans forward to say something. "The North End has never been a dangerous place. But it changed months ago. The same kids and the same gangs who wreak havoc in the south, they are coming over here, causing trouble. And we, this commission, did nothing to stop that. Nothing to help these people here. As you know, when it comes to this sort of trouble, we can't even help ourselves."

I want to yell.

Commissioners shake their heads, throw up their hands.

I want to scream.

She says, "So these people here did something to protect themselves. Why shouldn't they? Why wouldn't they? Wouldn't each of you have done the same?"

Still I want to scream.

• • •

I'm at the overpass the next day, taking pictures for the paper, when the two police officers arrive. The two who've been here a few times before.

Cars and trucks, an almost overwhelming flow of traffic, race underneath us. The highway is eight lanes wide here, the traffic moving incredibly fast, as if the travelers beneath us are fleeing a flood or a war, and the sound of it leaves me slightly short of breath, the noise seeming still to always rise without ever reaching a peak.

The police officers are talking to the guards. Their car is parked to the side of the overpass. The guards have already opened the gate but the police seem uninterested in the gate or the barriers. If anything, the police officers seem to be laughing.

"Do you know how many of those commissioners live behind gated walls?" one of the police officers says to a guard, yelling to be heard over the sound of the traffic below us.

The guard is a scavenger, weathered and pale and thin, and yet, as big as each of the officers is, it's hard not to think this woman could easily knock down either of them.

She is smiling some as the officers laugh. Her many earrings flash in the light. They don't match, left side and right, but they aren't meant to and I can see that some of them are made of copper wire and some are tiny nails.

"Gated communities," the female officer yells, "with security guards and bars on their windows and alarm systems that go off every time one of their kids sneaks out at night to smoke some pot."

"I'm sure they do," the scavenger says and although she must be yelling to be heard, she doesn't seem to strain.

One of the officers says, "Will you stop everyone who tries to pass?"

"We are not vigilantes," the scavenger says. The woman. "We aren't looking for retribution."

The male officer nods. "Understand, though," he yells to her, "that some of those commissioners are."

The officers shake hands with the guards. The male officer waves toward me. "The writer," he yells. "Someone told me who you are. You're everywhere."

I'm not sure what to say. In a moment, I simply raise my hand.

I realize the minister is next to me. He is pulling a red wagon carrying food and water for the guards. He says, leaning close to me so I can hear him, "I forgot to tell you that those police came by. To the church. To talk to me about that body you found."

We watch the police car turn around, drive away into the South End.

The minister is still leaning close, yelling to me over the sounds of the traffic, "The cops made some noise about how I shouldn't have handled the body at all, how that was illegal." He smiles some, his small teeth showing. "One of them said I could lose my license. I asked him, 'To be a minister or a mortician?' Both of them tried not to laugh."

My head nods. I think maybe I have smiled. But it's hard to focus on the minister or the guards or even what those police officers were saying. I don't like being at the overpass. It is a block long, but even from the north side, you can see the South End. There are low buildings and there's a dingy gas station and there are trees.

Dead trees.

There is trash along the sidewalk too, and in the gutters in the street there are plastic bags that rattle in the wind, beer bottles, beer cans, a large paper bag from a fast food restaurant, all spread across the street, all having been thrown from passing cars.

There is very little trash in the North End.

I know that I should go to the south side of the overpass to take a photo of the gate and guardhouse and guards. The view that a visitor will see. But I can't do it. I can't get that close to the South End.

The minister is still standing near me.

In a moment, I say, "I need to take a picture from the other side." I'm standing still as I say this. Staring toward the South End.

It's a long minute. Maybe two. Cars scream out sometimes, a single engine roaring upward in high-pitched acceleration and how one noise could be louder than the others makes no sense to me.

I still have not stepped forward.

It's as if the noise of the traffic were a harbinger of something we all know will happen. A warning, maybe, that if I cross I won't ever be allowed back into the North End.

There's a hand on my arm. The minister holds my elbow, very lightly. "I'd like to see the guardhouse from that side too," he says.

He moves forward, still holding my elbow, and although we are walking side-by-side and he is hardly touching me, I am very much being pulled.

We cross through the gate and the concrete barriers meant to slow the traffic, the South End approaching me, it seems, and I can barely see beyond the low buildings and dark gas station right in front of me. Can barely see the tops of trees a few blocks away, thin and gray like the buildings beyond them and there are a million people there, so many people.

"Probably far enough," the minister yells, but in the sound of the traffic here it's like he's whispering and I turn to him and he's only barely smiling and I follow his arm on mine as he turns around and she was right, the commissioner, everyone does know my story, the minister does and the police do too and maybe the scavengers know it and maybe everyone I see on the street every day, maybe they all know the story of the family of six in the North End, five of whom died, their house burning down, the children and wife burned in their sleep as the dying city around them failed to respond.

But mostly I just try to step one more time.

"Take your picture," the minister says, still a whisper. "Go ahead. Take it now."

I turn around. Focus the camera. Take a picture. Focus again. Take another.

I see the North End beyond the gates. The lightly sloping neighborhoods and wide avenues leading toward downtown, the tops of buildings there, my building, my hotel and my room, it is one of them. I think, I can see the windows, very far away.

"That's probably enough," he whispers. Many minutes later.

The guards, the scavenger, they watch me. Very still. The scavenger, she has that stare.

And I turn to the minister. He's shorter than me, but compact and strong, and if I fell he could hold me up. I can't move. But he steps forward again, back to the North End, and I can barely see him, eyes so blurry now and wet, but the minister still is smiling his slight smile, arm on mine.

"Now another step," he whispers. "And now another step."

• • •

The South End is the suburbs to the North End. The sprawling, senseless suburbs that will also someday be abandoned. You can't build places of substance and duration only as an antidote to what you have for so long neglected.

I write this up for the paper.

In my memory, the South End is made of plastic. An amorphous mass of tan houses with flat and treeless yards, of low shopping centers with stores placed intermittently in plain boxes of one size. There is no height in the South End, the trees too young to be noticed, the buildings all kept to a few stories at most. And the surfaces of everything are like plastic, the neighborhoods finished along sharp lines and dull curves that are repeated, again and again, on every house, every block, every subdivision for many miles. Some neighborhoods are fading, not aging, that panacea of newness already crumbling as cracks show in the sidewalks and as potholes form in the side streets and as the surfaces of the homes and shopping centers all begin to peel, like the decal of a window on a small toy house, the decal lifting at the edges, sliding along the surface of that toy, now off center and askew.

I write this all up for the paper.

When I lived in the South End for that year after they died, I remember that I seemed always to be driving. I drove constantly along streets of six or eight lanes, stop lights, turn lanes, the exhaust of delivery trucks idling in traffic in front of me. To do the simplest thing, I drove, in traffic, waiting at traffic lights turned green, waiting for cars to complete their turn, waiting for trucks to enter the lane.

I think about the story of the woman and her boy. How that story makes me want to scream.

The people of the South End aren't aware that their own community is dying too, that their existence is colorless and indistinct, filled with tasks like navigating traffic and making money to pay for bigger plastic homes farther from the crowded neighborhoods they already want to leave behind as they keep pushing to build new places even farther to the south, always shutting down their own failed neighborhoods and driving good people away.

I write this up, read it again, and put it all in the paper.

I think about what the woman told me.

I think about wanting to scream.

The South End is based on fear, fear of anything that is not new, fear of the North End they want to forget, and fear of the death of their own neighborhoods, a death which, right now, spreads steadily among everyone who lives there.

. . .

The commissioner is asking me about the flooding to the north. She has read my article about the broken levees and the miles of flooding I found in the boat. She has come to the newspaper's office.

I tell her the things I wrote about, how I made my way from canals through broken levees and across so many flooded neighborhoods. And although she read the article, she continues to ask questions.

"The water reached to the second floor windows?" she asks.

"Yes."

"How could it reach that high?" she says. "The North End wasn't built that far below sea level."

"That area, all of it, is particularly low," I say. "I looked it up on old survey maps. But also the water levels in the bay, I would guess that they have risen."

It's a moment, then she nods. She sits in an old wooden chair on the other side of my desk. She wears a skirt, boots, a heavy sweater. She carries a black bag that she has set near her on the floor.

I think again, as I did when I first met her, that I can't figure out how old she is. She could be fifty. She could be forty.

I wonder, for a moment, if she is pretty. But I know that I can't tell. That part of me is sunk down somewhere, buried. Covered up.

But I notice she has blue eyes. A fact. *She has blue eyes.*

"As you know," she says, "there is very little will to help the North End and the people who live here."

I say to her, "There is no will to help." I am sitting back in my desk chair. Leaning to the left. I'm not bothered by talking to her, but I am exhausted by it. As always, it drains me fully.

"I have begun looking for someone to assess the levees," she says. "But there's a very deep lack of interest in the problem. As you can imagine. And there are people who would welcome the breaking of the levees," she says. "That's why I haven't mentioned it to the commission. Some of them, they'd want to blow them up. Flood the North End. Be done with this place."

I am not sure what to say.

She says, "The way you write about these things has changed."

I lean farther to the side.

"You're making a case now," she says. "You're calling for action. Why?"

I shake my head. "I don't know."

It's a while, maybe a minute, before she says, "I've read your books. From before. I read them."

I shake my head. I'm not sure why. It's like I'm trying to shake off what she has just said.

"I enjoyed them," she says.

I push my hand along the edge of my desk, very slowly.

"Are you still writing?" she asks.

"I write for the paper," I say, quickly, more quickly than I'd meant.

"I mean another book," she says. She is leaning forward slightly.

I remember this conversation, repeated many times, before they died. Friends and neighbors and family all asking what I was writing. What I was working on. What my next book would be.

It was never a comfortable conversation. It felt like I was offering inappropriate details of my life, details too secret to mention aloud.

"What are you working on?" she would ask, my wife, and I would shrug and shake my head and even with her I struggled to answer.

The commissioner says again, "Your writing in the paper. You're making a case. A very good case."

I shake my head.

"Was it seeing the water covering the airport?" she asks. "The water covering the neighborhoods?" She pauses, then says. "Your old neighborhood."

I shake my head. Can't answer. Say after a moment, "I don't know."

She shifts in her chair. Leaning forward. Toward my desk. "The death of things," she says, "the way the trees die and the grass dies and the animals all go elsewhere, it is spreading across the South End. It's spreading very rapidly."

"Yes," I say, because I need to say something. "That would make sense."

"And with all the people who were killed by that storm," she says, "maybe people will begin to take these things more seriously."

Her hands, the nails shining, rest on the edge of my desk.

I'm thinking about what she said about the commissioners blowing up the levees. It's happened. In other cities long ago. It could happen again.

"I think the people in the South End," I say, "the commissioners, everyone, they should remember that the South End is below sea level too."

She stares.

I've read a lot about these things. During my days sitting in the library.

"People in the south forget that," I say. "You're so far from the bay."

She looks around, oddly, as if to see if anyone else is hearing this.

"The South End wasn't built below sea level," I say. "But now that sea levels are higher, the South End is very much at risk."

It takes a moment for her to talk again. "I didn't realize this."

"If they even know about the water," I say, "people in the South End assume it's far away."

She sits back in her chair. I wonder how old she is. I wonder if she's pretty. I wonder why she comes here. I wonder why she seems to care.

"There are no levees in the South End," I say, and a tiredness overwhelms me, so that it's like I'm listening to myself talk. "No canals to capture the overflow, to channel the water back to the bay. If the water ever reaches this downtown, then the highway will become a river. And eventually the streets of the South End will run with water for miles and miles and miles."

She stares.

I'm not sure what else to say. I hope she'll let me sleep soon. Lie down. Close my eyes. And sleep.

"I didn't know," she says. "I'm not sure anyone does."

She has blue eyes.

"Our problems are theirs," I say, and I do close my eyes now, as if to sleep, and rising, rising from this room, asleep now, hearing myself say, "There's only so long for them to deny this."

She has blue eyes.

. . .

Still the sound of my own voice disturbs me. But this is not really new. In the year before they died, I talked less and less. Eventually the sound of my own voice began to surprise me, even bother me.

And so I talked even less.

I wrote at night, sleeping in the afternoon, waking up sometimes at eight or nine, writing in a small office on the first floor of our house till three or four o'clock in the morning.

Some days I did not see them. Other days I'd wake as they left for school and I'd see them tumbling out to the car where she waited, ready to drive, looking back at the house where I was still lying on the old couch in my office.

Something had gone wrong. With me and with writing and with how it was that I was living. I walked at night, after working, wandering the increasingly abandoned neighborhood. Streets with lights all out. Streets still populated by those few people committed to staying.

I could not find a way to focus again on the family. I no longer wanted to visit new places. No longer wanted to travel. Some days I spent an hour touching every item in my office. Wandering the room and letting my hands touch everything.

But I told myself this would pass. I told myself once I finished the book, I'd be myself again.

I hardly saw the children. They crashed into me when they saw me. Climbed on my back and on my lap and made themselves as close to me as they could, pressing, it's just how they were.

It's not that I didn't like it. It's not that I didn't love them. But my attention was somewhere else.

She would do a similar thing. Hold my hand, wrap her arms around me from the front or side or back. Hold me tight a moment. Ask how the work was going.

She had blue eyes, my wife. Palest blue and shining.

She was beautiful, my wife.

But my attention was somewhere else.

I slept through the day and worked into the night, thinking always about that book. Thinking about it as I walked the North End, as I lay on that old couch. Thinking about the words I'd write. The scenes that I'd create.

A book about this place. The North End. A book about life in an abandoned city and a man who chose to stay here.

Who will be the narrator? What will he do and think and say?

She had blue eyes, my wife.

I'd forgotten that. But I remember it now, alone, in this hotel room. Under blankets. On this couch.

I remember those eyes. I remember her voice. I remember what it meant to touch her.

I slept on that couch for months.

I lost track of the kids. Of her. Of the house itself.

I left her alone to parent them, to keep track of them, to handle everything they did.

My memories of the dinner table, before that last year when I disappeared, are loud and there is laughing and we felt a kind of joy, together, all six of us, laughing still at that round table.

She had blue eyes. I'd forgotten that. Because my other memory of her eyes is empty, her eyes burned out as she lay on the ground in front of the house. On the curb and she was as broken and black as the rest of them. But she was still alive. Still breathing. Whispering. Whispering my name and whispering that she was sorry. Sorry.

Sorry.

And then she died.

The story that was told, in papers and on TV, in the South End and beyond, was that all of them burned in our house. That no fire trucks or police or ambulances ever came. That this death was caused by the very place where we chose to live.

But sometimes, at night, I would light houses on fire. Back then, before all of them had died. I did it to see what it would look like. To learn how it was done. This would be in the book. A narrator, alone, in a city that has been abandoned.

I told no one that I did this. I just took notes as the houses burned.

Took notes as I started the fires in the basements of those dark, forgotten homes.

Took notes as I lit a mix of boards and gasoline in a bucket. Notes on how the shadows played on the basement walls and wooden beams. Took notes as the fire in that bucket died.

And then I headed upstairs from my basement. In our house. To write for another thirty minutes. In my office. Before I went to sleep.

Waking up an hour later, and the first floor was engulfed in flames.

Flames that were already up the stairs. In the halls. In their rooms.

Flames that I had started.

A fire that I had caused.

PART III

CHAPTER 9

I've been awake nearly an hour before I realize the power is out in my hotel room. I only notice when I try to heat some water and the starter on the stove will not spark.

The gas is not out, though, and the water runs, and so I use a match to light the gas, then make tea and soup, drinking it with a piece of bread I've toasted above the burner.

It is morning, daylight, so I can't see from my windows whether any other buildings have lost power.

I wonder if the commission has finally cut the electricity to the North End.

The power gives us choices. And yet any day it could be cut off.

I stand at my open window. The plant, the gardener's plant, is on a table near me and I touch it, absently, with my hand.

It's a few minutes before I see a traffic light turning red. The green and yellow bulbs are out and so, every few minutes, the light simply turns red, then minutes later it goes dark.

I watch as that light goes through its cycle, left to imagine the minutes when it is green, the moment when it is yellow. An imagined backdrop of normalcy and routine. How many green lights had I watched before I came to this hotel? How many red lights had I sat watching as the kids talked in the backseat, my wife in the front seat next to me?

Moments I can picture, dreamlike in how I remember nothing that was said.

I stand at my open windows. A lamp near me suddenly turns on.

163

The power, for whatever reason, it has returned to my building.

But I am only crying.

And I am only thinking about how I cry all the time. In my hotel room. Walking down the street. Sitting at my desk as I write an article for the paper. Lying on the couch after trying to work in the old library.

My breathing breaks and tears come and it goes on this way for minutes.

I am not always particularly conscious of this happening.

I do not think about it all that much.

But, for a moment, I picture all that crying.

Crying as I lie under the heavy blankets on my couch, still cold and wet from a shower.

Crying as I look out at the flooded airport in the North End.

Crying in front of each house, as I sit and watch it burn.

I try to stop myself now. I hold both my eyes, pressing against them with my bare hands.

But it's morning. And I am always much weaker when I've just woken up.

• • •

The press begins to roll in the basement beneath my office. The floor shakes and there is the distant sound of machinery in motion.

Twenty minutes and it's done. I hear the press shut down. I hear the lift that brings the papers up from the darkened basement. I hear the pressman, once again, driving away to deliver the papers.

Soon I'll turn the lights off. Leave. Walk back to the hotel.

But for now I just sit still.

• • •

The minister and I are in my playground. He is drinking from a glass of what he says is bourbon. "Do you want any?" he asks.

I shake my head. "No, thank you."

164

Still I allow myself just the one drink, at night, alone at the windows in my room.

It begins to rain, very lightly, the drops touching my hands and face. We are both sitting on one of the park benches.

"I remember once giving a woman money after sex," he says now, looking toward the pond and trees around it. "Not paying for it. Although I would have. I mean, I'd done that before. More than once. But this time, the woman I was with, I just knew she needed money."

I don't know what has started this thought for him. Maybe the bourbon, I think. Maybe the rain.

"I am starting to replant the courtyard behind the church," the minister says. "With the help of the gardener."

I find myself tapping my hand lightly on the arm of the bench, affirmation, though I don't think he needs that.

The minister fills his side of the bench, yet his bare feet barely touch the ground and his arms, I realize, are short as well.

Bare feet, even in this cold and wet.

He is nodding, to himself, I think. "I've done things I would rather not remember," he says, "So in my mind I am constantly changing the subject, trying to keep myself from remembering."

His feet swing, the soles just touching the grass underneath us, a silent metronome to his talking.

"I paid her that money," he says, his small fingers wrapping around his glass as he lifts it to his lips. "Just twenty dollars. And she began to cry." He sips again. "But the thing is, she took it. She took that money. Put it in the pocket of her long dress. We had sex other times. But I never handed her money again. Instead, I left money on a table, wrinkled up, like it had fallen from my wallet, so that it looked forgotten, looked like I wouldn't notice that she left with it each time."

Rain touches my hands, lightly, and I look up, squinting, and can see each drop as it falls toward my cheeks.

"Don't you think," I ask, "that the lie was as much for you as for her?"

It's a moment, but he smiles some. Barely. He says quietly, "Yes. I'd never thought about it that way. But yes."

When there's no wind you can hear even the faint drops landing on the leaves of the garden around us.

"There are much worse things I have done," he says. "To others. To myself."

In a moment, I ask him, "Where did you do those things?"

He is still looking away from me, toward the plants growing along the base of the stone benches along the wall. "Back there," he says. "In the South End."

It's a long while before I respond. "But not here," I say. "You haven't done them here."

His feet swing. He smiles slightly again. "That's right," he says.

There's a smell to a rain like this. Something warm and close and not bad at all.

"Why haven't you written about the gardener?" the minister asks me. "Or about this playground or the other gardens he has helped the scavengers plant for themselves?"

I shake my head. "I'm not sure."

"It's quite remarkable," he says. "What the gardener has been able to do. I would think it's worth a story."

And of course he's right. And I don't know why I haven't done this.

We are quiet for some time. The rain falls so lightly that my hands are barely wet and the water hasn't reached through my hair to my scalp. I drink from my coffee and the minister sips from his bourbon and I watch his feet swing, slowly, evenly, brushing drops of water from the blades of grass.

He shrugs, as if responding to something I've said. He smiles again. "I don't really know why I moved myself into that church," he says. "Of all places, a church. But I grew up going to church. I grew up believing a place like that had meaning. I grew up believing a place like that brought out the good in people."

I press my finger against the arm of the bench, the finger sliding, the beads of water collecting on the skin and fingernail.

166

"I guess," he says, pushing his hand across his eyes, "I guess I grew up believing in the idea of redemption."

My finger is wet to the knuckle with the collected beads of rain. Water that is so clear. It's surprising, really, that the water here would be so clean and clear.

I raise my hand, touch the water to my tongue.

"Write an article about the gardener," the minister says. He's looking from the pond to the paths to the ivy crawling so very slowly up the red brick walls. He wipes his eyes again. "There's hope in this," he says. "There really is. People should know. Everyone needs to know."

• • •

On the third floor of a small building, I find an old photo studio. There are cameras and many lenses and large hooded strobe lights on tripods and tall, curtained backdrops in white and black and green. There is a darkroom too, much bigger than the one at the newspaper, and in the darkroom is a large vault, its shelves filled with boxes of film. Hundreds of small, tightly sealed containers. Far more film than I've used in all my years at the paper.

It's a while, many minutes, before I go ahead and take some boxes. Five boxes, then another five, I put them in the pocket of my coat.

I find various lenses that will fit my camera. I take two of those as well.

And within days, I'm taking more pictures than before. Of people near the corner store. Of commissioners at the table during their meetings. Of the view from the open windows of my room as the fog moves across the surface of the many roofs below me.

• • •

The scavengers strip the homes down to bare studs in what seems like minutes. Others they strip down all the way to ground level, leaving only the flat, concrete outline of a home.

The scavengers work on twenty houses at a time and even then there are ten or twenty people working on each house.

There are more scavengers, this means. They are gathering more workers.

I'm taking notes for a story about what direction the scavengers are moving. I've written these stories every few weeks since I started at the paper. But it has been many months since I've come to see them work. Usually, I just watch them from my window.

Music plays, loudly, from a set of speakers set up on the back of a truck. Speakers six feet tall, four of them, so that the music is as loud as a concert, booming and grinding, and it's a few minutes before I'll realize that, like the last time I was here, the music has no voices, no words.

Brokers in their panel vans catalog what they load into their trucks.

Scavengers move, quickly, into the front doors and windows of the homes.

I keep a map of the areas where the scavengers have worked. I run it with the stories I write. The scavenged area now covers most of the southwestern corner of this place, forming a wide finger wrapping its way around the oldest neighborhoods and the grand boulevard and slowly approaching the overpass.

I came here today because, looking at my map, I realized the scavengers are moving with purpose through the newest neighborhoods in the North End. The square mile of cheap homes that were built when the vast urban park was cut in half by the highway.

These houses are indistinguishable from one another, the landscaping around them barren, barren even before everything died.

Soon, all these new homes will have been scavenged.

I don't know how this decision was made. I'm not even sure who to ask. For now, though, I am only taking pictures as they work. A scavenger emerges from a hole in a roof. He pulls the ends of a group of cables behind him, then throws them, one by one, to another scavenger suspended above the roof on the hook of a crane. The cables are attached to the hook and the first scavenger slides down the roof, then drops to the ground in front of the house. As he walks away, the crane begins to tighten the cables and, in a moment, the house collapses in on itself, the cables pulling in on the four corners of the structure, on the load-bearing walls in the interior of the home, on the beams in the roof, and with a crashing barely louder than the music from the speakers, the house is flattened onto itself.

When the cables are detached from the remnants of the home, a scavenger on a bulldozer comes to the pile of materials and begins to push all of it back from the street, shoving the wood siding and the roof across the backyard until it is pressed up against the house behind it.

They do this another ten times while I watch, methodically moving down one side of the street.

I begin to realize they've done this nearly a hundred times already. I am walking back along the areas where the scavengers have already been. Along one side of the street, they've flattened a row of houses, then pushed them through the backyard onto the neighboring house. In a few places there are low, cheap strip centers of two or three abandoned stores. These are flattened too, so that a line of flattened homes and buildings winds its way around the area that's been scavenged.

A border, it seems, that starts a few miles from the overpass.

They're not just scavenging. They're clearing this place.

"Why?" I ask a scavenger when I've made my way back to where they work. He drinks water from a spigot on a barrel on the back of a truck, his lips wet and his mouth wet but the rest of his face is covered in dry, black dirt.

The truck sells food, too, and another ten scavengers are here eating and drinking water. They all watch me.

The scavenger says, in a moment, "A few months ago we decided there wasn't much else worth scavenging in this area. And it certainly isn't worth keeping."

I write this down in my notebook.

The music is not as loud here, but it still grinds on from the truck a few blocks away.

I have watched the scavengers work many times. How they skip one house then choose another, how they turn away from one street, moving south instead of crossing an avenue or a canal. It has always seemed unplanned, the almost accidental decision to pick one house over another, the collected group then moving in a new direction.

I hold my map of the scavenged areas out to the man with the dirty face. "Where will the line of flattened homes go?" I ask.

He looks at the map for a moment. He drinks again from the spigot. Then he points to the overpass. "To where these neighborhoods, the new ones, they end there at the overpass. That's where we're going."

I nod. But I'm still confused. "So you'll have outlined the area that, you say, isn't worth scavenging anymore?"

He nods. Another scavenger has come up next to him, a woman covered in a white, fluffy powder, insulation from an attic maybe, and only her mouth and nose and eyes aren't covered in the fluff, having been covered by a mask she now holds in her hand. She takes a drink of water before speaking.

"You're the writer," she says to me.

I nod. We stare. It's a moment before I look around at the rows of demolished houses. I ask her, "Why?"

She stares at me for a moment, then says, "It's the gardener's idea."

"To do what?" I ask her.

"To cut off this whole neighborhood," she says, looking at the map and tracing its outline with a long finger covered in fluff.

"And then what?" I ask.

She turns to me again and now she smiles, her eyes bright and her lips bright and even in her alien form, nearly every surface of her covered in the dusty white fluff, even still there's a hard and surprising beauty to her.

"Then," she says, "we burn the entire neighborhood to the ground."

• • •

I'm walking through yards and open lots and courtyards that the gardener has helped scavengers to plant. I had not imagined anything this big or complex. But there are twenty of these elaborate gardens in a small section of one of the oldest neighborhoods. Streets I don't go down because for years, as I've walked, I've stayed clear of houses that might be occupied, stayed clear of so many of the few other people who are here in the North End.

There are front yards green with shrubs and grass and small trees growing upward. There are open lots lined with wooden benches and long boxes in which row after row of small plants are growing. There are small parks repopulated with chairs and tables and flowering vines and arbors strung with plants and small trees lining the pathways.

It's overwhelming. The effort it took. The normalcy it has created.

As we walk, the gardener answers my questions about the universities where he studied and about the places where he did research on plant life around the world. Some of this he's told me before, in his courtyard mostly, but with fewer details. Fewer names.

Now, though, I take notes as he talks, then ask him more questions, simple ones, about what trees and vines he's brought here and about why it is possible that some plants will grow when everything else has died.

"It's a matter of shifting the plant life to meet this new environment we are in," he says. "The changes in soil and temperature and weather patterns and light." As he speaks, he walks quickly, I realize. His hands move faster and his talking is faster than when I first met him in his courtyard. "This has long happened, these shifts. The transporting of seeds by birds or other animals. The introduction of new species via hurricanes or tsunamis or even forest fires and flooded rivers. What we're doing is making the same changes that nature has always made."

We walk through a series of connected backyards, which together form a space as green and overgrown as the gardener's courtyard.

I take notes. I ask questions. "So you're saying this is all a normal process?"

He smiles. He says in a moment, "Does anything about this place seem normal?" He shakes his head. "No. This is not normal. It's simply a response to something that absolutely did not have to happen."

I write, quickly, my words and letters scrawled across the pages, indecipherable markings that only I can read.

"Could the entire North End be replanted?" I ask.

He thinks about this for a while. "There's no reason it couldn't. But I'm not sure there's the will to make that happen."

We pass through a large iron gate covered in more ivy.

"And understand," he says, "that everything we now plant, if it is neglected the way we neglected and abused this place in the past, then it will also eventually die." He turns to me, smiling only vaguely. "And know that the climate, the weather, the way it is changing, that may inevitably kill these new plants as well."

The tip of my pencil scratches across the paper. Blunt lead dragging across the dry, bleached fibers.

I stop to take a picture of the diagonal brick paths leading to a park on a corner. There are small trees. Wooden benches.

"These plants here," the gardener says to me, still with that slight smile as he runs his brown hand along a swath of tall, flowering grass, "in India, where these are from, people long thought of them as weeds."

I turn to a new page in my notebook. I can hear the sound of the pencil on the paper and once more, for a moment, I have a sense that it's not the words I write but the sounds of the pencil, the shape of the markings, that I am here to create.

And the notes I take, the sound of the pencil, all cover my surprise and confusion that I've never seen any of this before. It's as if it took till now, till I wrote this all down, for me to understand this place is real.

The aura of so much that is growing and alive. The shock that I have never seen this.

"When you wrote," the gardener now asks, "what did you like about it?"

The question makes me wince, very suddenly, but I don't think that he sees me. Even though he is looking right at me. The question, about writing, reminds me of another time, when people would ask that sort of thing. *What do you write? When do you write? How do you know what you'll write about?*

In a moment, he says, "It's okay. You don't have to answer."

It's apparently been some time since he asked the question.

I'm still writing in my notebook. But I stop. Shake my head. "I can answer," I say. "It's just that it seems so long ago."

We walk again, along a stone fence bordering a house.

"What were you working on?" he asks. "Before," he says.

It takes a while for me to answer.

"A book," I say. I say, "A book about this place. The way it has become. And a man who lives here."

"Why?" he asks.

We're in the backyard of a brick house, where nothing around me looks dead. Scavengers, two of them, sit on the back porch, watching us. The gardener raises his hand to them.

"I lived here then," I say. "We did. We watched as this place finally died." I stare up for a moment, toward the sky. Gray and the clouds are low today, solid, that indistinct layer, uniform, flat. "It was a setting," I say. "A place where anything might happen. Where people would have had to make a choice to stay."

I've stopped walking.

"Are you still writing?" he asks.

In a moment, I shake my head. *No.*

"Did you keep it?" he asks. "Do you still have what you'd written?"

I'm staring up. It's a moment before I nod.

"How would you end it?" I hear the gardener ask.

I shake my head. Standing still and staring up and speaking to the sky. "I really don't know."

• • •

Portraits on the wall stretch nearly from the floor to the ceiling. They are photos, life-size, eight portraits lining the walls, a woman and her daughter, a man and his son, some in green fields, some in bright playgrounds, others standing by a swimming pool or a shiny yellow school bus.

I've found my way into a doctor's office. A pediatrician.

The people in the photos smile perfectly. The parents hold the hands of their brightly lit children. The children laugh, in their eyes, as they stare into the camera.

The floor of this room is littered with trash and pieces of broken furniture and empty boxes of medical supplies thrown everywhere.

The lights turn off. I'm left in darkness, my eyes still flashing with the memory of light, the suddenness of the darkness seeming almost to have created a noise, my ears for a moment ringing with an echo of the room going black.

I see a window then, with faint glimmers of light coming through the glass. I walk to it, slowly, hands forward, and with each step I carefully test where my foot will go.

The noise, if it is a noise, still rings in my ears.

At the window, the glass is cold and there is very little light outside. No streetlights. No traffic lights. No buildings or homes. The only light is the glow from the South End.

The power to the whole North End is out.

It seems unlikely this has happened by accident. The commission, it seems, has finally shut us down.

And then the lights blink on, blinding and white, and I have to sit down on the floor and close my eyes tight, cover them with my hands, and when I do open them, barely, the people are there again, all of them, life-size, eight parents and their children all smiling and holding hands, standing against the walls above a floor thick with debris, and all of their faces stare down at me.

• • •

Something bad is happening at the overpass. I feel it before it happens. The minister, he does too.

We've been talking about the power. About how it went out the night before and whether it was an accident or a plan. "If it was an accident," the minister says to me, yelling as he leans close to my ear because of the deafening sound of the cars underneath us, "it was a happy one for the commission."

There are two scavengers here, along with the minister and me.

But now the minister and I both turn toward the guardhouse on the overpass. Despite the noise of the cars, there's a sound, it seems, or the absence of sound, or a disruption of some kind that leads the two of us to turn and see a black van pulling forward from the South End, moving slowly toward the gate, and it's only a moment before men, dressed in black and with masks over their faces and carrying blond baseball bats in one or both of their hands, ten of them pile out of the back of the van, now headed toward the guardhouse and the assembled people there.

Those who don't run are beaten badly.

The ten men are taking their bats to the guardhouse and the barrier and the chairs where people were sitting. The ten of them pound on it all, busting everything into pieces. The minister and I and the scavengers drag away the five wounded people. There are bloodied faces and broken arms, and the people we've dragged away are moaning or yelling, at least their faces show they are, because still at the overpass it's too loud to hear anything but the cars.

The men in masks do their work in the deafening silence created by the traffic.

They move quickly but with a purpose. A plan. They've been sent here with a plan.

Soon they are burning everything they see.

We watch them, the minister and me and the two scavengers all standing above the five wounded people on the ground. We're barely half a block away. If the men cross to us, I'm not sure how we'd fight them off. Not with the injured people on the ground. Not with those bats. Not with the rage they carry and the freedom their anonymity gives them.

For minutes, we can only watch them.

Their anger and violence, it clearly spawns in them a kind of joy.

That a storm can cast shadows on a landscape without sunlight is surprising, disturbing, even breathtaking as I turn to see the wall of black clouds approaching us fast.

Lit with lightning and filled with rain, thick and swirling sheets of rain, the storm rides on a base of dirt and debris and rainwater spraying back up from the ground.

It's a minute before the roar of the traffic is overwhelmed by the rising sound of the storm.

The men in masks, one sees the storm now, stopping where the group had begun to move from the overpass toward the four of us and the wounded people at our feet. Another man drops his bat. Still another man turns and runs. Soon all of them are running. Toward the van that brought them here.

But there is no way to find safety.

The minister is dragging a wounded person toward the high concrete wall that lines the highway. I drag another, by the leg, quickly and roughly and I see this person screaming as she slides across the street and up a curb and I stop dragging her only when we're both pressed against the high concrete wall.

The scavengers pull the other three, two by their arms, one by his leg, and now the nine of us are turned to face the storm coming onto us as we press back against the wall, the wounded lying down and the rest of us standing, backs flat against the concrete, and the air is shaking with the storm that's so high, a wall itself that goes straight up, erasing my building from sight, and the other downtown buildings are gone and even the homes on the ground just a few blocks away are disappearing from view as the mass of wind and rain and lightning approaches.

It's on us.

The storm has weight, pressing down on us with rain so thick that I am within seconds soaked through to the skin. Lightning strikes nearby, a blast that blinds me and leaves me deaf for a moment so that all I know is the wall, behind me, that I've pressed myself against in a world where otherwise my ears only ring and my eyes are white with light.

Debris now, I feel it crashing down near us before I can see it or even hear it, but when I can, there are objects falling, the boards from a fence and a tire and dirt and so many shingles, black and green and some are made of tile, the shingles seem suddenly to be the very source of the storm, dancing among the wind, swirling in every direction, till finally they slam into the wall at our backs.

I drop to the ground, debris exploding against the wall, the wounded woman trying to cover her face but with her arms broken she can't, and so I crawl to her, cover her with my body, her face is in my stomach and she uses her bare arms to grasp at my legs and still the objects slam endlessly into that wall.

I've never been in a car wreck or a plane wreck or an earthquake or tsunami. But this must be the same. The ground shakes and I shake and the wall behind us seems to bend against a wind thick with rain and objects turned horrendously violent.

I see the minister near me. He covers a wounded person, like I do, he covers the person with his body, his own hands and arms over his head.

The other wounded people are near my feet. Pressed against one another. Covering each other where they can.

The two scavengers are still standing. Against the wall. Hands at their faces, the rings of pipe and wire on their fingers and their forearms wrapped in aluminum and leather, arms they hold up toward the wind and the rain and the monstrous force pressing onto us, but, still, the two of them stare out, up, directly into the storm.

This goes on for some time.

When it's done, it ends as quickly as it started, the storm moving south still, we can see it, and we stand, soaked and bleeding and covered in dirt and rain and pieces of debris so varied I can't identify it at all.

We move away from the wall, the four of us who can stand. We see the storm where it has crossed into the South End.

On the overpass, the black van is turned over. The driver's door is open. I see a man in the driver's seat, another in the passenger's. Their eyes are wide open but they don't move and we don't move and it's only when the minister walks forward that I follow him.

But there's another noise now. A sound I can hear as the storm continues to move farther away. It's the sound of car engines. But there is no driving, no roar.

What I hear is the absence of that highway roar.

I go to the side of the overpass, then look down.

Cars, hundreds and thousands of them. Four lanes each way, filled with vehicles that don't move. Jackknifed tractor trailers. Trucks slammed into buses. Cars that are wrecked or simply stuck in place.

People have begun to emerge from their vehicles. Standing. Looking around.

Some scream. Some wail. Some hold their bloodied heads in their hands. Some are waving their arms, frantically, to other cars and people around them.

There is water too. On the highway. Collected there. Covering the bottoms of tires and the soles of the shoes of people standing dumbly and injured beside their wrecked cars, and the water makes it look as if everything is sinking, descending into the rainwater that has collected in that deep and wide trench.

Behind me, on the overpass, I see that the minister has reached the van. I watch him. He checks on the men in the front seat. Goes to the back. Yanks on the door till it opens. There is moaning inside, loud enough that I can hear it. The minister enters to help.

I turn back to the highway. Staring down. The two scavengers are next to me. Staring down as well. We are so far away, it seems. We watch from a distance I can't quite measure.

A woman below us, just one among the thousands of cars and trucks and people all down there, this one woman sees us and now she's screaming, cupping her hands and screaming.

"Please don't," I hear her yell, but there's no volume up here where the sound reaches us. It's more of a whisper. A pleading. "Please," her voice says. "Please don't hurt us."

CHAPTER 10

We watch the people in their vehicles down on the surface of the highway, all of them stuck in place still, a few hours after the storm. It rains lightly and it is very cold, though I think the wind probably doesn't reach down into the trench formed by the high walls. Most cars are idling, the engines creating a low, rumbling sound, the smell of exhaust strong and fragrant and dizzying as it rises up to us.

It is so strange for the highway to be this quiet.

The closest ramps to and from the highway are a few miles in either direction from this overpass. Most people sit in their cars, waiting for the traffic to begin to move. But I have seen a few people walking. Some going west, others walking east, their feet sloshing through the inch of standing water on the surface of the road.

But otherwise there is no motion down there.

I'm standing on the overpass with the minister and gardener. Others from the North End have come too.

"I'm not sure what we could do from up here," the minister says. He's sitting on the guardrail, his short legs and small feet dangling over the cars and trucks on the highway. "Doesn't it seem like help will come at any moment?" he asks.

I say, "It seems like it would have to."

The gardener says in a moment, "You would think."

We've already put the wounded people from the attack into the back of a scavenger's pickup truck. A scavenger and the minister took them to a hospital not far away in the South End, but then returned with them just half an hour later.

"There were already too many wounded people at the hospital," the minister says. "From the storm."

And so instead they put the wounded in the community center, near the overpass. Others from the North End have arrived and some have begun to tend to them.

Four of the masked men died in the van. Most of the rest were hurt badly. They too were offered a ride in one of the scavenger's trucks. But the masked men hurried off instead, wounded but living, leaving behind the four dead men in the van.

The minister and two scavengers loaded the bodies into the back of the truck, then took them to the morgue.

The van, the masked men's van, is turned upright by the scavengers, twenty of them, who then proceed to strip it down to nothing but its steel frame. It takes them just thirty minutes.

A wonder of motion and purpose and skill.

There are now no wheels, no windows, no side panels, no seats or interior finish at all. The scavengers slide the skeletal steel frame to the south end of the overpass, then hoist it, with their hands, onto a block of concrete.

A pedestal.

One scavenger smiles, slightly, as the group returns from the monument they've created.

A reminder. And a warning.

And, by the next morning, we've already rebuilt our guardhouse and barriers and protections at the overpass.

But that same morning, nearly twenty-four hours since the storm hit, there is no change on the highway. The hundreds and thousands of vehicles are still motionless below us. Except now, fewer cars are idling. And a few more people are walking, sloshing through the water on the surface of the highway.

Water that is, clearly, a few inches deeper.

I've been at the overpass for an hour, again watching the highway with the minister and the gardener. Taking notes, taking pictures.

The minister is sitting on the guardrail, again his small feet dangling from the overpass.

"It did seem like, by now, help would have come," the gardener says.

Other people from the North End are here. The guards at the overpass, scavengers, others. Thirty or so people. Many of them staring down.

A communal helplessness.

Not disinterest. Not disdain. But we seem to have been placed here as nothing more than accidental observers.

"Why isn't the water draining?" the minister asks.

"Sea level," I say. "The highway is far below sea level."

"Built that way?" he asks.

"Yes," I say. "But the water should be pumping out. The highway, in its way, is an engineering wonder."

The minister's dark eyes follow the trail of vehicles.

"From the newspaper," he says, part question, absently, to himself. "You wrote that in the paper."

The gardener says, "Maybe the power to the pumps went out in the storm."

I have a feeling of heat on my neck. I say, "Maybe another levee broke in the storm." It's a minute, and I say, "One that's maybe now releasing water into the highway."

The minister says, a moment later, "Could all of them be flooded?"

It's as if he is going to say more. But there's a shared stupidity among us. A sense of waking from a dulled and empty sleep.

"I mean, flooded," the minister says. His feet continue dangling above the scene below. "I mean," he says, and still there's that sense that we are all waking up, "I mean, could all of them drown?"

"I'm not sure," I say. I lean forward against the rail, then back. Look from the minister to the gardener. I say, "It seems impossible."

The gardener smiles slightly, barely glancing at me, but it's a sick and distorted smile. "Of course it does," he says.

"How far below sea water are they?" the minister asks.

"Many, many feet," I say. "It's a tunnel, really, an open air tunnel."

181

The minister says, "They should start to walk."

The gardener is leaning forward now, looking down over the guardrail. He cups his hands to his mouth. He yells, "Why did you come back?" He's pointing at a man and boy now, the two of them sitting on the hood of a car. The gardener yells again, "Why did you come back?"

They don't answer. They seem not to hear.

The gardener turns to us. "I saw him walking last night," he says. "With that boy. Going east. Coming from the west. But now they're back."

The gardener cups his hands to his mouth again and, once more, yells down to the man.

The man looks up after a moment. He yells but we can't hear him. The gardener shakes his head. The man yells again. And this time we can hear it. It's a quiet sound, barely audible through the low rumble of the idling engines and the wind that blows past us and as I hear this man's words I'm awake, I realize, now I am awake.

"Because of the water," the man has yelled. "The water, in each direction, it's too high to walk."

The minister swings his legs back over the guardrail, landing on the overpass, heading now to a group of scavengers near the newly rebuilt guard-house.

And I realize that, once more, it is raining. It rains so much here, so hard, that it often goes unnoticed. But it is raining. It hasn't stopped since the storm.

"My oh my," the gardener says and another time if I'd heard that I'd have thought it was a joke, his joke, an effort to make light. But it is not. "My oh my," he says again, quietly, almost whispering. "My oh my."

Within ten minutes, scavengers have brought two ladders that they drop down to the highway. It's sixty feet from the overpass to the surface of the road. The ladders all have three sections and some seem to have come from fire stations or fire trucks. The scavengers use heavy rope to secure the tops of the ladders to the guardrail on the overpass.

No one on the highway moves toward the ladders. They stare at them. Some people roll down their windows and lean their heads out, staring, and other people just sit in their cars, pointing at the ladders. Talking. They discuss.

A man and his two children step forward, the man helping his daughter, then his son, onto the ladder, then following them close behind. They climb for a few minutes, the ladder bouncing lightly but steadily with each step, the children pausing often, motionless as they speak back to their father, the man talking, coaxing, and then they climb again and even from the guardrail I can see that the boy's eyes are closed and the girl's hands shake wildly and the three of them are now fifty feet in the air and at the top of the ladder is the minister, smiling. Talking. "It's okay," he says. "Almost there. It's okay."

Others have moved closer to the base of the ladders.

Another child gets on a ladder, a woman behind him. A man behind her. They climb.

And soon people by the hundreds are lined up at the ladders.

And soon it is clear that the water on the surface of the highway is rising faster. Nearly a foot deep. Covering feet and ankles and the bottoms of tires and the bottom rungs of the ladders themselves.

A levee must have broken. Somewhere far from here. But the water from that levee is bleeding into this trench

The scavengers bring more ladders. Drop them down to the highway surface, secured at the top by ropes tied to the guardrail on the overpass, and how it's possible the scavengers could have so many ladders is a question only the people down below would ask.

Ropes are run down the center of the ladders, tied tight to the top rung and the bottom, and makeshift climbing harnesses are dropped to the people waiting and not all the people use them but some do strap themselves into the harnesses, then clip themselves to the safety lines.

Ten, then fifteen, now twenty ladders are in place. They form a wall almost, a nearly continuous surface on which the people climb, three or four at a time, spread out across the length of ladders that bow and bounce with the weight of so many people climbing up them. It's as if a fort or castle is being stormed by invaders. And the scavengers, in their worn clothing and hair stained gray and their skin that's white with paint and gypsum,

183

they stand at the top of the ladders, defenders awaiting the soldiers who've mounted their attack.

Except these aren't soldiers or invaders. They are just survivors. And when they finally reach the overpass, grasping at the guardrail as they reach the top, it's clear these are not just survivors, they are refugees, who the scavengers and others from the North End must help from the ladders, talking to them about where to put their hands on the guardrail, where to step, holding the refugees by the hand, and others they lift, screaming, as they can't get themselves free of the ladders, and others they have to help stand up as they fall forward over the guardrail, sprawled out onto the surface of the overpass.

Some refugees hug the people who've helped them, weeping, arms wrapped tight around a tall and weathered person from the North End. Other refugees only nod. Still others turn quickly and run away, fearing what might happen even as they are saved by people from a place that they've long ago learned to fear.

The scavengers and others from the North End just nod. Help each person stand up straight. Point them toward the south.

And the refugees keep climbing. Gathered in a massive group on the highway floor. Pressing inward toward the ladders.

And the water, it still rises. I see a man who's submerged nearly to his knees. I see people lifting children to the hoods and roofs of cars.

And I see that more and more people are coming from the east and west. The water there is getting higher, even higher than it is here.

Many more people from the North End have gathered at the overpass. A kitchen of sorts is set up under a tent. People make soup and they make coffee and at first they serve this just to the refugees who've made it out of the highway. But soon brokers arrive, the brokers who buy from the scavengers most days, and with them they've brought huge boxes of containers of all sizes. Soup and coffee and water is put into the containers and taken to the guardrail and put into wooden crates that are lowered to the highway.

More brokers arrive, their panel vans loaded with loaves of bread and cases of water and blankets and tarps to use on the overpass and to drop to the surface and the brokers also bring more rope, it seems there cannot be enough rope, as a group of scavengers sits in a large circle making harnesses, making safety lines knotted every three feet for grip, making large nets from the rope that are then used to wrap the food and water and blankets that are, again and again, dropped down to the highway.

There are the disabled and elderly among the people down there and they've moved to the north side of the highway and it's soon that the scavengers, not far from the highway, have built a kind of cage, a steel basket they've welded together in the street using the pipes and gear in the back of their trucks and now that cage drops down from a winch and boom they've set up, in a few minutes the cage rises up with an old man in a wheelchair, then an old woman too pale and weak to even walk and again that basket is dropped back down to the surface.

There are buses I can see in both directions from the overpass. Passengers are unloading into the rain and water. Cars unload. Motor homes. A school bus, bright yellow, the students file out, two by two, holding hands, the teachers at the front and back of the line, there's a decency in the crowd as the students are allowed to make their way to the very front of the mass of people.

The climbing has been going on for hours.

There are animals then, moving among the cars and people. Livestock released or broken free from massive trailers, so that chickens and pigs and cows move aimlessly between the vehicles, the cattle in water up to their bellies and the pigs have their snouts up in the air and the chickens hop from roof to roof and it's not long before I see a man on a horse, riding slowly from the east, taller than anyone who walks this way and he does not stop at the overpass, does not even seem to notice the ladders or the people massed on them or around them, instead he only rides steadily forward, searching, I assume, for another way to get free, and it seems now to me that all has broken down in this timeless scene of desperation and escape, all who are on the highway living on the edge of a madness or chaos they can barely recognize as, still, the refugees only push slowly toward those ladders.

And still it rains.

And still the water rises.

And still no one from the south has come to help.

In the evening, the streetlights turn on, flooding the highway in a coldly green and barren glow.

The rungs of ladders break and the people on them scream and the people above the break manage to get to the top and the ones below, saved by the safety lines strung along the full length of the ladders, they are forced to return to the bottom. The broken ladder is pulled up and a new one is immediately dropped down to the highway, the scavengers taking the broken ladder to yet another workspace they've established, mending or discarding the broken sections they've just salvaged.

I see the office manager and the garbage man, both in the community center, two of many tending to the wounded on their cots.

I see the pressman and the woman from the water pumping station, two of many loading food and water into a crate, then helping to lower it down to the highway.

I see the gardener helping to build more tents near the overpass.

I see the minister, still, at the top of the ladders, I don't think he's left the guardrail yet, instead he's been talking endlessly to the people who climb away from the surface. "You're almost there," he says, again, once more. "It's okay. You're almost there."

I see the commissioner arrive. Running from the South End and looking down at the rows of ladders and the mass of vehicles and the people all making their way toward the overpass.

The gardener goes to her. "When will help come?" he asks.

She stares at him. He touches her arm, pulls on it lightly, but still she only stares.

"Help," he says. "When will help come?"

Her face is wet with rain but she is crying, I realize, I can see that she is crying. She stares at the gardener, shaking her head. Only shaking her head.

No one will come.

The minister has been watching her. He turns to me and there's a low, bad smile on his face. A smile of sadness and despair and probably disgust and he turns back to the guardrail, moving from one ladder to the next.

186

"You're almost there," he says, to the people climbing. "You'll be fine. You're almost there."

I mostly help as people climb over the guardrail or help the frail emerge from the steel basket on the winch. But I take time to move among everyone on the overpass. To take notes in my notebook. To take pictures with my camera.

"Document this," the gardener has said to me. "You really must document what is happening."

I take photos of faces as they climb up the ladders. Photos of the scavengers. Of the people who cook. The livestock between the cars. The men and women who've come to help. I load new film into the camera, more often than ever before pulling the plastic rolls from a knapsack, one filled with the film I found in the studio some weeks ago.

People fall from the ladders to the highway surface. A few have done so in the twenty-four hours we've been doing this. They've not worn a harness and their hand slips from a rung and they fall to the ground and die.

There are screams when this happens. Family and friends go to the body where they've fallen. The crowd moves away. And, soon, the family and friends do too.

There is, really, nothing else they can do.

Because still the water rises.

Still, people climb.

There are forty ladders now. The water is nearly four feet deep. The animals swim east or west. The people on the highway make their way through the water, hundreds of them from both directions, slowly approaching the crowd at the ladders.

People from the North End still converge on the overpass, helping people over the rail, helping people in the tents, helping the scavengers with their ropes and cages and winches.

And at some point in the night, some sixty hours since the storm first hit, I realize that it's not just that no one from the South End has come to help. I realize that no one, from anywhere, has come to help.

A fight breaks out at the base of a ladder. There is screaming there, and pushing, two men shoving their way to the front of a group. I watch a scavenger see this happen. She steps up onto the guardrail above the fighting, leans over as if she's going to dive but instead grabs the side of the ladder, swinging around to its underside, where she begins to slide, down, past the people still climbing on the top side of the ladder, and the scavenger slows just barely at each of the sections where the ladders meet, and when she nears the bottom she lets go, landing now on top of one of the men pushing forward.

He falls. She kicks him in the head. She turns to the other man who'd been pushing forward. She hits him in the face. Hard. One punch. He falls too and she kicks him in the head also.

The mass of people steps back. But only slightly. They are packed so close together. The scavenger watches the two men where they lie on the hood of a car.

Then the scavenger grabs hold of the underside of the ladder, climbs upward, two rungs at a time, it takes her twenty seconds to reach the overpass again.

Soon the crowd moves forward, over the men she knocked down, the bodies pushed into the water by the collected movement of the people.

Fog descends. It spreads across the overpass into the trench, the cars and trucks and the people and animals all soon disappearing and there is a moan that becomes nearly a scream as the people on the highway can no longer see the walls of the trench or the people around them or the ladders they need and the overpass above them that they want so badly to reach.

For a few minutes, the tops of the ladders are empty. The climbing has stopped. But then the people begin to emerge from the fog, rising to the top of the ladders, now even more panicked and wide-eyed than those who preceded them, looking back into the thick mist, shaking as they try so hard to stand, grasping the hands of anyone on the overpass who can help, the gardener is there and the minister and the commissioner too, the commissioner as panicked and wild-eyed as the people she helps over the rail. Not one of us in the North End, after all, has so recently lost so much.

And hours later, when the fog dissipates, it's clear that the water is deeper. Five feet now. And rising still.

I take more pictures. I pull more people over the guardrail. I hand out water and coffee and food as men and women and their children finally stand, dumbly, on top of the overpass.

I move through the medical tents where people lie out on cots, their heads bloodied and arms broken and some spit blood into containers at their sides, many injured from the wrecks that happened in the storm so long ago. People from the North End move among them, offering water and food and whatever medical attention they can. The minister comes through, helping with the injuries; he was a mortician once and is now the best medical help we have.

And now I see the woman and her boy. They go from cot to cot offering blankets and water and I'm frozen, crouching, camera in my hands, knowing the two of them left many months ago, they aren't here anymore. But I can see them. Near me. And I wonder for a moment if I've only imagined their absence.

The boy runs into me, as I stand from kneeling, putting my camera away. The boy looks up, sees me and there is panic in his eyes as he pulls away and then he looks at me again and, for a moment, there is something like a smile. I touch his head. Before I know what I'd meant to do.

"How are you?" I ask.

He only stares up at me. Eyes dark. Blinking. It's a long moment, stillness in the fray of so much motion and worry and suffering around me, but now he pats my hand. Then points to his mother. Behind him. She stands near a set of cots filled with a mother and father and their many, many children.

I stare toward her. The room is loud, filled with the noise of motion and moans and the cries of people in pain.

I turn to look down at the boy. He wipes his mouth on the back of his hand. Looks around the room. Then he pats my leg, lightly, and he moves on to get fresh blankets for the new people who have entered the tent.

The woman is watching her boy, as he goes to help others around us.

She glances at me. I hear her voice. "There was nowhere to go," she says, staring right at me. "Nowhere better to be."

189

I am back at the guardrail. Taking pictures. Then helping a man and a woman over the rail.

There are people from other places who climb up those ladders. People not from the South End. Some get to the top and look north, with a fear similar to what they'd felt on the highway. "That's the North End, right?" I hear a man say. "My god," he says, "what if they come down here," he says, pausing. "And see what you are doing?"

The minister smiles at him. "Welcome," he says. "Welcome to the North End."

But some of the refugees turn north, not south when they've reached the overpass. Scavengers point them the other way. "That's the South End," they say. "Don't you want to go south?" But these few refugees shake their heads, point north. "No," they say. "No. There's nothing in the south. Nothing for me. I want to go north."

The brokers bring more tents, large military tents that they set up on the north side of the overpass, in the remnants of a park across from the community center. The tents are meant for the people passing through, people who don't live anywhere near here, for whom the South End is not home.

The water has covered the windshields of cars. And still people are coming. Fewer now, but those who do must jump from vehicle to vehicle or simply swim in the spaces between the cars, even though the animals now, the cattle and chickens and pigs, they fill the spaces between the vehicles with their wild movements, their panicked noises, so that it is safer to move from rooftop to rooftop, bypassing the livestock who will very soon drown.

I see a woman on a ladder with a baby stuffed into a backpack on her chest, the baby's head sticking out, looking around in wonder and confusion. I see people moving toward the crates and nets that, still, drop food and supplies to the highway, to a flatbed truck where the supplies are stacked before being given away, and now a man tells his children, four of them, to get into the net to be raised to the overpass, and they cry and they scream but they get into the net, bundled up, smashed together, their faces pressed against the ropes as all four are now raised to the surface.

Air-raid sirens lift, screaming across the North End, and for a moment the people on the highway stop in place, look around, thinking this is the moment when help has finally come.

But of course it is not. Instead the sirens are again only sounding off on their own schedule, as always disconnected from the reality of the scene.

There's a current to the water now. It flows, quickly, from east to west. The cattle stand still, the water pressing against their chests and snouts, the small cows already beginning to fall. The pigs can't fight it anymore and, soon, all turn with the current and sink. Chickens float toward the overpass, from the east, a body floats with them, a woman or a man and those few hundred people still left on the highway step slowly aside, letting the body pass, silent, and when it's gone the people all move forward once more, waiting their turn to climb up those ladders.

CHAPTER 11

A week later, the cars and trucks and buses still lie ruined and abandoned in water three feet high. It peaked at six feet. Now it's a liquid junkyard strewn with empty crates that once held food and water, with shreds of rope and crates and safety lines, with the still-swollen carcasses of dead cattle and pigs and chickens.

The ladders are all gone. The winches and tents that had been set up on the overpass, they're all gone too. The scavengers and brokers have taken their gear back to wherever it is they store their things.

The quiet on the overpass is still jarring. The absence of that solid, seemingly unbreakable sound of traffic.

I lean over the rail, looking down, taking a photo of a man's body bent horribly across the roof of a car, one of at least ten bodies I can see, and I feel like the sound of the highway will return any moment, rising up from below, as if the sound were disconnected from the traffic that once passed.

But it doesn't.

• • •

I am looking through my photos of the night with the ladders. I used nearly twenty rolls of film. Now I stand at one of the big wooden layout tables in the office. Photos, hundreds of them, are spread out across this table and another next to it.

The rows of ladders strung down from the overpass. The scavengers in their circles building more ladders to replace those that had broken. The sparks from the welding gear as large baskets were being built. The winches to drop the baskets to the surface. The stripped-down frame of that black van now placed on its pedestal at the southern end of the overpass. The stretchers and cots in the tents where the injured had lain. The faces of broken, frightened people emerging from the fog.

I've been sorting through the photos for hours. Trying to narrow them down to just the ten or so that will fit in the paper.

I see the pressman is near me, at the other table, looking over the photos. I'm not sure how long he's been there. I glance at the old clock on the wall. I'm an hour late getting him pages for the paper.

"I'm sorry," I say.

I've never seen the pressman up here in the office.

He's a white-haired, small and strong man wearing reading glasses. He shakes his head lightly.

Not a problem.

Still he looks at all the photos. I've arranged them in groups of eight or ten. Trying to find some order to the photos. Some are sorted chronologically. Some are focused on the types of people—scavengers versus the refugees, those who work and those who run to the south. There are scenes of night and of day. Images of the highway chaos and the loosely ordered kitchens and medical tents and sleeping areas built on and near the overpass.

I say to him, "Trying to figure out which photos to run."

He touches the pictures lightly, at the edges, shifting them slightly, gently. Studying each one.

He says after a minute, "Why do you need to choose?" He turns to me. He pushes his glasses onto his forehead with thick, worn fingers stained gray with ink. "We should run them all."

There are extra paste-up boards in large bins along the wall. I've never put together a paper bigger than eight pages, but the pressman now sets up the boards for a forty-page edition. We begin to place the photos on the boards, the pressman pulling a razor blade from a drawer and cropping photos on a mat, his hands moving quickly, cutting in perfect lines without a guide, turning the photos three times, three cuts, and then placing that

194

photo on the board. The office manager is at the table now, next to him, and she begins to glue the photos to the boards and I am still grouping photos together, eight or ten to a page, and as I see the pressman and office manager work, I realize I don't need to worry about any sense of order.

The order is there, in the madness of the scenes these photos have captured.

We don't finish the boards till midnight, the three of us then carrying them down to the pressroom and the pressman first converts the boards to film, then to metal plates that he wraps around the press drums, and the office manager and me, we help some, where we can, but this is the pressman's work.

He has the press set up and running in less than an hour, all five units now turning in sync, the paper pulling through the rollers, and soon papers of forty pages are coming off the end of the line. Pages that include a photo of the office manager, I realize, and of the pressman, each of their faces like the hundreds of others, all racing through the rollers on the press before being folded and cut and turned into a newspaper.

He prints twice as many copies as usual. The office manager and I help him load the papers into the delivery truck, then ride with him around town, daylight breaking behind the thick layer of seamless clouds, all of us loading the news boxes, there are nearly fifty of them across the North End, and the office manager and I sit together with the pressman in the front seat of the truck as we drive through the city.

The three of us hardly talk all night, even as we put the last of the papers into the last of the boxes.

All the papers will be picked up within a day. We print again, a second edition, more copies this time.

All those are picked up as well.

I see people reading the paper. Standing in front of the corner store. Sitting on the steps of the church downtown.

I had time only to write a single story, about the storm and the aftermath on the highway. It runs across most of the front page. But the rest of the paper is photos. Uncaptioned, all black and white, that's what people are looking at, slowly turning the pages, the photos, page after page after page.

...

The minister tells me that the storm caused massive damage across the South End. Hundreds killed. Power cut to most of the area. Within an hour of the storm moving out of the South End, looting began, bands of kids and adults attacking shopping centers, restaurants, car dealerships, a school. Police chased and fought them, using water cannons and helicopters and SWAT teams in full attack gear. Looters were killed. Police were shot. Even a commissioner was beaten to death. As many people were killed after the storm as during. The conflict went on for two nights and days.

"It was a civil war almost," the minister says to me. "A full battle between armed and opposing forces."

More than a week later, the South End remains under curfew, with a massive police presence on the streets and with store owners and security guards camped out in the wreckage of their buildings.

"It's martial law, I suppose," the gardener says. "It's their only response."

We stand, the three of us, at the guardrail on the overpass.

The water on the highway has receded another foot. Now the tires of cars are visible again, though still the water must be at least a foot deep. The highway's engineering, its water pumps and drainage system, seem to be working. At the height of the flood, the water reached throughout the highway trench that borders the North End. In some places, the water covered everything, even the roofs of the cars and tops of the pickup trucks, the water flowing as if it were in a canal.

No one goes down to the highway, even now as the water recedes. I have a thought that there should be owners looking for lost items and insurance adjusters readying claims. There should be reporters documenting what happened. Emergency workers retrieving the dead bodies I can see and those that I cannot.

But there's no one.

I ask a scavenger why they do not go down to the highway to gather things from the wealth of items in the miles of deserted cars and trailers. But it's a place of no interest to them, the scavenger tells me. She's working at the guardhouse. "It's an awful, haunted place," she says, looking down at the highway. There is thin, knotted rope around her neck. She stands taller than me, it seems, but then I realize she is on her toes. I don't know why. "All those dead animals," she says, "men dead, women killed, children who drowned in their seats. The highway is diseased and decrepit and it will to us always be a place of decay and abandonment and death."

• • •

There are more people here now, in the North End. People from the highway who went north not south. And people who have made their way across the overpass since the storm, escaping the violence and disorder in the South End. They come to the guardhouse on foot mostly, some pulling carts filled with their belongings or pushing wheelbarrows filled too and some even pull red wagons stacked high with bags and food and water.

A few people an hour. Not a tide. Not an exodus. But, every day for two weeks now, they have arrived in the North End.

I've come to the gardener's courtyard. It is greener than I remember, maybe greener than it ever was, the tree in the center seeming taller and fuller and the leaves so brightly fertile that it feels like they are growing, now, as I watch them.

I find the commissioner is here, not the gardener.

"He's gone to talk to the scavengers," she says to me. She is sitting in one of the chairs near the table, a blanket across her lap. There are newspapers on the table, I see my photographs on a page, but there are papers from elsewhere too.

I don't want to get close enough to see even a headline.

I'm sitting near her, the water in the fountain pouring quietly nearby, the water rolling lightly onto itself.

"The scavengers are planning to burn down that neighborhood soon," she says. "The one they've scavenged and cut off."

I nod and we are quiet. Flowers have bloomed, growing high enough that I can't see from this side of the courtyard to the other.

197

It's a minute before I realize something's different about the commissioner. She is usually fast to talk, to ask questions. To try to get information from me and everyone.

But now she sits in the chair, cross-legged under the blanket, and I realize she looks different somehow, her hair down across her shoulders and she leans back as she sits and she wears a man's jacket. The gardener's, it must be, and it's another minute when I realize that she's been here since the storm.

"There are people crossing the overpass," I think to say. "From the South End. Escaping, it seems."

She stares down at her hands in her lap. Nodding slightly. "I'm sure they are," she says. "The South End is coming apart. The chaos, the violence, it was something I'd never thought I would see." She looks up at me. "It's dying there. In a way that can't be undone."

Some part of me does wonder if, were I a different person, the commissioner would have come to stay with me.

But the thought is distant. A question, not an emotion.

"I thought I could come here to the North End to help," she says. "I thought the South End had something, much, to offer you here."

I reach down to pick up a leaf, green, that's blown from the tree. "The South End has been dying for many, many years," I say.

She nods. She has blue eyes and is quite beautiful. More so now, here, in this courtyard and without the questions and the need to find a solution.

But that too is not an emotion. Only a thought that comes to me. Like how I wonder also if, in another place, I would have gone to her.

The gardener arrives and he pats me on the shoulder and sits down near the commissioner and smiles at her, only slightly, and begins to talk about the scavengers, their plans for the neighborhood, but I'm not able to listen. Because I am having more than a thought now. I am having a feeling that rises in my chest, to my neck and jaw.

Happiness, in this moment.

Happiness, for this man and woman.

Things have started to change. The pace of things. The pace of life here in the North End.

Weeks go by and those weeks now seem like days.

A small outdoor market opens near the church, across from the corner store, selling vegetables and bread and meat and cheese. Food of a type and quality we've never had here. It is run by a scavenger whose left leg and left arm are cut off. "Lost them in some house," he tells me. "Tangled in the cables that lifted the walls from their foundation."

He has a prosthetic arm and leg, though, and makes his way around his market with relative ease.

Most of the food he sells is grown here in the North End, he says. They've been expanding their gardens as quickly as they can. Even the dairy products come from animals that a group of scavengers are raising. Only the meat comes from elsewhere. "But we have a plan for that too," he says to me.

The corner store closes within a week.

It had never occurred to me that food could be grown here. I had only just begun to accept the presence of trees and plants and flowers.

"Don't the animals, the cows," I ask him, "don't they try to get away?"

"They did," the scavenger says and he has the monotone voice all of them have and he stares right at me as he speaks. "Until we put them near a garden. Let them move among the plants. That's what calmed them down. Being among the living."

A young man shows up at the paper, standing in the doorway as I work on an article. "I can write," he says to me after a moment. "I can help."

The office manager turns back to her typewriter.

It's a few moments before I nod, then I tell him to come back the next day with a story.

He does. A story about new people moving into the neighborhoods along the grand boulevard. Refugees from the storm have taken over some of the oldest houses.

The reporter, he comes back every day now, with stories about people who are new here. About where they are from and where they've now chosen to live.

He cleans up the office as well. "Can I clear out these files?" he asks me, standing next to a set of file cabinets filled with old advertising contracts and accounting records. After a moment, we say he can.

He cleans the windows and scrubs the blinds and wipes down the desks and tables and chairs, carefully, slowly, using cloths he rinses every ten minutes or so.

It's hard not to be surprised by the care he shows for what he does.

The gardener tells me that more people come to him now, asking for help with planting things, and soon he sets up in a vacant building near the church. It's an old brick building, one story high, with no roof anymore so that when you pass through the front door you enter a space filled with shrubs and flowers and trees and the tools to plant those things. But you don't realize you're still outside until you look up and see the sky.

The woman and her boy work here. The woman, the gardener tells me, has an instinctive understanding of vegetables and fruits and flowers especially. "It's quite remarkable," he says.

The boy works with her, moving quickly to stock and restock shelves, to bring plants in from the back of the building where they are dropped off by scavengers. He pushes a cart filled with plants, he carries bags filled with seeds, he organizes shovels in piles that are grouped by type and size.

The woman smiles some as she watches him, then turns back to helping to load plants onto the cart of a person who's asking her for help. She tells this person about spacing the plants apart, about watering, about digging holes of the right depth.

She sees me near the front of the building, writing quickly in my notebook, and she smiles some to me as well, raises a hand, then turns back to her customer.

I write this all up for the paper. The gardener's store and the new market nearby and the scavengers' plans for more food.

The paper is bigger, now sixteen pages to accommodate the other reporter's stories and the number of photos I like to run, and the papers, we print more of them now, but still all of them are picked up within days.

I see them, these people who read the paper, watching them from the windows in my hotel room, high above it all.

It's much later that I realize I forgot to wave back to the woman.

· · ·

I'm in the small boat from the warehouse. Once again heading out into the canals, this time to check on the flooding and the state of the levees. The gardener has come with me. He sits on the wooden seat in front of me.

We leave little wake as we move through the canals and into areas flooded by breaks in the levees. I see the airport control tower ahead of us to the west and, in twenty minutes, we have reached what was once Runway 2. The water has covered another half mile of the airport. I see small waves lapping silently against the base of the control tower.

We turn back east, toward neighborhoods north of downtown that have now been flooded.

The gardener suggests going farther north. But I shake my head. "We can't go that far," I say. I'm picturing the neighborhood where I lived. Maybe the gardener is too, because he nods.

In a moment, I say, "It's just more of this."

There is a broken levee only a mile from downtown. A few square blocks of three- and four-story buildings are now flooded up to the middle of their second floor windows.

"The water gets closer," the gardener says, as much to himself as to me.

We move along one of the original canals, heading again toward downtown. I can see my building just blocks away. There are houseboats, three old wooden houseboats, lined up along the canal. Although they are old, they haven't been here till now. Then we see people. Coming out the door on the back of the first of the houseboats, a bright blue house with lights on inside, and the other two houseboats are painted bright green and bright yellow and other people come out from those houseboats as well.

The gardener points toward them and I realize he wants to speak to them. I turn the boat that way and soon we slowly pull up alongside the first of the houseboats.

A man, younger than us, leans down as we approach and I realize he's ready to help us tie up. The gardener tosses him a line, in a moment reaches up as the man helps him onto the houseboat. I kill the engine, nodding slowly as the man now helps me up too.

There are eight of them, living in these houseboats. There is handshaking and they offer up their names and they ask how long we have been here. Where we live. What brought us here.

The gardener answers. He smiles some, nods, asks questions too.

An unexpected normalcy, the pleasantries of greeting newfound neighbors.

I'm standing behind the gardener.

"It seemed, at this point, that a houseboat was the safest choice to make," one of the men says, smiling widely, nodding toward the north. "What with the levees breaking not far from here."

They are from the South End. "She and I were in the storm," the smiling man says, though his smile does fade some as he speaks. "We climbed out of the hellhole on the highway and decided right then, that night, that we would go north. Found this houseboat. Made contact with our friends who were still in the south and soon we were all here."

His wife is looking at me as he speaks. "You were there," she says, eyes bright and she steps forward, holding me, a hug, and I'm slow to raise my arms. "You were there," she says again.

I'm in her arms and it's not clear to me why.

Her husband, smiling again, slaps my shoulder. "Yes, yes," he says. "Goddamn. You were there at the top of that ladder. You helped us over the rail. Goddamn."

"He was there the entire time," the gardener says. "Seventy-two hours."

I look from the gardener to the people around me. The woman kisses the side of my face, damp and warm and I'm frozen in the moment. She is wiping her eyes.

In a minute, I say, "Anyone could have been at the top of that ladder." I'm still looking around at them. "There were lots of people there."

The gardener starts to talk, about that night, and I still feel where she pressed her lips against my face, how she pressed herself against me, and it's been many years since I've felt another person near me.

Two children appear on the roof above us, leaning their faces over the edge and peering down at us. The woman, she absently reaches her hands toward the children on the roof. The boy jumps and she catches him, staggered only slightly by his leap, then she swings him down to the floor. The boy runs inside. The girl, though, stays up top, still leaning her head over the edge. Peering down at the group, particularly the gardener and me.

I'm staring, I realize. And I'm silent. The others are all still talking, I hear the sound of voices, but I am only staring. At where that boy disappeared into the houseboat.

My eyes drift up to the girl still watching all of us below.

I suppose I remember helping these four over the guardrail. Four faces among thousands who climbed, desperately, upward on those ladders, wet and filthy and falling down as they reached the overpass, so many would fall down, gather themselves, their wife or husband and the children around them, thousands, each one staring upward as they climbed and these people were among them and in some way I remember each person I helped even as each person became one in the mass of movement and salvation that occurred in those hours.

The girl is staring at me from the roof, crouching now, on her feet. She nods at me and I don't know why but I lift my arms, instinct, as she jumps to me. She grips me tightly as I catch her, then taps my shoulder, and I release, all of it is one motion, and the memory of lifting and catching and tossing children for those years is back on me at once.

The gardener holds my arm as I turn away, stepping down into the boat, sitting now, staring at the rope tied from this boat to the houseboat, it's slack then moments later it goes tight, slack again, then tight, and I sit there, silently, I mostly close my eyes, until a few minutes later the gardener has gotten in the boat, started the engine, and then we turn and leave.

· · ·

More people move into the neighborhoods along the boulevard leading from downtown to the old neighborhoods.

More houseboats are reclaimed. Groups of three and four people, all now living along the canals in and around downtown.

More people make their way to the market downtown, to the vendors set up at tables nearby. Tables that are now stacked with more goods for these people who've come to the North End, more vendors who sell clothing and hardware and supplies that could be found in many of the abandoned homes.

A vacant lot near the market downtown is being turned into a park. Scavengers help the people who are clearing the land of refuse, then begin to plant and shape and form a park with benches and brick walkways.

I stand watching this in the street, making notes in my small notebook.

Walking back from the newspaper toward my hotel, I hear something, sound, just a half block from the downtown corner where the market is and the church.

The sound isn't loud, but it is steady and it takes a minute for me to realize it is music.

There is a bar, maybe, or is it a restaurant, set up between the brick walls of two buildings. Yellow lights like Christmas lights are strung in the air and there are tables, some wooden and others metal and chairs of every kind, hard wooden chairs and low deck chairs and a couch and a love seat and an ottoman and beach chairs that sit just a few inches off the ground and there is even a chair still attached to a school desk, in which the minister now sits.

He's one of fifteen people here.

The minister offers to get me a drink. I say no, but sit with him and the people nearby.

"He's the writer," the minister says, introducing me. "For the paper."

And people, five of them, they nod and say hello.

I have my notebook out and ask one of them about what they left behind in the South End. He shakes his head, confused. He says in a moment, "No, I didn't come from the South End. I came from hundreds of miles from here. Trapped on that highway in the storm. But the city I left, we left," he says, touching the hand of the man next to him, "it seems that it will be abandoned next."

He drinks from a coffee mug. Others drink from glasses of all sizes. A man behind a makeshift bar made in part from the hood of a car comes over, pouring some sort of whiskey into all of their drinks. The minister pays him money.

"The rats," the man in front of me continues. "The roaches. The animals that left this place, they didn't all just die. They went to other places. Like the city we are from. Huge packs of dogs. Feral cats. The failed efforts of the city to wipe them out with poison, so many dead animals that they had to leave carcasses in piles on corners and overflowing from dumpsters and still the animals roamed the street."

"What you have in rain," the man's friend is now saying, "others have in heat and drought. Rivers turned to creeks or dried up completely. Lakes emptied of water, now dead valleys or dry plains. Uncontrollable fires and not just in the forests. Whole neighborhoods destroyed on the edges of big cities. Hillsides that should have never been occupied, even before the drought began, finally the fires could not be stopped, so that now those hillside neighborhoods are turned black and white, burned flat to the ground, they look like the landscape of some moon."

• • •

The gardener has many questions for me about the canals and the levees and how they were originally designed. We meet in the atrium of the old library, where I pull old maps from the files of public records. Survey maps and schematics showing the emergency plans, showing how levees were built to funnel water away from the city. I mark as best I can the levees that are broken, the places where water has advanced.

There are news articles from decades ago, some from newspapers and others from engineering journals. The gardener stacks them all up. "Can I use this table?" he asks me, then smiles some. "Right," he says. "Of course I can."

. . .

The woman and her boy have a large yard behind their building. It's along one of the main canals downtown, so that the grass they've planted and the shrubs and ivy, it grows right up to the edge of the water. The yard is bordered by brick walls on both sides, the building on the other. There are archways in each brick wall, with iron gates swung open, and I see that the yard on one side has started to be planted.

"I'm helping them," the woman says, looking through the archway.

The other archway opens onto a small playground. A swing set and monkey bars. "The scavengers have been very kind to me," she says.

There is a rope swing, too, strung from a heavy, dead tree that stands along the edge of the canal. The boy swings on it, standing, his feet on a big knot at the end of the rope, he can pump his legs and swing over their yard, then out ten feet above the canal.

The woman and I stand watching him. It's quiet here.

"The places we went," she says now, quietly. "They offered no better escape."

I nod.

The boy swings. Forward then back.

It's a while before she nods too.

"You should tell my story," she says now. "My boy's story. How we ended up here. What they did to us in the South End."

I say in a moment, "I thought you'd want that kept private."

She nods. Pushes her hair behind her ear. Blinks her dark eyes. "I did. But then I saw those photos. Your photos. Of the night of the storm. The highway and ladders. People will never forget that night. And they'll never forget those photos."

The boy sways, silently, the branch reaching out over the canal.

The woman has turned to look at me. "They should know what was done to people like us. And they should never forget that either."

· · ·

The commission meets. For the first time in many months. The community center is filled with a few hundred people from the North End.

I stand near the side of the room, notebook open. There are scavengers along the wall behind me. The minister is near the front, sitting next to the gardener and the commissioner. There are people from houseboats and from the market downtown and faces I've seen walking along the streets of the North End.

The woman is here, with her boy, the two of them standing near the back.

I wrote up her story this past week. Her story of this commission, these men and women, moving to take her neighborhood, her home, her boy.

"You'll see us return the South End to normal," says one of the commissioners, an old, bald man who now calls himself the chief commissioner. "You're already seeing the highway reopen. And then you'll see the overpass to this place and the power we provide you, you'll see that all cut off completely."

There is silence from the crowd. In a moment, the gardener stands. "Why is this place of any concern to you? Why do you want so badly to shut this place down?"

"Because," the chief commissioner says, loudly, nearly yelling, and he leans forward, his hand up, finger out, pointing at the gardener, "it is places like this and people like you that distract us from the work we should really be doing. The support of good people and good places, that's what we should be providing."

"Like the woman and her boy?" says the commissioner, from her seat next to the gardener.

The commissioners all turn to her, staring with looks of disdain and surprise and in some cases it seems they look at her with hatred.

She was one of them once, turned now to the other side.

I doubt the commissioners know about the woman and her boy. Certainly they've not read my story about them.

"I don't care about some woman or some boy here in the North End," says the chief commissioner, again leaning forward, staring angrily toward the commissioner and the gardener and now looking around at everyone in the room, trying, it seems, to meet the stare of all three hundred people here, all of us in a room that just three months ago was used after the storm to care for people from the North End and South End and places far away. "I don't care about them," he says. "I don't care about you. All I want is for all of you to go away."

He's met with silence, which seems to make him angrier. He leans back, then leans forward. He seems to try to find more words that will better express his hatred for us, this place, for everything he sees and feels.

The minister stands up, next to the gardener. He's smiling slightly. A crooked smile crosses his dense face and he cups his small hands to his mouth. In a moment, he says loudly, "Boo!"

The chief commissioner leans back, staring at the minister in his black shirt and black pants.

The minister says again, with his hands still at his mouth, "Boo!"

The gardener, standing next to him, can only stare at the minister, slowly looking him up and down, this compact man in black, his dark eyes bright as he continues to boo the commissioners.

And then the gardener starts to laugh. He laughs loudly. He slaps his hands against his knees, bent over.

The minister has it going steadily. "Boo!"

The gardener joins him. The commissioner and the people around them, standing all of them, they join too.

Boo.

Others begin to stand and the commissioners at their table at the front of the room, they lean back, staring from person to person in the crowd, all of whom are also standing.

Boo.

Yet there's no anger in it. No hatred or mass aggression of the crowd. People smile, stand, and boo.

The noise, it gets louder.

The commissioners lean back farther, pushing their chairs away from the table, and one of them stands.

The noise is still louder, shaking the windows and the floor, and the crowd is all standing, booing, and the booing is changing. It's a kind of yell, happy, a sound guttural and instinctive and there is clapping now and cheering and all the commissioners are standing up, looking from the crowd to each other, and in a moment one of them begins to leave the stage, moving forward toward the aisle and the cheering now, the screaming, the clapping and shifting in place that almost seems to have become a dance, it all rises with the roar of the voices.

The commissioners are leaving, the aisle kept open for them, there's no jeering, no taunting or anger. There is only the still rising cheer of the crowd.

A celebration, I write down. *You can only call it a celebration.*

• • •

The water on the highway continues slowly to recede, though even three months later there is an inch of filthy water on the surface of the road.

The cars and trucks and the rotted carcasses of dead animals, they are all still where they were left. The human bodies too.

But word spreads that a set of bulldozers and cranes is beginning to make its way along the highway. I go to the overpass to see them. Moving through the center of the vehicles, slowly making their way toward us.

Cars are pushed to the side. Cranes lift trucks and even small trailers, then drop them onto vehicles in the neighboring lanes. Bulldozers pair up and begin pushing against massive buses. The highway is so packed with abandoned vehicles that the bulldozers and cranes can barely move forward.

Dead people are removed. By men or women in hazmat suits, hooded and wearing gloves, they put the bodies into bags and slide them into a van behind the crane and bulldozers.

Slowly, over many days, two lanes are formed. One in each direction.

Why forming lanes would be a priority for anyone in charge, I don't know. But a great deal of effort is being made.

In another few weeks, traffic starts to move on the highway, cars and heavy trucks and sometimes buses. The traffic moves slowly, starting and stopping often, reaching just ten miles an hour at most, the drivers and passengers all staring to the left and then right, studying the landscape of destruction through which they now pass.

• • •

"I'd like to take you somewhere," the woman says. "Show you something. Something the scavengers have been working on."

We walk down the street. The boy is in front of us, tiptoeing carefully but quickly on a faded yellow line in the street. He follows it to the right, toward a set of taller buildings, three of them eight stories high.

"There are many more scavengers," the woman says as we walk. "There have always been more of them, maybe five hundred or six hundred, more than anyone knew."

The boy leads us to the middle building, one of three old brick buildings, each with windows six across.

Inside, the building has been gutted, the floors removed, by rain or a storm or the efforts of the scavengers who have taken over the place. The basement is exposed, three floors deep, and we stand at the edge, a set of heavy horizontal bars forming a railing. I look down and then up, leaning against the rail, seeing scavengers, twenty of them at least, climbing up and down a mass of beams and the thick black branches of dead trees, branches brought here and attached to each other and to the walls, and there are cables stretched at angles too, strung from one brick wall to the next, the coordinated tangle rising to the very top of the open building where a set of nets covers the opening.

"There are birds here," I say, dumbly, because that is most obvious to anyone who enters.

I can't tell how many birds there are. Hundreds, maybe a thousand, of all types, and I realize that there's a thin, nearly invisible net strung up in front of us, reaching from the basement to the ceiling, and I see that parts of the building, horizontal sections, are cut off from one another by more thin nets, segmented into separate areas of separate types of birds. I see finches and I see blue jays and I see robins and high above there is a hawk.

I step back from the edge. Arms at my sides, mouth open, not sure I can breathe.

There are trees and shrubs and flowers planted throughout the carefully tangled structures that rise up to the eighth floor. Platforms have been built to hold beds of dirt, and ivy curls its way up various beams and a huge tree trunk, slick and black like all the dead trees here, it is suspended midway up the building and has been carved out in places to let other plants grow from it.

"They've been working on this for years," the woman says, standing near me, and like me she stands back, staring up. "All of them, the scavengers, they spend time here, tending to this place and to the animals they've brought here."

The boy begins to run along the edge overlooking the basement, his hand brushing against the bars. He tumbles and rolls now, but soon he is only running, his arms out straight from his sides, and as he runs the birds begin to make even more noise, whistling and squawking and some launch from their perches below us, the motion spreading upward from section to section, the birds flying in circles or sometimes swooping toward the boy, and as they move and whistle, the force of their motion fills this massive space, shaking the thin net in front of us, which moves slowly, lightly, the boy now smiling and soon he is laughing, a high-pitched silly giggle that if you close your eyes sounds almost like he's crying and so I don't close my eyes, just watch him as he circles, smiling, the birds rising from the basement or descending out of view, so that the boy now seems to fly among them all.

Scavengers stop their work, the ones digging holes along the walls and the ten of them spread out through the scaffolding above, each adding to the framework that will eventually lift the nets and plants and birds even higher. But now they have stopped. All of them looking at the boy as he runs.

All of them smiling. Some of them laughing. And I've never seen a scavenger laugh.

They've worked on this for years, she said, but it's obvious anyway that the people who built this have been at it for so long, tending this place, tending everything here that lives and grows.

The woman is smiling, watching her boy next to the birds, her eyes wet, but she is laughing as he moves, in circles, the trees and the flowers beyond him and the birds ducking and dodging next to him, crying out, probably in warning or in fear, but here, now, it sounds to everyone like the birds are simply laughing along with the boy.

CHAPTER 12

The office manager tells me there are a few hundred teenagers at the checkpoint on the overpass.

I ride my bike there from the newspaper's office, moving quickly through the streets of downtown, then through the old neighborhoods before coming to the overpass.

And it's clear immediately that this is something different. These aren't kids in lit-up cars. They aren't kids coming here because of boredom or disdain.

These kids are homeless. Castoffs. These kids are children.

There are nearly two hundred of them, teenagers mostly, but some are younger, all carrying backpacks or small duffel bags. They are dressed in layers of clothes, items clearly accumulated over months or years of time. Hair long and thick and some of the boys have thin, bad beards across their faces, and some of the girls are tattooed across their necks and arms and the backs of their hands. Rough, colorless and elaborate tattoos done by themselves or a friend.

"They shut down the shelters," a girl says to the gardener as I listen. "Which is maybe a good thing. But now we had nowhere to go."

The gates to the overpass have been opened, but the kids are all gathered, pressed together, on the south side of the overpass. None have crossed into the North End.

The minister puts his hand out and, in a moment, the girl shakes it. "Welcome," he says, and smiles. "Welcome to the North End."

The kids begin to move slowly forward. The commissioner and others meet them as they cross, walking through the crowd, shaking hands, welcoming them, telling them where to find food and where there are places to stay. "There are homes," I hear the commissioner say. "No one lives in them. And so you can live there. Those places can be yours."

The gardener steps up to a boy, sixteen or seventeen, who walks with a dog, more like a puppy, who stays at his side.

"Your dog," the gardener says, leaning down, scratching the short, tan hair on the dog's thick neck. "Your dog does not run away."

The boy shakes his head. "Never once."

The dog circles the boy, then sits.

"They say it's not violent here," says the boy. He's looking at me, if only because the gardener is still leaning down, staring at the dog.

"It's not," I say.

"Can I believe you?" the boy asks.

"How old are you?" I ask, aloud I think, but I'm not sure.

"How old?" he repeats. He's got brown hair and blue eyes and he stands almost six feet tall. "I'm sixteen," he says. He pauses, looks around. In a moment, he asks quietly, "Is that okay?"

I nod. I stare. I've done the math without meaning to, instinct. The boy is the age my oldest son would have been.

I say, in a moment, "Yes. You can believe me."

• • •

"I think there's a way to fix the levees," the gardener says.

The gardener and I are in the library, standing over his table with the maps and the journals focused on the levees.

"Or at least to keep any more from breaking," he says. "And to keep the flooding from coming any farther."

I can't think of a response.

"So many levees have already broken," he says, smiling slightly. "There really aren't that many we need to fix."

"Who will do the work?" I ask him.

He smiles again. "The scavengers."

What the levees need after years of inattention and years of more and more water pushing up against them is to be reinforced. The gardener shows me drawings, detailed schematics of how all the levees were built.

"I could never build a levee," he says, still smiling some. "But I can read a plan. And these plans all lay out the maintenance to be done. Beams that must be added or replaced every ten years."

The stubs of his fingers trace lines on the plan. He opens a file of public records he's retrieved from the archive in the basement. There are only five small levees holding back the water.

"We can find a way to insert new beams," he says, turning to me and smiling some. "Can't we?"

The work begins within a week. The scavengers cut large steel beams from the insides of warehouses in the industrial zone. They find beams that aren't corroded or rusted, then cut them to size with blowtorches. Fifteen feet each, they are stacked onto trucks that begin to haul them north toward the levees.

"How long will this take?" I ask the gardener where we stand watching the scavengers lower a beam into slots built into the levees, slots that have been there since the levees were first built.

The gardener turns to me. Says in a moment, "I think it will take forever."

There are teenagers, the kids who crossed the overpass, helping the scavengers. Ten of them at the warehouses helping to cut down the beams, another ten at a canal, helping with the unloading, with digging, with bringing beams to the scavengers.

"Truly," the gardener says now. "It will take years to reinforce the levees, and by the time the project's done, it will be time to start over again."

I'm taking notes.

"But that was always the point," he says. "These levees, this city, it was never meant to fall dormant. It has always needed constant attention and care."

· · ·

The playground blooms one morning. There's a force to it, in the suddenness with which it happens and the color that reveals itself and the sheer volume of the flowers themselves. I see it first from my windows, leaning out, and it has transformed the place I look at every day.

The gardener has a box of frogs. "The scavengers," he says, smiling. "They can get me anything."

He puts the frogs in various green spaces, his courtyard and my playground and a few of the places the scavengers have built. He says, "We'll see if they can even live."

I see more houseboats reclaimed from farther north, pulled closer to downtown, lashed to houseboats that are already lit and repainted and occupied again.

The population of the North End, it has grown by a thousand or more.

Through the dim window of an abandoned store near the church, I see an old calendar on the wall. *December 2009.*

"I assume they come here for the same reasons we did," the minister says to me. Along the wall behind him, bright yellow flowers, tiny and in the hundreds, have bloomed in a swath reaching up at a slow angle from the ground to twenty feet high. "To make a life for themselves," he says.

"What kind of life?" I ask.

He shrugs. He sips tea. "Maybe something quiet. Maybe something satisfying and simple."

When the air-raid sirens go off the next day, I realize there are fewer of them. Someone has disconnected some of the sirens.

"Strangely," the minister says as we walk through his growing garden behind the church, "I have become my best self here."

In another week, when the sirens go off, only three sirens scream out. I look toward the bell tower near my hotel, where a siren had until now screamed out all of these years. I see a man standing there.

It's the minister.

I see him smile.

216

Traffic barely crawls along the two cleared lanes of the highway. The minister and I stand at the guardrail. Watching as the vehicles move in fits and starts and how could it be that anyone would need or want to drive through there?

"I wake up," the minister says now, as he sits on the steps of his church, "and look forward to the day."

Only one siren goes off, near the library, I can barely hear it from where I walk.

"What is it," the minister asks, sitting with me in my playground, "that I find so pleasant about this place?"

And in another week, I realize, the sound of the sirens is gone completely.

• • •

I've found a record player in the library, hidden in a cabinet I'd never noticed near the library's collection of old albums. The albums are all classical or old jazz.

It's been a very long time since I've chosen to listen to music.

I bring the record player back to my hotel room. Plug it into a socket along the base of the walls. I've brought a few albums, ten maybe, the first ones I saw.

The music starts from the wide black speaker in the front of the record player and it does not seem right. But I did not ever listen much to classical music and combined with not having listened to music for so long, I think I'm just not hearing the sounds the right way.

Soon, though, I realize the record player is turning backward, the needle arm moving out toward the edge of the record, not in toward the center. I adjust the knob that controls the speed of the turntable, but the player still turns the wrong way. At full volume, the music makes for a mess of noise, the record screeching and nearly howling from the speaker. But when I've turned the volume down, still trying to figure out what is wrong, I realize that the sound now fills the space. I reset the needle to the inside of the album. The sound comes quietly. Simple, long notes, faint beats coming without rhythm or expectation, all of it very quietly echoing out into the room.

A lifting and falling of sounds. All of which fills the silence.

I see the box of things from the house. A small box, wooden, sitting atop a photo album. I touch it with the palm of my hand. Don't open it. Don't move it. But I press my palm against the box for a full minute, feel the rough texture of the wood, the sound from the record filling the silence.

The box and photo album sit on top of a stack of paper. The manuscript. About this place.

The music lifts then falls and at some point I'll have to restart the record.

Because, still, I do so hate the silence.

• • •

The minister and commissioner tell me that the South End is still under curfew from the storm. The commission has not met in months. Every day, people cross the overpass to the North End. Walking alone, coming sometimes in a car, a whole family of four making their way with their suitcases and whatever they've fit into their backpacks.

"The breakdown," a woman says, her children leaning close to her legs, her husband resting a hand on her shoulder. "A total breakdown. Among the police. Among neighbors. Everyone is coming apart."

The commissioner meets them, all of them she can, and tells them about the North End.

"I don't know how long we'll stay," the husband says to the commissioner. "We have family far west of here. We just need time to regroup. Then we'll go to them."

I stand near them, writing this all up for the paper.

"It doesn't matter," the commissioner says. "You stay as long as you want."

"Is it safe here?" the man asks. "Will we be safe?"

The commissioner leans down and talks now to the children. "All of you," she says, "will be safe."

I watch the boy swing out over the water of the canal, then back again on his rope swing.

The woman and I sit in the courtyard, green with ivy and grass and plants not yet ready to flower.

"Someone told me who you are," she says.

I turn to her.

"The fire," she says, slowly. Pausing. Her brown hair is pushed off her face and her eyes blink as she stares at me. "I remember," she says, "I remember it was on the news. Five people killed in a house in the North End. Video, from a news helicopter, of the house still burning. Of bodies laid out on the street and a small crowd nearby and the man, the father and husband, leaning over those bodies. And no police ever came. No ambulance or firefighters." She's quiet. I hold a small, waxy leaf. "And I saw that video," she says slowly, "and I thought what everyone thought, that the North End was the most frightening place I could imagine." She turns to me. "A barren, abandoned city where people were left to die."

I'm watching her. She moves her hand to her face, then away. She looks up at the sky before turning back to me.

I'm replaying what she's said. I know it is true. Know that people saw the stories. Know that, even now, it's a memory in people's minds of a horror incomprehensible.

But I've never spoken to anyone about it.

"I'm so sorry," she says. "I'm just not sure what else to say."

Never. Never once.

It's a long while that we don't speak.

"And when you saw that man leaning over those bodies," I say, slowly, staring past her at the grass, long grass, that grows a foot or more high along the base of a brick wall, moving slowly in the very light wind here in the courtyard and wet, I'm sure, from the lightest rain that falls. "When you saw that man, what did you think of him?"

She doesn't answer for a minute. The boy swings out over the water, again, twisting some as he does, his eyes closed and if he pushes his legs or leans his body to continue the motion of the swing, I can't see it, and instead it seems that the dead tree gently swings him back and forth in a steady, endless arc, toward us then back out over the water in the canal.

She says to me, "I wondered, how he could have possibly thought something so horrible as that wouldn't happen?"

It's a moment, longer, I'm not sure, before I find myself oddly smiling. "No one," I say, then pause. "I've always known people would think that. I know I thought that. But no one has ever said it to me."

She looks away, toward her boy. "I'm sorry."

I shake my head. "No. Don't be. There's no reason to be sorry for saying that."

The boy swings. My hand, laid out on the table, the palm is damp with rain.

"I've never seen you smile," she says.

"In my mind," I say, "there is always the fire and the desperation of that moment when I realized what was happening, and the screaming, my screams, because their screams were already done, but my screams are always somewhere in my mind." I close my hand on the rain. "And so no, I don't often smile."

The boy swings. Eyes closed. Head back in the wind. The branch of that slick, black tree swaying back and forth.

She says in a moment, "You should. You have to. You have to know it's not your fault. Even," she says, leaning toward me, blinking, "even if it is. Even then, there has to be forgiveness. Of yourself. Of what happened. Of anything you have done or didn't do. There's no other way for you to live."

• • •

The scavengers have been building small farms for the past year or more. In greenhouses hidden behind the many homes they've scavenged, they've planted rows of all sorts of vegetables and fruit. They have chickens too, in large open pens made by linking together the backyards of stripped-down homes, and there are cattle there and dairy cows from which they bottle milk and make cheese.

"It's amazing," I say, quietly, as I walk through one of the greenhouses.

The gardener is with me, and around me there are scavengers tending the plants.

"It's about to become even more remarkable than this," he says, smiling at me. Outside one of the greenhouses, there is a group of twenty of the teenagers, the homeless kids who arrived here weeks ago.

"We're going to create a farm," the gardener says. "A full-sized farm, a hundred times larger than these greenhouses and pens."

I look at the kids. A scavenger is talking to them, staring upward as she speaks. She's telling them how hard something will be. "You will be more tired than ever before in your life. And then you'll work some more."

The gardener and I keep walking. "The aviary," I say. "It's a remarkable place."

"Yes," says the gardener. "I saw it when I was still a scavenger. It made me realize so much is possible."

The heat in the next greenhouse we pass through, this one filled with tomato plants, squash, vegetables I can't identify, the heat is overwhelming.

"At some point," the gardener says as we step outside, pointing upward, the hand with the missing fingers reaching toward the clouds above us, "they plan to release some of the birds."

"Why?" I ask.

He smiles slightly. "To see if they will stay."

We come out from behind a scavenged house. Across the wide street is the row of flattened houses. The outline of the neighborhood the scavengers plan to burn.

In a moment, I turn to the gardener.

He smiles wider. He seems like he is about to giggle. He nods. "We're going to turn that neighborhood into a farm."

● ● ●

I look at the new people who've come to the North End, seeing them on the street or seeing them answer questions as I interview them, or seeing them as I watch from my room in the hotel, and I wonder. There must be bad people among them. There must be, somewhere, a history of darkness, wrong, even just a deep sadness. There must be people crossing the overpass who come not for some promise of hope or possibility, but who come here to escape all the bad that they've done.

This must be true.

Maybe they can make a new life. A new self. A new world in which all is different. All is better.

But I'm not sure.

I see one of the police officers near the church. She isn't in uniform. It becomes clear soon that she now lives here in the North End.

"There are bad people," she says, answering my questions as I take notes. "Everywhere. I don't tell myself otherwise. Even now that I am here. There are bad people. Always."

I nod. I thank her. She doesn't know why and I'm not sure either.

But I thank her.

● ● ●

We've come to the overpass for the start of the fire. Hundreds of people are here, scavengers spread out along the length of the neighborhood, water trucks lined up and two old fire trucks the scavengers found in some warehouse in the industrial zone.

Other people have simply come to watch. The minister and me, other people I've seen in the North End for years. But there are also others who seem new to this place, the way they stand back, look around, nervous and unsure about what is happening.

Not that the people who have long lived here have ever seen something like this. But we're beyond a point of being surprised or unsure.

The preparations for the fire have been elaborately coordinated. It's not just the long line of flattened homes that will keep the fire from jumping to the old neighborhoods, but also there are firebreaks the scavengers have built every few blocks to keep the flames from spreading faster than they want. Heavy, industrial balloons have been lofted along the side of the neighborhood, measuring the direction and strength of the wind.

West.

The fire will be lit here, near the overpass and community center, then move west through the neighborhood.

The gardener is talking to a scavenger holding a walkie-talkie. The scavenger then talks to others via the same handheld radio.

The neighborhood was built badly, cheap houses thrown up to replace the massive park that had been here, fields and woods and playgrounds and a large, empty field, a green whose only purpose was its openness, the simplicity of a wide and open green space, all of it once used by thousands of people every day. All of it destroyed by a highway. Cars. Replaced by poorly built homes of little value at all, disconnected from any schools and any jobs and even built without sidewalks in order to save money. This neighborhood was in decline the moment it was created.

A precursor to the South End.

And so now we will burn it down.

I take notes for the paper, standing to the side.

I notice that the frame of the van at the end of the overpass, the one left there by the scavengers after the storm and the attack at the highway, it has been painted. It is striped with yellow and red and orange and blue and the minister says there's a smiling face on its front. Pointed toward the South End. "The kids painted it," he says. "They did quite a good job."

There are teenagers here too, the shelter kids, some helping the scavengers, others watching the scene.

The gardener smiles as he listens to the scavengers on the walkie-talkie. He turns to the minister and me. "We need help lighting the fire."

I stare. The gardener smiles and nods and the minister steps forward, his hand on my arm and I'm following the gardener too now, a group of scavengers and vendors and the commissioner is with us.

The gardener hands out heavy sticks whose ends are wrapped in oil-soaked cloth, torches for each of us that he begins to light, some ten of us from the North End all lighting one another's torches here under a dark, evening sky, the rain barely falling, I notice it now only because of the hissing around me, drops turned to vapor as they touch the fire I hold near my face.

We spread out, fifteen feet apart, and move forward, the gardener in the middle of our line as we step up onto the curb and walk over the row of flattened houses and the houses behind await, the collective destruction of the North End continuing again.

But this time for the better.

The gardener touches his torch to the window frame of a small house.

I think maybe he expects the house to ignite. His body leans away from the flame, ready to step back, jump back, even run away.

We wait.

I know that what he's doing won't work.

It's a long moment, minutes maybe, I don't know for sure, before I step forward. Opening the door of that same house, walking to the center of what seems to be a living room, and then I begin to spread fire in that home, to a chair, to a table, the curtains nearly explode in flames, the carpet now burning toward the bedrooms and as I walk back toward the door through which I had entered, I light the sofa and a chair, the heat from behind me building with the light, yellow and orange and shining red on the walls, and I leave through that front door, outside seeing the rest of them with their torches all staring at me.

I feel the house I lit behind me, burning bright against the sky.

A scavenger near me, the wire jewelry around her neck shines bright with the flames, and she smiles some at me, then moves toward the front door of the house in front of her, enters, and now all do the same, because you have to commit to the effort, you have to put yourself at risk, the realization is obvious as this row of small houses sheds ashes and embers that gently alight on the ground all around me, watching houses burn, all of them burning and all of these people emerge, turning around, seeing the fires they've started, and like me every time I've burned a home to the ground, fifty, a hundred, I don't know how many times, like me they now stare, there's nothing to do but to stare, stunned and horrified and awed by what you've managed to do.

It's been many weeks since I burned down a home. Many weeks since I cried. It's as if I haven't had enough time.

There has to be forgiveness, she says.

There has to be.

• • •

Drinking then. Even me.

Many people have made their way back toward downtown after the fire. Some sit drinking on the wide steps of the church. Others are in the small park that's being reclaimed. Others simply sit in the street.

We sit in the restaurant, the six of us. It's nearly morning. I sit at a wide, wooden spool turned on its side to form a table. The gardener and commissioner and the minister and the woman are sitting here too. The boy sleeps curled up in a low chair next to his mother.

The burning of the neighborhood took hours. Even now the entire neighborhood smolders and smokes and burns, groups of scavengers and others moving slowly through the scene like rescuers searching the ruins of a crash site, fire trucks stalking the edges of the neighborhood, ready to respond if the fire tries to jump from where it is allowed to burn.

The other four adults around me all smile, drinking some sort of liquor the owner of this place has served us in mugs and wide, low jars.

We're outside, the ceiling having fallen and been cleared away and only heavy wooden beams cover us, the beams strung with small yellow lights in all directions, and above that is the sky just hinting at a sunless daybreak.

My face and hands are dirty, I realize, only because I see these other people dusted and streaked even after we all tried to wash ourselves before leaving the neighborhood.

The fire was loud and rolling and the heat drove most everyone a block away from the flames and even when we left, after the neighborhood had been leveled to the flat, blackened ground, still the heat reached a few blocks away.

I drink. We all do. The four of them laugh and talk about the fire we started and the possibilities of what can come next.

"I have a plan," the gardener is saying, smiling. "For all of the North End."

He is rolling out a map on the top of the table, using people's drinks to hold down the sheet, two feet by two feet, showing all of the North End. He begins to draw on it, roughly, creating large areas of green ink.

"Parks," he says, still smiling, almost laughing. "More room for farms. And over here," he says, carefully holding the pen with the short nubs of his missing fingers, now drawing on the industrial zone, quickly covering it in green, "here we'll put a forest."

The commissioner touches the map near the gardener's hand. "A forest?"

The gardener is laughing again. "A small one, yes."

The minister finishes his drink, turns and waves at the bartender. Another. "So are we doing this next week?" the minister asks.

"Well," says the gardener, looking around the table, "let's just see how far we get."

The commissioner kisses him on the side of the face.

The minister sips from his new drink.

I wonder, somewhere in my mind, how much of this can happen.

"What is that?" the woman asks absently, as the gardener draws a series of sticklike markings in the industrial zone.

"Yes," the gardener says, "right. Those are windmills."

The minister's eyes get wide. He takes another drink.

"You know," the gardener says, "for power."

The minister shrugs. "Oh, right," he says, nodding rapidly. "Of course. 'For power.'"

"At some point," the woman asks, "won't some of these things have to be paid for? The people doing the work. Doesn't there have to be money?"

The gardener is smiling again, again on the verge of laughing. "Yes," he says. "I've got a plan for that too." He looks around at each of us, then says, simply, "Taxes."

He is laughing almost wildly now. The commissioner holds his hand as she laughs too. The woman smiles as she watches them. The minister finishes his drink, waves to the bartender for another as, silently and repeatedly, he mouths the word *taxes,* and the wildness in the gardener's laugh is the drinking and the wiry exhaustion of being up all night and it's the neighborhood we've burned down and the vision he's laid out matter-of-factly for us, and all of it, here, at this hour with these drinks with these people in front of me, I wonder if it's possible that the gardener's plan will come true.

It doesn't seem possible. But I know what I want. I want this to come true.

"Once more," the woman says to me quietly, "I see you smile."

I nod some and feel myself smiling, then stopping, and I sip from a new drink. "I suppose," I say, not sure what other words to speak.

"What about an amusement park?" the minister asks loudly. "Or a roller coaster? Do your plans contemplate that?"

The gardener smiles at him.

"Or a zoo?" the minister continues. "Personally, I'd love to be in charge of the zoo."

I drink again, a third drink probably or maybe it's a fourth and now I laugh at the prospect of the minister running a zoo, laughing like the gardener is and the commissioner is and the woman near me too.

The minister says, "Maybe the scavengers can find us a hippo."

I drink again, in the laughter of these people around me, drinking now and leaning back and above us the sky is turning brighter with daylight above those clouds, but for a moment it's different, here under the old wooden beams above my head and the hundreds of yellow lights strung everywhere around me and it's as if I can see sunlight, finally, there is a sunrise now, it was inevitable I suppose that these clouds would finally break and maybe now we'll be a place that doesn't always have rain and doesn't always have clouds because there is sunlight, here, above me where I sit, and at some point all had to lift and all had to change, like words on a page that I can write and rewrite as I drink again, near the end, where all of this has been written in a manuscript in my hotel high above the ground where I sit, a manuscript, a book, and outside those finished pages everyone is still alive, she is and they are, all of them once more running in from the backyard, crashing into a house that is not underwater, that has never been burned, the girls Ellie and Carmen and boys Cole and Sam too, blue eyes and brown eyes and blond hair and brown, and Nora is here, in the house, our house where we always have been, only the darkness in my thoughts manifested on the page keeps them from being real, real to the touch and real in their sounds, their laughing giggling eruptions of sound as they climb onto me again, cling now to me as I hold her, each day, again, because as I look up at that sunlight and drink here in this chair, I know where they are now, exiled from me or me exiled from them, as it's my choice to stay here, it always has been, to live in these ruins apart from my life that goes on, it's only written this way, by me, my choice, their deaths only something I have put into words, nightmares on a page from which you inevitably awake, leaving behind my fault and my blame and a turn of plot too sad and dramatic and awful to be real.

"What happened?" she asks and past her head I see now a calendar on the wall. The date, today's date. Clearly visible to me.

The others are here. Also staring at me. "What happened?" she asks.

And next to the wall I see the water, as always, seeping down through the cracks in the mortar and bricks, this building like all of them bleeding endlessly with rain, the same rain that falls lightly on my face and my arms and my hand where it holds that drink.

"Tell me," she says, leaning forward, and the boy is awake now, still curled into a ball, but staring up at me like all of them stare, though the boy doesn't blink, instead simply knows, and understands, and the sunlight I see is only a yellow bulb on a string, suspended so delicately above his small, fragile body.

"Tell me. What happened?"

228

And this is why I can't sleep more than an hour and can't be among people and can't drink any more than the one drink I allow. Because it takes me somewhere else, a place where I'm forced to use names I've created, fictional representations of the people who died.

That's how I know this moment is real, here in the rain under another gray sunrise over this place where I live. I still can't say their names.

EPILOGUE

We thought there was something in the ground that was killing us. But what's killing us is ourselves.

The minister tells me this. The gardener agrees.

I write this in my notebook. Even though I'm not sure it's true.

Water, icy, I drink it from the tap, rinse my face and push it through my hair into my scalp.

The office manager doesn't come to work one day. I see her near the market. I see her headed toward the neighborhoods to the east. We nod when we see each other. But there's no need to speak.

The new reporter, the young man, he begins to do the work she did. To enter my stories and his own into the Linotype machine. To find paper and office supplies in buildings nearby.

I'm not sure how to pay him. He says he doesn't care. But after a week I realize that there is money in a bank account down in the South End. My account. I can't go there to get it. But the minister volunteers to help me. And so, each week, I now put a small amount of money in an envelope for the reporter, leaving it on his desk, and money for the pressman, I leave it on the heavy wooden cart down in the basement.

They thank me, both of them, each week.

I never once thanked the office manager.

The reporter goes through the file cabinet filled with my notes and files. He asks if he can use them and it's a moment, I have to stop and think if he's asked me this before, then I tell him that yes, of course he can.

Standing at the windowsill of my hotel room, I find a spider web. I touch it, very lightly, and the motion spreads through the thin white strands immediately, the tiny spider in the corner clenching, retreating, then in a moment stretching out its legs again.

I see birds, half a mile away, released suddenly from the aviary, a small mass of flying bodies lifting up into the sky.

The minister has started sprinkling seeds on the debris and abandoned vehicles down on the highway. Plants grow in places, from the hoods of red cars and the broken windows of huge trucks and from the pale and sunken carcasses of cattle. Passersby in their vehicles all stare at these plants and if they were able to go faster I think that they would, but instead their cars crawl forward, stopping and starting and to walk would be faster I'm sure.

I hold a dead frog in my hands. Found in my playground. Among the ivy near the wall.

I bury it. Quickly. Not ready to tell the gardener. Or anyone.

In the library, I wake up in the atrium, and there are other people here, working, reading, some just wander, and I realize I can't sleep here anymore.

I load the boat with an extra can of gas. A set of blankets. Water and food. I'm headed north. I can see the first of the windmills in the industrial zone as I pass, tall and white and turning steadily in the wind that does never seem to end here. The scavenging has moved into the factories nearby. They hold a wealth of materials, mercury and iron and copper and even gold, in small amounts that, once accumulated, have tremendous value.

The brokers tell me that their buyers wonder where all these things could possibly be found.

The woman and her boy are with me in the boat. The boy rides in the bow, leaning over the edge, dragging his small fingers across the surface of the water.

We cross through broken levees. Follow the bare outlines of canals. We pass through neighborhoods flooded to the second story windows. It's a full hour before I can hear the sound of the bay. The low waves, the sea smell, a sense that the horizon has finally emptied of all its distant objects.

The neighborhoods here are almost completely washed away. Few houses or buildings still stand, the street signs bend down to the surface of the water, or are submerged completely. Streetlights and old trees are all pushed at an angle, worn down by the water and constant low waves, everything losing its fight with the tide.

The dark bay stretches off as far as I can see, disappearing where it joins the equally gray clouds at the horizon.

The tall cranes at the port still reach high up into the air. They were built on high ground. But one crane is bent sideways, sinking toward the warehouses and stacks of containers that all drift slightly to the side.

The zoo is still here, and the small amusement park too.

I'd thought they'd been torn down. But they remain, half flooded, at the far end of the port.

A huge ice-cream cone sticking out of the water. The metal arms and seats of a Ferris wheel whose base is lost to the waves. The wooden scaffolding of a small roller coaster now sagging down upon itself. The concrete walls between each animal's cage, cages filled with water that flows easily through the rusted bars along the front.

She tells me her boy has never been to a zoo.

I tell her I have always hated the zoo.

He stares from the bow, his chin on the edge of the boat.

We circle the zoo again.

Circle again.

We spend nearly an hour only circling.

Still I live with the box of things I don't touch. And the photo album I can't open.

I look down toward the people moving toward the market and the church.

My world is not theirs and theirs is not mine.

But I go down there, for just one drink, that's still all I can have.

And if I'm down there walking and I hear the sound of music and people behind me, I'll find myself walking into the dark and unlit streets that lead home, and I'll think that I have to move. Farther north. Away from all of this.

233

Finding a new place to live. Another city that's been abandoned. A place like this once was, the city where I've lived for the six years since they died. My place. My purgatory. It can continue.

I am crippled, really. By what happened to them in the fire. But maybe even more so by how I have chosen to live since they died.

I don't move on, though. Instead I stay here. Alone in this building. I see the church and market and the playground, my playground, once more blooming again. I go down there sometimes and live among those people. I find I can write better in a place that is loud. And now, sometimes, they even come here. To my hotel room, the six of us, a gardener and a commissioner, a minister and mother and with her there's her boy, all broken, shattered people, standing here, silent, as we look out at our city through these tall and open windows.

ACKNOWLEDGMENTS

The author wishes to thank Elizabeth Trupin-Pulli for her commitment to and belief in this book. Thanks so very much. Thanks to Maxim Brown and Cal Barksdale at Arcade Publishing, and a special thanks to Emily St. John Mandel, who's always been so supportive of the author's writing, and Minna Zallman Proctor, editor of the *Literary Review*, who has published so many of the author's short stories, including "Why I Stay," parts of which made their way into this novel. Thanks also to the journals *Mud Season Review* and *District Lit*, which also published short stories that appear, in part, in this book.